REVENGE OF THE BROBOT
A Steam Room Story

JC Calciano

175 Publishing

Paperback Edition ISBN-13: 978-1-7364463-0-0

Cover design by: Miblart
Printed in Los Angeles, California, USA

To the sixty-plus actors over the years who have appeared in the Steam Room Stories series and movie (aka "The Steam Room Guys"), who brought their own unique personality and sense of humor to the show

.

I've learned something from every single one of you and, collectively, we've shaped the Steam Room Stories Universe into what it is today. You made a tremendous amount of work into a joyful and amazing experience.

Author's Note

Revenge of the Brobot is another chapter in the Steam Room Stories universe.

    Steam Room Stories began with the sketch comedy series on YouTube, then jumped to the big screen with *Steam Room Stories: THE MOVIE.*

    For more adventures, visit SteamRoomStories.com.

Table of Contents

Chapter 1

D r. Herbert—famed chief robotic scientist and programmer ("Herbie" as his colleagues called him at Hot Bot-y Robotics Corp)— looked through the one-way mirror at the pulsating pile of writhing bodies. It was hard to tell where one body ended and the others began from where he stood. Like a human game of Twister, the mound of lust-engaged bodies licked, petted, and fornicated their way into a ferocious five-way.

Soaked and sweat-saturated, the bodies were moments away from their second and third orgasms. All but one—the hunk at the center delivering the physical pleasure to the promiscuous pile, ROB.

ROB (Robot with an Organic Body) was a masterpiece of manhood, a mountain of muscle with piercing crystal blue eyes and sun-kissed blond hair. He had smooth, squared pectorals and round, ripe buttocks. ROB was spectacular in every way—and eager to please as he jubilantly jack-hammered the last of his orgy partners into delighted delirium. Herbie couldn't be prouder of Rob and loved him like the son he never had.

Herbie watched and smiled at his creation's performance. *The statue of David wasn't as perfect as this robot*, Herbie gloated. Michelangelo himself would be impressed by ROB's physique.

The viewing area had a thick, soundproof, one-way

mirror barrier that separated Herbie from the test subjects. The room was specially designed so Rob and his horny harem couldn't hear or see the spectators. As Herbie reveled in his accomplishment, the metal door behind him flung open with unnecessary force, slamming against the wall. Herbie jumped.

"That just took another ten years off my life," he yelled, attempting to calm his beating heart, lodged in his throat. Herbie was by nature a nervous soul, the kind of man people referred to as a "nerd" or a "dork." He was a slight-framed man who'd been pushed around by bullies his whole life. He had soft, almost feminine features and an undeniably kind face framed by white, unkempt hair. Herbie was past due for retirement, and with his failing health, he couldn't afford to lose any more time.

"What the hell is going on in there?" said a deep, booming voice. "It reminds me of when I went to Woodstock!"

Herbie blinked as his eyes adjusted to the harsh, bright light. He sighed heavily as several men entered the small room. One stood out more than the others — a General in the United States Marine Corps with a full adornment of stars and stripes. He was stoic and barrel-chested with a precise, military haircut that made his silver hair and weathered, austere face all the more imposing. He had a strong jaw that jutted out with dark, almost black eyes. The General's scraggly, bushy gray eyebrows made him look more like a villain from a James Bond movie than a war hero commanding a battalion of Marines.

"Explain yourself, Bentley," the General began a verbal onslaught on the man standing next to him. "I flew in for a demonstration of my billion-dollar soldier prototype, and all I see is a mound of buttholes and mouths, all of which have something in them!"

Bentley Burns was the CEO of Hot Bot-y Robotics Corp. and Herbie's boss. He was a sharply dressed, silver-haired fox of a man who only knew the taste of the finer things in life. Bentley was what an aged Superman would look like at fifty-five years old, that is, if Superman could've aged.

Bentley addressed the General meekly. Herbie couldn't remember when he'd heard his boss so apologetic. "The point of this demonstration is to show how our state-of-art pleasure-bot is indistinguishable from a human. And how dexterous it is. It's able to satisfy five people at a time. More, in fact, all of them are unaware that it's a robot or anything short of human. He has all the physical and social skills of a man in his mid-twenties and is, in many ways, the perfect human being. He is called ROB - Robot with an Organic Body."

"I don't give a shit what its name is and how many people it can fuck at the same time. The United States government gave you a blank check to develop the perfect soldier — and you gave me a dildo with a body. If I wanted a sex toy, I would have called Doc Johnson."

Bentley attempted to explain further, "It's just a software adjustment at this point; we can program him to do whatever you want him to."

The General turned to a soldier standing quietly beside him. The young Corporal was a strapping, corn-fed Midwestern man with a mixed ethnic background. His dark, bedroom eyes and strong, chiseled jaw made this handsome Marine both seductive and intimidating. "Corporal Matthew, see that this man is given a full breakdown of the weaponry every soldier in my army should be able to handle. Also, make sure he has a full briefing of the basic training that every recruit goes through. When I get back here in two weeks, I want to see a killing machine, not some porn star made of aluminum and rubber. Do I make myself clear, soldier?"

"Sir, Yes Sir!" the Corporal replied. The General once again turned his attention to Bentley. "I want that six-foot-six sex-doll reformatted, reprogrammed, retooled, re... whatevered, until you have the picture-perfect prototype of a super-soldier. If you can do that, I'll get Washington to sign off on another one hundred, perhaps a thousand of them. You've got two weeks." He turned to the macho Marine beside him. "I'm leaving you in charge, Corporal. See to it that my mechanical soldier is properly trained. Two weeks," he repeated fiercely. "Don't disappoint me or your country." With that, the General turned and left with Corporal Matthew behind him.

Herbie and Bentley turned back to the demonstration, which was now over. They watched Herbie's assistant, Kyle, hand out cold compresses and Gatorade as he thanked the participants. The performers were exhausted. Twenty minutes of passion with a literal love machine had taken its toll on them. And even better, not one of them had suspected that Rob was a robot.

Bentley turned to Herbie, wasting no time in laying blame.

"Herbie, what on God's green earth was that display about?" he exploded. Herbie recoiled at the outburst. From an early age, he'd never been good with confrontation. His prowess in robotics could be directly attributed to him making his own mechanical friends, simply to avoid other kids. Flashbacks of being pushed around when he was younger flooded back, and he couldn't take it. Herbie snapped.

"I was told to create the perfect human specimen — physically flawless. You said my job was to demonstrate *all* his skills and how Rob is indistinguishable from other humans, and I did just that! I've created robots for this company for twenty years, from vacuums to domestic servant prototypes. This company was built on mechanical sex toys. Our number one seller is Dan, the dancing dildo! How was I supposed to know that the perfect man you paid me to create was not actually a love machine but a soldier, and that the demonstration was for a top U.S. General?"

Bentley was taken aback. Herbie had never spoken to him like that before.

"I'm sorry, but up until now, all our clients were adult toy vendors," Herbie muttered.

Bentley was silent for a moment, then sighed. He opened his mouth and did something Herbie couldn't ever remember Bentley doing before. He apologized. "You're right. I'm sorry. You did what I asked you to do, and you did it perfectly."

Herbie's jaw dropped, and his brain buzzed. This was certainly an unexpected outcome. Herbie managed to find words to reply: "Thank you for saying that. Now perhaps you can tell me exactly what it is you want Rob to be other than a sex-bot."

Herbie felt a sense of satisfaction at having stood his ground. However, he couldn't help but feel a growing sense of foreboding, knowing that the military had its sights on his creation.

Chapter 2

After seeing the General to his car, Corporal Matthew returned to have more words with Bentley. He knew that if he didn't get Herbie's love-bot properly trained and reprogrammed, he'd be on the short end of the General's temper, and that was something he did not want.

Matthew thought the General had done himself a disservice storming out of the factory so hastily. He hadn't even made time to take a tour of the facility. It was an impressive operation. Long conveyor belts whirred as robotic body parts were pulled off the line and assembled onto their torso chassis. Matthew had never been to war, although he had seen his share of gory movies. The body parts lying on the belt and hanging from walls resembled scenes from a battlefield. Although he was a soldier, Matthew had a healthy fear of fighting. It was a departure from many other soldiers in his squadron who longed for the day they could go into battle. Matthew thought compassion was the key to making a good soldier.

Body parts filled bins and shelves as far as the eye could see. Robots resembling men, women, animals, and aliens were everywhere in various states of assembly. Some robots were created for household chores, others as companions for the elderly, but most were designed for pleasure.

***

Matthew entered Bentley's impressively large office with a soft courtesy knock on the door. The finest of fabrics adorned the walls. It was first-class—every stick of furniture custom made by an artisan's hands. Bentley insisted on having only the best of everything, and as the CEO of Hot Bot-y, he felt he deserved it.

Bentley glared at Matthew as he entered. He'd instructed his dutiful assistant, Mrs. Habershed, not to let anyone or anything disturb them. Time to sort this damned mess out.

The tension in the room was thick. Matthew didn't expect Herbie to be with Bentley, arguing about ROB's future.

"Bentley, you explicitly instructed me to create the perfect robotic companion, programmed with skills ranging from domestic, emotional, compassion, and sexual. I made you a state-of-the-art robot fitting that description. Of course, my assumption was it would be our best-selling sexbot. I'm not going to allow Rob to be a soldier or killing machine." He scowled, irritated.

Bentley sighed as he leaned forward to punctuate the point. "I know what I said. I told you ROB would be a game-changer that would revolutionize the industry and ensure that Hot Bot-y remained the leader in humanoid robotics. This military contract will ensure we get there."

Most of the robots in the warehouse were made of metal, wires, crude skin, or hair. Rob, however, was different. He was a multi-billion-dollar prototype designed specifically by Herbie. Herbie had spared no expense making Rob perfect. It was a true labor of love.

"I am not making soldier-bots," Herbie vehemently

asserted again. Matthew cleared his throat loudly to make his presence known. Bentley had forgotten he was even there. Before he addressed the Corporal, Bentley needed to calm Herbie down. He decided to take a different tack than his usual bullying bravado. "Herbert, you're a star, a true genius, and you did everything right. But now we've got to deliver what was promised to the government — a soldier, like this fellow here." He gestured to Corporal Matthew, who didn't look too pleased with being thrust into the middle of this disagreement.

Bentley looked at the soldier, uncertain of his name.

"Corporal Matthew," the Marine muttered.

"Like Corporal Matthew," Bentley continued. "Make ROB like him. It's just a software thing now — programming... so easy. Something I have every confidence that you can accomplish in fourteen days."

Herbie was silent for an uncomfortably long amount of time. He didn't seem sure where to begin or even how to reply to Bentley's demand to change ROB from a lover to a fighter. Bentley stared down at him with his steely gray eyes. Herbie chose simply not to answer him at all. Without a gesture or indication of what was going on in his head, Herbie turned and left the room. The large, heavy wooden door thumped behind him.

Bentley looked over at Corporal Matthew. "He'll fly right. Trust me — artists... geniuses... they're all the same. They need to work things out in their heads. At the end of the day, he knows he's here to do a job, and he has no choice. Let him cool down, and you'll start working with him. In the meantime, I've got work to do. Why don't you go get yourself a soda and kill an hour on your phone until we're ready for you?"

Matthew glared at Bentley coldly, "Way to be

condescending. A soda—look at my phone? I'm a fucking Marine, not some teenage girl." Matthew left the office offended. A few minutes later, Corporal Matthew found himself sitting at a table with a Coke, playing what appeared to be a quick round of Candy Crush on his phone.

Chapter 3

Herbie barreled into his laboratory on a mission. A naked ROB stood in the corner of the lab, awaiting his creator. Unlike Bentley's plush and opulent office, Herbie's workshop looked like the bridge of a starship. Stark and sterile as lights flashed and diodes glowed. Wires, circuits, and mechanical parts were impeccably placed with precise planning.

At the sight of him, ROB smiled with happiness. Herbie returned the smile, albeit a little forced, and greeted ROB with a hearty "job well done" pat on the shoulder. "You did great," Herbie muttered. "Really great." His smile dimmed when he noticed ROB was naked. He reached into a cupboard and handed Rob a skimpy towel to cover himself up.

I know ROB is nothing more than synthetic flesh, steel, and wires, but I can't help but feel he needs to be more modest about his impressive body.

"ROB, I need you to listen carefully now. Obey the instructions I give you without question. Trust me, and no matter what your programming tells you to do, make sure you heed what I say to you now." Herbie pleaded.

ROB nodded, eyes wide. He sat down on a stool and waited for his instructions.

"You need to escape—hide—and never tell anyone

you're a robot under any circumstances," Herbie said urgently, his heart breaking. But it was the only thing he could do to keep ROB safe. "You must blend in with humans and never come back to Hot Bot-y or look for me again. You must find your way alone. You'll be a castaway on the run from now on. If the government finds you, your very existence will be in jeopardy."

Herbie opened the iron security door that led from the factory to the outside back alley. He spotted a sample wardrobe from a domestic male robot across the way and pulled it into his office so ROB could get dressed before escaping out into the world. As Herbie started to grab the shirt, pants, and shoes, heavy footsteps approached from outside. Tap, tap, tap—the sound of leather dress shoes on the faux marble floor echoed through the hall.

Panicked, Herbie implored ROB to run. "Don't look back, go, go! No time to get dressed."

***

ROB fled into the bright, warm sunlight outside without taking the clothes from Herbie's hand. The door closed, locking ROB outside in the back of the factory. He stood for a second in the warm California sun, confused. Wearing only the small towel around his waist, Herbie's last orders replayed in ROB's head.

"Don't look back, go, go!" He was programmed to take a direct command and did what he was commanded to do. Without direction or any knowledge of where to go, he ran.

***

As Herbie stood grieving over Rob's sudden departure, the office door swung open to reveal the owner of the tapping leather-soled shoes. Herbie's excited assistant, Kyle, entered gleefully.

"It's fixed! It's perfect." Kyle couldn't contain his excitement. Herbie waited in confusion for the punch line. *What the hell are they talking about?* he wondered.

Kyle was lean and tall with wispy, short, black hair. He was oddly adorable in an unconventional way. Kyle was an unabashedly confident, sexually fluid millennial who, in many ways, was more brilliant than Herbie. "You know ROB's power cell, the one we removed that was giving us trouble? It no longer overheats! By changing the conducting coils from copper to magnesium, the hydrogen cell will run forever without going up so much as a degree in temperature." They both beamed proudly.

Herbie's excitement at this incredible and necessary breakthrough quickly gave way to dread and concern.

Fuck. If ROB's power cell is in Kyle's hand, what the hell is powering ROB?

***

ROB kept running as car horns honked and women and men alike yelled, "Whoo-hoo!" ROB was puzzled at first but then realized it was no doubt unusual for a large, muscular, and semi-naked male specimen to be seen on the streets of Encino. ROB had run for blocks and decided he was now far enough away to relent. *My next step is to blend in within the community, as Herbie instructed.* ROB engaged his Infra-red scanners. He was seeking a place where he wouldn't be found—a place where he wouldn't raise suspicion. ROB had only one mission on his mind: Hide.

Chapter 4

Chase walked out of the double glass doors from his downtown design firm. He was making his way towards his car but couldn't resist glancing back at his building. As with everything in his life, his workplace looked perfect — a giant glass and steel structure that would impress even Tony Stark.

As he walked over to the valet, Chase felt bone-tired. The pressure from his job weighed heavily on him. There were only two weeks to go until the grand gala opening of a new museum exhibition. Chase was the head creative director on that project and was about to get thrust into the spotlight.

His project was a state-of-the-art exhibition of Los Angeles' most important art collection. A veritable Hollywood who's who of society elites would be there to judge his work. It was a make-or-break occasion, and he wasn't sure he was ready for it.

As he waited for his car, Chase eyed himself in the shop window across the way. His reflection showed a good-looking man in his early thirties in a custom-tailored suit. He knew he was an attractive man, as evidenced by the number of women in the office who continually dropped hints about how much they'd like to be with him.

Chase was not vain, but proud of his looks. He was

tall and ripped with big, blue eyes and tussled sandy brown hair. Although his job preferred him to be clean-shaven, he kept a bit of scruff, which he felt was a nice contrast to his boyish appearance. Chase enjoyed his fitness routine and religiously hit the gym. He and his buddies affectionately called themselves "the steam room guys." His group was a rag-tag, motley crew of 'bros' — most of them barely employed. Each of them was from a different social or economic group, but that's what made them all so awesome to Chase. The steam room was a judgment-free zone where everyone was welcome, no matter where you were from or what kind of things you were into. He grinned thinking about them.

Of all the places in the world, Chase could think of no place he'd rather be right now than a steam session. He pulled out his cell and sent a group text to the guys. He used the steam emoji (some called it the fart emoji, but everyone in the group knew what it really meant). If they were available, they'd assemble in the steam room and talk shit about their day, their lives, their loves, and each other. *Perfection*, Chase thought — just what he needed after a day like today.

By the time his navy-blue Range Rover pulled up to the Gym, one of the guys had already texted back with a "thumbs up." *Sweet*, Chase thought. *At least, there'll be someone there.*

The steam room was located deep in downtown Encino in an old converted Spanish mission. Chase had no clue when it was built or how long it had been there. It was a whitewashed stone building covered in outdated posters of boxing matches fought in the two rings inside. In the back were an old-school gym, sauna, and steam room. The steam room was nothing special. Just past the lockers behind a frosted glass door, it had dark blue square tiles and old wooden benches. The room was relatively small, comfortably seating only about eight.

The building stood across from a strip mall brimming with state-of-the-art workout facilities with fancy names like Techno-Sport and Ultimate Boot Camp. Inside these glass and chrome gyms were tanning beds, electronic stair climbers, and other such luxuries for their bourgeois clientele. Chase and the guys preferred the old-style workout facility aptly called, The Mission Gym.

Chase prepared to strip from his custom-tailored pin-striped suit. He would lovingly hang it in the pale blue locker numbered "thirteen." It was his locker of choice, and all his buddies respected that. First, he removed his jacket. Next, his shirt and pants. And finally, his white boxer briefs. Chase chuckled to himself as he grabbed a towel to wrap around his waist. *Why bother putting on a towel at all? It's just us guys*, he thought. The towels provided by the gym were impossibly small. Chase's tight, toned mid-section barely allowed the towel to be folded around itself. The towel was more of a gesture.

Once in the steam room — reclined, legs open — there was nothing left to the imagination — everything was on display for anyone who wanted to look. *It's not like we haven't all seen each other naked in the showers. Heck, most of the guys in this steam room have already slept with each other.* Nothing was off-limits in the steam room — at least for the other guys. Chase knew they saw him as a bit of a prude. He admitted he was notoriously vanilla when it came to his love life. Some things were private, and he believed they should remain that way. Chase rarely talked about his girlfriends — he always felt bedroom talk tacky and off-limits. However, tonight would be different. Tonight, he needed friends to confide in. He wanted the advice and insight of his steam room bros.

***

Chase was a sweaty mess by the time the door to the steam room banged open. He shook his head in amusement. His favorite bro Bolton slammed through the door; seemingly unaware it was made of glass. Bolton was ex-military and currently a CrossFit trainer. His muscles had muscles. Chase had often wondered if it was healthy for a person to have such low body fat, but Bolton had assured Chase he knew what he was doing. And if Bolton decided he was going to do something, there was no changing his mind.

It was strange that they were such good friends, being so different in every way other than both being fitness freaks. Bolton had a hair-trigger personality and was always up for a good time. Chase was meticulous, calculated, and precise. Bolton was impetuous and foolhardy. Chase was fascinated by Bolton's wild, carefree nature.

"Damn, bro, this feels good." Bolton sighed. He gave Chase a quick fist bump before flopping down next to him. He breathed steam in deeply. "Are the other guys coming?"

"I think it's just us," Chase replied.

Bolton nodded. "I figured you needed some bro time. What's up?" he asked, already guessing what the answer would be. "Rebecca split today," Chase muttered. "Woke up, and all her stuff was gone. She slipped out in the middle of the night while I was sleeping — who does that?"

"Seems like all your girlfriends," Bolton teased. Chase winced. Bolton's comment was too true to be funny.

"Sorry, dude," Bolton was quick to remedy. "I liked Rebecca. In fact, I liked all of your girlfriends. You have great taste. How come they don't stick around, bro?"

"Honestly, no clue. Guess I just choose girls that are duds." Chase confessed.

Bolton blurted out, "Maybe it's you?" This statement stopped Chase in his tracks. Bolton had his shortcomings, but mincing words wasn't one of them. He was a straight shooter and never one to sugarcoat anything.

"ME?" Chase defended. "I'm a catch!"

Bolton's giant arm — an arm that probably weighed twenty pounds — wrapped itself around Chase's shoulder.

"Dude, we all know you're awesome with the guys — we couldn't ask for a better friend — but with the ladies, you're batting zero. I can't say that I blame Rebecca for moving on. You're either working late hours, or you're here with us. Everyone wants to be with someone who wants to be with them. You've got to put something into a relationship to get something out of it."

Chase sat quietly. First, his defenses went up, ready to convince Bolton that he didn't know what he was talking about. But rather than launching into all the reasons Bolton was wrong, Chase decided he'd consider if Bolton was right. Steam hissed through the vents as the warm, moist air circulating around them. Bolton retracted his arm from Chase's shoulders and gave him the space to process. Chase looked Bolton squarely in the eye.

"Dude, I'm obviously doing something wrong, but I have to be honest; I have no clue what it is."

Chapter 5

The sky had turned a brilliant display of purple and pink—hues that Rob had never seen before. The world was indeed a spectacle of colors, he marveled. Soon though, the darkness would set in, and he'd need to find a place to recharge. The simple lithium cell he was running on was severely depleted from the demonstration at the factory. Sexually satisfying five people would drain anyone's battery, he supposed.

Rob's indicators registered that he only had six hours of operation left before he shut down completely. As Dr. Herbie had designed Rob to be the perfect domestic companion, he'd installed scanners to enable Rob to see through walls to check whether his human host needed anything. Tonight, though, these scanners would help Rob find a safe place to hide and recharge so that come morning, he could continue to locate an area of long-term lodging.

As Rob wandered the streets of Encino, he came across an older, more remote neighborhood. Trees and open spaces semi-obstructed an old whitewashed building, different from the others in the area. It looked like a building that had stood for ages and repurposed several times. Torn, faded boxing posters gripped onto the stone exterior in a futile effort to appear relevant. As Rob studied the venue, few people entered or exited the establishment, but he could hear a smattering of activity inside. His infrared and body scanners made out several men through the walls—all resembling him in size, age, physical fitness, and prowess. He noted: This would be an excellent group to assimilate into. Within those walls, he could be unnoticed, just "one of the guys."

Through his scanner, he could see two men sitting—both in towels, both similar to his muscular build and resembling his perceived age range.

Rob entered the building.

Time to blend in.

A gruff, older man immediately greeted Rob. He wore an ill-fitting yellow polo shirt with "Mission Gym" embroidered on it. The man's 1980s "gym teacher" athletic shorts were very short and tight and revealed a significant amount about him.

"Can I help you, son?" the old man asked gruffly. "You look like you're ready for a steam dressed like that." He gestured towards the towel Rob wore.

"I'd like to gain access to this establishment," Rob replied, his eyes fixated on the old man's appendage, visible through the thin shorts. He surmised; that he must be an older model sexbot with a love log like that. The older man stepped forward and held out his hand.

"Name's Harry, but they call me O.M.J. or Old Man Johnson around here."

Rob smiled as he shook the hand of his new friend. "Nice to meet you, Harry Johnson. I'm Rob. Pleased to make the acquaintance of another sex machine."

OMJ's eyes widened, but the way he smiled, he was no doubt flattered that Rob acknowledged him as a fellow sexual dynamo. "It's usually five bucks to work out here, but we're closing soon, so enjoy. You can pay the next time you're here."

Rob thanked OMJ for his assistance and quickly moved past him to find his place somewhere in this establishment. He heard OMJ mutter, "Crazy kids," as he spotted a sign that read "Steam Room" with an arrow pointing to the left.

Good. I'm designed to be watertight and fully submersible so that the steam won't affect me.

He entered the small tiled space located behind the frosted glass door. The steam room door squeaked open as Rob entered.

Seated inside the steam room, Chase and Bolton stopped talking as their gaze lifted to see who entered. This was a strange hour for any of the regulars to arrive.

Damn, you're one built bro, was Bolton's gut reaction. "Wow, way to make an entrance. Looking good man!" he joked at the handsome stranger wearing a tiny towel.

Rob smiled, "Back at you, you're seriously swoll yourself," he replied, taking note of this ridiculously ripped man in his late twenties. Rob couldn't help but scan Bolton's body fat index. Rob was unaware that a human could be this buff and lean at the same time. Bolton's strong facial features, along with his light brown, hip haircut and hazel eyes, made him strikingly handsome.

Bolton laughed at Rob's compliment. Bolton considered himself the unofficial steam room welcome wagon. He felt it was his duty to make the new guy comfortable. He patted the bench, inviting him to join them.

Rob sat down, expending a sigh, "This heat is good for my circuits. I've been walking miles today, and my battery is pretty drained. I'm called Rob, by the way."

Bolton wasn't sure what Rob was talking about, and from the look of confusion on Chase's face, neither did he.

"I'm Bolton, and this is my buddy, Chase."

"Hi," Chase muttered softly. "Nice to meet you."

Bolton (and Chase, he noticed in amusement) watched with an open mouth as the humidity created droplets of condensation on Rob's super smooth skin. It ran down his chest and stomach towards his hidden delights.

This fellow is flawless, observed Bolton, licking his dry lips. "You from around here? Haven't seen you work out here before."

"Yes, I was created not far from here, but unfortunately, I can't return." Rob looked sad. "I'm looking for a place to recharge."

"We've all been there," Bolton said, nodding. "I'm from Encino. Chase and I are here for the same reason. It's been a long week."

The guys settled in and continued to exchange pleasantries. Bolton was glad to see Chase getting drawn into conversation. It was a welcome break from Chase worrying about his broken heart. It wasn't that Bolton wasn't sympathetic. It was because it was the same old story with Chase. He dated great women, but he never clicked with any of them. Often Bolton would even pick up Chase's exes. Bolton could count on two hands how many of Chase's exes said the same thing about him.

Chase is rarely around. He never seems to want to spend time with me. Sex is infrequent, and when it happens, it was rarely anything to write home about.

This made Bolton feel good about himself, although

he hated to admit it. Chase was his bro, and he'd never wish anything bad for him. If Bolton were, to be honest with himself, Chase had everything he could want; whereas Bolton was a scrappy guy from the proverbial wrong side of the tracks — a latchkey kid brought up by a single working mother. It had been his athletics and his stint in the service that had gotten him scholarships and access to life outside the trailer park. He still struggled with money and his place in the social strata, but he'd never admit or let anyone know life was tough for him. For all Bolton lacked in his life, the one thing he knew he could do better than anyone else was rock someone's world. Bolton was a proud bisexual man. He was attracted to either sex, depending on the day or the mood. He didn't care to think much more about his sexuality other than the fact that everything was on the table for him.

Anyway, Chase seemed happier now. The chatting had helped, plus he'd lit up when Rob entered the Steam Room. Hmm, Bolton thought, these two get along remarkably well. He found Chase's nervousness around Rob oddly endearing.

"I gotta split. It's getting late," Chase announced. "It's going to be weird going home and finding no one there tonight." His statement wasn't really intended to elicit a response; it was just one of those things that flashed through his head and slipped out of his mouth. Chase hated to be alone. He was always happier when he was working. He loved his work, maybe a bit too much.

I'm either crazy passionate about what I do for a living, or I'm using it as an excuse to hide from life. Truth be told, it's probably both.

But he wasn't expecting what Bolton blurted out

next.

"Rob, Chase's got a big, empty place, and since you're looking for a spot to crash—why don't you room with Chase till you get settled?"

Chase's jaw dropped. Was Bolton insane? Sure, he had an impressive place with a spare room, but they didn't even know this guy. What if he was a thief, a murderer, a grifter? Every day there were stories about people who let strangers into their house. Chase wasn't about to make the same mistake as all those people who ended up on the nightly news.

But before he could say Hell no! to Bolton's grand idea, Bolton doubled down on the suggestion. "Chase's all alone with a huge deadline coming up. He's never home, plus having you there to get his mind off his work will be the best thing for him."

Chase could hear the ring of truth and logic in it. The memory of his ex would just be constant reinforcement to his fears that he lacked the ability to love anyone. He feared that he was incapable of intimacy, and thus, he would grow old and die alone. He rolled his eyes at himself. Drama Queen, much?

Chase saw that Rob lit up like a Christmas tree at the thought of having a place to go that night. For such a muscular, handsome man, he had deep, loving, almost puppy-dog eyes. Eyes that could hypnotize you into complying with nearly anything he desired. Yup, he's a serial killer, Chase thought, and tonight he's going to suffocate me with his pillow. Rather than saying no to Bolton's insane plan, Chase found himself saying, "Ok, fine, but just till you find a place of your own."

And please, please, don't murder me in my sleep.

Chapter 6

Rob stood confused in the locker room as Bolton and Chase dropped their towels and started dressing.

What the heck am I going to wear other than this towel?

Rob dropped his towel almost in sync with Chase and Rob, but unlike the other guys, Rob had nothing to change into. He stood there naked, awaiting the next opportunity to follow their routine, as he conspicuously and curiously checked out Bolton and Chase's people parts. Bolton didn't seem to mind. In fact, it appeared he thrived on it and deliberately turned to give Rob a healthy view. On the other hand, Chase seemed shy by nature, so he turned away casually. Although in truth, he did not need to be bashful.

When both men caught full sight of Rob's full-frontal, Chase reacted with a gasp. Bolton's eyes widened as he exclaimed, "Geezus, man. Is that real? Do you make the poor person on the other side of that thing sign an insurance waiver?"

Rob didn't understand what Bolton meant by that statement. His personality scanners indicated that it was humor of some sort, so he laughed. That seemed to do the trick.

Bolton was amused at his response. "I mean, me and

Chase sized each other up ages ago. We're pretty similar, right down to our boy berries, but you add a whole new meaning to the phrase 'hung like a horse.'"

Rob watched as they changed into their clothes. He wasn't sure what to do, seeing as he had nothing else but the towel on the floor, so he stood there naked.

Chase was a boxer-briefs guy who seemed to prefer the casual look of jeans and a soft tee. Bolton went commando and threw on a pair of loose sweats and a tee.

Someone else came into the steam room. It was OMJ, holding a mop and spray bottle of 409 cleaner. He stepped forward, placing the cleaning products to the side, and handed Rob jeans, a tee-shirt, and trainers.

"I've got all kinds of stuff in lost and found. Guys leave their crap in these lockers all the time. Take them. They're yours." His gruff, deep voice had an unexpected kindness to it.

Rob appreciatively took the clothes and began to slip them on.

Bolton grinned. "At first blush, OMJ could easily be that crusty, old neighbor who yells at kids running across his front lawn. But that isn't the case. He's a champion to all the guys who work out here."

OMJ raised an eyebrow as Bolton continued.

"Sure, he can be cranky at times, and he looks the part of an old boxing trainer, but he's a softy at heart. He knows what we need before we do."

Chase joined the conversation. "He's like a guardian angel to the dudes in the gym. He always seems to be in the right place at the right time to lend a hand."

OMJ waved a hand impatiently. "I ain't gonna ask why you appeared from nowhere in the steam room wearing nothing but a towel. That isn't my business."

"He needs clothes if he's coming home with me," Chase muttered.

OMJ narrowed his eyes. "Well, still, just in case, best lock your bedroom door tonight so you don't get murdered in your sleep. I've seen those stranger-danger movies." And with that chilling statement and a mischievous smirk, he turned and left the room.

Rob noticed Chase had turned a bit pale at OMJ's statement, so he hastened to reassure him. "I'm not programmed to kill yet," he promised. "So, no worries. You'll be safe with me."

Bolton laughed out loud while Chase simply looked dumbstruck. "Thanks—I think," he said finally. "Ready to go then?"

***

Chase pressed his code into the front door to his townhouse. The ornate wooden door swung open, and the entrance lit up. He turned to Rob.

"My world is all about automation. I love tech. Anything electronic with flashing lights and circuits fascinates me."

Rob's excitement peaked at seeing the place. The vastness of it was a stark contrast to the cramped box he'd been regularly stored in. He found it impressive that humans could create such inviting habitats. It was decorated with large stuffed leather couches and classic, turn-of-the-century inspired furniture, looking like a page out of a Pottery Barn catalog.

"I'm critically depleted. My internal sensors indicate I only have 10% power left. I need to recharge."

Chase looked puzzled. "Uh, sure. Are you, like, one of those Star Trek science fiction fans?"

Now it was Rob's turn to look puzzled. He didn't know what Star Trek was.

Chase shook his head. "Never mind. Let me show you to your room." Chase pointed up the marble staircase with a reassuring nod, indicating where Rob would be sleeping.

Rob's room was fantastic. It had all the works; A large bed, a modern desk with a laptop computer, and a spacious bathroom. He was excited to make the most of all the fantastical things provided him (all except the bathroom, as he had little need for that, but he knew he'd make good use of the king-sized bed).

"I'm out of here by six in the morning to hit the gym, then head to work, so that you know." With that, Chase bid his final goodnight and disappeared into the room across from Rob's. A slight but audible click told Rob that Chase had locked his door.

Rob entered his room. First things first—recharge. He made his way to the large black desk across the room— a high-back leather chair with wheels made for the perfect recharge station. Rob made himself comfortable in the chair and pulled the computer in front of him. From the tip of Rob's index finger, a USB jack emerged. Dr. Herbie had provided Rob with several ways to recharge—one being a conventional plug with two brass prongs that could fit comfortably in a standard wall socket, as well as a USB interface for programming updates and power.

The surge of power through Rob's finger was a welcomed sensation. He'd grown concerned at his low battery levels. His battery had never been powered below 50% in the past. He wasn't sure what would happen if he went into reserve mode. No matter now, though. He was well on his way to a full charge. Once his power cell was fully fortified, he'd power down and set his internal timer for five a.m.

While he absorbed the energy he needed, he thought he'd take time to learn more about his new roommate. Rob could quickly learn all about Chase from everything available online.

He grinned to himself. The internet provided business backgrounds, government census, and social media files. All these, in addition to photos, painted quite the complete picture of someone's life.

***

"Go, Go, Power Rangers," chimed Chase's phone. He reached across groggily to his side table and silenced the tune. He knew it was a silly alarm, but he didn't care. It reminded him of his favorite show when he was a kid. Chase loved heroes. He was a fan of the underdog, and the idea that five ordinary kids could come together and defeat evil was awesome.

He didn't function on all eight cylinders when he first opened his eyes. In fact, Chase instead coasted through his morning rituals on autopilot until he got to the gym. Powerlifting was the thing that got his body and brain pumping and primed for the day. Chase didn't want to think about waking up alone, without his ex, Rebecca.

Truth be told, she'd been emotionally absent from the relationship for a while. While the relationship wasn't passionate, it had been okay. He cared for Rebecca, but he wasn't in love with her. She was just someone who kept him from being lonely.

Chase slipped into his workout gear, grabbed his neatly prepared gym backpack with clothes for the day, and headed downstairs to make coffee. He was completely unaware of what he was about to find.

The first of Chase's senses to be greeted was his sense of smell. It was the aroma of bacon, fresh ground coffee, and pecan toffee pancakes. It hit him like a sucker punch from the past. He hadn't smelled the mouthwatering aroma of pecan toffee pancakes since his Nanna had made them when he was a boy. And bacon hadn't been present in Chase's diet since he could remember. It was a favorite food, but something he'd eliminated a long, long time ago for health reasons. His curiosity piqued as he made his way downstairs.

He wasn't sure what to make of the sight in front of him. Rob had found Rebecca's apron and was wearing it as he stood at the stove. Only the apron.

Now, Chase knew that Rob had no clothes with him other than the ones OMJ had given him. But he didn't expect Rob to be only wearing an apron this morning as he prepared breakfast. He was even more convinced he'd let a crazy person into his house. It was an incredible sight to behold, for sure, but he wasn't sure what his next steps should be.

Rob turned and smiled so brightly that almost every perfect tooth in his mouth could be seen. He held up a fresh-off-the-griddle pecan hotcake with one hand and freshly tapped maple syrup in the other. "Morning," he chirped.

Chase blinked. *If this is going to be my last day on this earth, I'm certainly going out with a full stomach.* He pulled out the chair from under the table and sat down as the plate of gourmet food was set in front of him.

Before Chase could take his first mouthful, a piping hot mug of coffee slid next to his plate. Across from him, Rob stood expectantly, no doubt waiting for

Chase's response. He bit into the pancakes and was instantly transported to his Nanna's table. The kitchen he'd sat in when he was a child — a place where his Nanna fussed about him in a manner not so dissimilar to the way Rob was attending to him now. The placement of yet another hot cake and more syrup snapped Chase out of his reminiscing. He figured he was in some kind of surreal dream. The thick-cut fresh bacon was crisped to perfection; the pancakes, perfect. Both triggered warm memories of when he'd sat down with his Nanna and eagerly gobbled down pancakes that made him feel loved and adored.

And the almost naked man wearing an apron was something of a tasty treat too. Chase caught himself admiring Rob's perfectly shaped, muscular, tear-drop ass, evident each time he turned from the table to refresh Chase's coffee. Chase had never in his wildest imagination thought he'd find another man appealing. But there was no doubt, given the growing erection in his sweatpants. The sight of Rob naked in the kitchen preparing breakfast turned him on.

What the hell is going on with me?

Chapter 7

The instant Herbie hit the delete button on the master files for ROB's construction, he regretted it. He still carried the blueprints on creating another Rob in his mind. That couldn't be erased. But the software to track him was now gone. In his hands, Herbie held Rob's new heart, the hydrogen power source that would enable Rob to run for an indefinite amount of time.

How the hell am I ever going to find him and replace the battery that is no doubt beginning to fail?

Rob had been gone only a day now, but Herbie missed him like crazy. Kyle rushed into the factory's laboratory, flushed and flummoxed.

"Bentley's on the warpath," Kyle announced. "He's expecting results about the whereabouts of Rob by now, and so far, we've given him nothing. Rob's been gone for over 24 hours."

Herbie scowled. "I thought I'd been clear in my position to that man that I'd continue creating domestic robots and factory workers, but killing machines are out of the question. Rob is gone. He can't be found, and I can't help them trace him."

Rob's escape was something Bentley and the General would not accept lightly.

Corporal Matthew entered the lab with a barely muttered, "Morning." He sat down and started to look through the computers, fingers tapping furiously.

"It's gone. Don't bother looking," Herbie snapped at him.

Matthew kept digging through the files on the screen. "Pardon me if I don't believe you. I'm sure you installed some form of tracking device. If you're not going to tell me where he is, I'll just have to find him some other way to locate him."

Herbie found Matthew's tone abrasive, if not condescending. "It's all gone, all the software. Anything remotely able to disclose Rob's whereabouts has been scrubbed clean. Search all you like, but no one is going to find him."

Matthew barely looked up from the terminal screen before replying snidely, "We'll see about that."

Standing nearby was a partially assembled prototype of Rob. The earlier model lacked the capabilities of Rob; it was for all intents and purposes as sophisticated as a Roomba, but it did resemble Rob in physical appearance. With a quick flip of the wrist, Matthew snapped a photo of the robot's head with his phone. Without further words or interactions, he slipped out of the laboratory. He was clearly on a mission. Herbie knew he needed to find Rob first—but how?

***

Flat on his back at the bench press, Chase's forehead was less than a foot from the bulging bratwurst of his spotting partner, Beau. Chase thought himself fortunate that Beau was wearing tight gym shorts that kept his sizable sausage secure. At five feet eight inches tall and weighing in at one hundred and seventy-five pounds, Beau was still small compared to the rest of the bros—

—but his package was not. Chase couldn't help but fear Beau's apt appendage would fall out from his workout gear and hit him in the face. He could easily be blinded if that beast were to fall unfettered into his eye.

Chase was benching an impressive three hundred pounds. Up to this point, he'd never given any of his friends' crotches a second thought when they spotted him. Today, however, was different. He was wholly preoccupied with his amorous thoughts about Rob.

"You good down there, man?" Beau inquired.

"Yeah, yeah," Chase said, attempting to convince him he was mentally present.

"Screw this, let's steam," Beau said playfully.

Chase was satisfied with the work he'd done so far this morning, so he conceded. He pressed out one more set with a mighty guttural grunt, then proclaimed, "Let's do it!"

Bolton was already mid-stream by the time Beau and Chase joined. Ryan and Tad were also there. Like clockwork, they arrived at seven each morning. And today's topic of conversation—just like yesterday and the day before—was all about sex.

Chase rolled his eyes as he sat down and caught up on the chit-chat. To the best of his knowledge, Chase was the only straight man in the steam room. Each of the other guys comfortably identified as somewhere in the middle of the fluidity spectrum. All but Ryan, who emphatically and proudly identified himself as an authentic "gold star gay." This defined him as a homosexual man who had never touched a vagina. He was a true gold star because he'd been born by Cesarean and wore the badge proudly.

Ryan was old-school hip and liked clothes that were either vintage or that he hoped he'd start trending. He was a man with a mojo very much his own. Clothes that shouldn't work together somehow became stylish on his lean, toned frame.

He was a confident, sexy man with deep hazel eyes and rich dark skin.

Ryan loved being a man as well as making love to them. Moreover, he was eager to sample as many of them as possible.

Tad was athletic and well-defined with a hairless swimmer's build. He had thick, straight, black hair with amber eyes to complement his pristine complexion. Tad wasn't sure what his ethnicity was since he was adopted. Whatever it was, though, it was an excellent combination. Tad identified himself as "vibe-sexual" and explained it as, "If I dig your vibe, I'm down with something sexual." He had a propensity for wearing bright, tight clothes — especially spandex. There was no such thing as "too tight." He had impeccable taste and wore only the most expensive of brands.

The men all relaxed as the steam hissed through the vents. The moist, hot air hugged their muscular, sweat-glistened bodies. Today, Chase's breakup and the addition of Rob — the burly, bright-eyed stranger — seemed to be the hot topic of the day. Chase knew that he'd be interrogated about both subjects, so he braced for the onslaught of questions to come.

"Is it too soon to ask if I can ask Rebecca out?" was the first question out of the gate from Tad. Chase grimaced. No surprise there. Tad, like Bolton, had a habit of picking up Chase's ex. But the difference between Tad and Bolton was that where Bolton seemed to always fail with Chase's exes eventually, Tad excelled. He dated them for a while, then moved on to his next conquest. Unlike Chase, Tad wasn't looking for love. All he wanted was a good time. His favorite saying was, "There's plenty of fish in the sea, and I'm a master fisherman."

Chase didn't know how Tad could do it. Chase himself wanted love in the worst way but could never find it. Perhaps I'm broken. I seem to lack the ability to connect emotionally and physically with anyone.

"You take Rebecca, and I'll take the stud Chase is living with. I hear from Bolton that he's hella hot. Can you put in a good word for me?" pleaded Ryan.

"I'll bring him in tomorrow to meet you guys," quipped Chase. He thought for a second about telling them about the insane and excellent breakfast Rob had prepared for him this morning. Chase knew that if he brought up the breakfast, it would prompt a litany of speculation about Rob he wasn't prepared to sit through at this time. His Apple Watch gently chimed. The chime saved him.

He stood up and tightened his towel around his waist. "Time for work, guys. It's going to be a hectic day."

***

Even though Rob was wearing worn jeans and the tee-shirt given to him by OMJ the day before, his good looks still stopped traffic in West Hollywood. He'd researched where to shop in Los Angeles for the best men's clothing, and Melrose Ave seemed the place to go.

An eager salesman spotted Rob right away outside the shop as he glanced casually into the window. Without missing a beat, the salesman made a beeline toward Rob.

"Wow, look at you, a six-foot-something of hunky hotness. How can I be of service? My name's Bryce, by the way. It rhymes with nice. And I assure you I live up to my name," chimed the thin, young man, batting his eyes as if in the presence of his favorite teen idol. Rob quickly scanned the salesman. He had a unique and attractive vibe: a trendy haircut, skinny jeans, leather designer shoes, and a breezy pullover. The salesman's observation of Rob's "hunky hotness" revealed to Rob that this young man had a sexuality geared towards other men. Rob produced the credit card Herbie gave him and handed it to the enthralled millennial.

"I was given this credit card. I need to look stylish and attractive. Can you help me get there?"

Bryce was quick to take the card and look at the name on it. "Herbert McAlister? This is you, right?"

"No, it's my owner," answered Rob.

Without missing a beat, Bryce understood. "I've got a 'daddy' too. I just work here for the discounts. Let's get you out of those old clothes and see what we can do." He winked, then escorted Rob into the largest of changing rooms, where he proceeded to help Rob disrobe.

Rob stood in the changing room as if he were a gift sent just for Bryce. Bryce's uninhibited nature impressed him. He was confident that this young man would enjoy the package he was about to unwrap. First, Bryce opened the top rivet of Rob's jeans, then kneeled in front of him. "Let's get these off you so I can take a proper measurement," he playfully joked.

Rob wasn't sure how professional this was turning out to be, but he wasn't going to complain. After all, this was why he'd been designed.

The pulling down of his zipper was soon accompanied by the clerk's hands wrapping around Rob's ripe rump. Bryce loosened the tight jeans that clung to Rob's rock-hard glutes. As the jeans fell, Bryce was positioned precariously close to Rob.

He grinned sultrily. "Ooh, I expected to find briefs or boxers underneath, but I'm pleasantly surprised that you're commando today. Every boy's dream." He licked his lips. "You came out of a wonderful mold, honey."

Rob nodded. "My master didn't skimp on anything when he assembled me. Especially the parts designed to please. He told me that parts of me were inspired by his favorite movie star, Jeff Stryker."

"Lucky me," Bryce murmured.

As the jeans fell, Rob's mighty man member was released from its denim dungeon. As if Babe Ruth was taking a swing for the outfield, Rob's boy bat bounced out from behind the zipper and swung like a perky pendulum in front of Bryce's face.

"Careful! You could give a guy a concussion with that thing!" he squealed with delight.

"Sorry," Rob apologized. "Maybe it would be best if I put it someplace else for safekeeping?"

Bryce's eyes lit up. "I have just the spot." He leaned and whispered his directive to Rob. Rob's primary directive to please was engaged. Under Rob's skilled hands and with the mechanical precision of a Swiss watch, Bryce's skinny jeans were removed and catapulted over the dressing room door. Bryce was pushed down and splayed across the dressing room bench, ready for the taking.

"I'm ready," Bryce gasped.

Rob knew that Bryce wasn't remotely ready for what

Rob was about to give him, but he would receive it anyway. Given the groans of delight and constant squeals of surprise coming from the young salesman's mouth as Rob pounded away, Bryce hadn't been prepared whatsoever.

Chapter 8

B ack at work, Chase sat at his desk reviewing his emails. He scowled at the screen. Every day seemed to create new challenges and problems for him and his team. Every new email arriving in his inbox threatened to delay the big museum opening he was preparing for next week.

Chase had worked for five years on this Los Angeles Museum. It featured the most extensive and impressive private art collection in the world. It would be America's Louvre. Chase had always been inspired by all things French. He looked forward to the day that he could take the time to immerse himself in a cultural tour of France.

From behind him, he heard the soft fluttering of his assistant, Jane. She was a cute girl, pretty and wholesome looking. She had shoulder-length brown hair and wore trendy eyeglasses to give her otherwise ordinary appearance some pizzazz.

Jane was smitten with him, and she did her best to look good in hopes of catching his attention. Chase certainly appreciated her as an assistant and was pleased with her work, but nothing would ever happen beyond work. Jane had a nervous tic around Chase. She rambled incessantly about the most random and curious things whenever he was nearby.

It could be endearing learning about how she'd had a

pet chicken named "Clucky" when she was growing up or how her elbows were double-jointed. But with Chase's deadlines looming, he didn't have the time to engage in her adorable drivel. He'd asked others in the office if they noticed her flirty chatter, but no one seemed to know what he was talking about. Apparently, it was only him who caused her strange mannerism.

"Exciting, isn't it?" she said. "The big day, less than a week away. Black-tie no less. I've got your tickets—two of them. It looks like you're bringing a date. Is Rebecca coming? I'm so excited about this opening. It's a huge accomplishment for you. We are all so excited for you."

Chase chuckled to himself, wondering how many sentences she could get out without taking a breath. Jane inhaled, ready to launch into another string of nervous ramblings. Chase needed to stop her before the next onslaught began. He took the two tickets from her hand and derailed her with a heart-stopping smile.

"Thank you for these, Jane. I'm not sure who I'll bring yet, but I appreciate you dropping them off." Chase refocused his attention on the computer, hoping Jane took the hint that they were done with their interaction. To his relief, she giggled gleefully and left his office.

Chase was quite flattered by how flummoxed she became in his presence. What to do with this extra ticket. Jane?

No, he decided. Her sweet, innocent heart probably couldn't take the excitement of being on a formal date with him. Chase wasn't conceited; he just thought it was cute how Jane behaved in his presence. And, it couldn't help giving his failing ego a little boost.

One day he hoped to feel that way about someone. He

wondered what it would be like to have butterflies in his stomach and feel his heart racing from being near someone who thrilled him. Chase feared that he just wasn't built like that. He was sad that he probably would never know those feelings. He wondered if he was incapable of being in love.

***

Back at the shop, Rob and his new friend Bryce had completed getting to know each other…as well as shopping. Bryce had equipped Rob with bags of clothes ranging from casual attire to man-killer sexy. There were over a dozen outfits for any occasion that could arise for a single man on the make.

Now was the moment of truth—time to ring up the purchases. Rob had never shopped before and wasn't sure how it all worked. But the gasp of horror at the tally from someone standing beside him was an indicator of the high cost.

Bryce smiled coyly at Rob. "I've given you everything for 50% off—the friends and family discount. All I want in return is your promise to come by again and see me."

Rob didn't understand what the fifty percent off really meant. He did, however, understand that Bryce had thoroughly enjoyed himself in the dressing room earlier and wanted another go-around at a later time.

"Sure—happy to," Rob gleefully replied, with the full intention of giving Bryce another pounding at a later date. After all, that was what he did best.

Bryce lit up like a five-year-old at the promise of Christmas approaching. "Here's another top that I know will look amazing on you," and with a quick wink, Bryce peeled a beautiful button-down dress shirt off the rack, folded it, and placed it in the already full shopping bags. Rob thanked him for his generosity and made haste home. Chase would return soon, and Rob wanted to make sure he walked into a clean, perfect place with a hot meal on the table. As Rob turned and left with his overstuffed bags, Bryce beamed at him, watching Rob's rear as he walked away.

"See you soon," Bryce called out.

***

Chase retrieved his car from the valet and wondered briefly where he should go. Should he head home, or perhaps buy some time at a movie? Was Rob still at the house, and if so, what was he up to? Chase still wasn't sure about what had happened this morning. It seemed odd that Rob would wake up super early, go shopping and make Chase's favorite breakfast. It was also weird that Chase had felt a strange arousal at the sight of a nearly naked man making pancakes. Deciding he was too tired to stay awake at a theater and too beat to work out; Chase became a little agitated.

I can't become a stranger in my home. I need to go back to my place.

Chase pointed his Range Rover towards home and made his way through the busy city streets, resolved in his decision.

Whatever weirdness I arrive home to, I'll deal with it.

***

Rob had been busy in Chase's apartment. Earlier, he'd topped off his battery and downloaded a Martha

Stewart book about creating the ultimate dining experience. Rob had sliced, diced, and sautéed his way through the lessons he'd learned from Martha Stewart's videos and cookbook. He'd prepared a culinary masterpiece for Chase. Rob was determined to create the ultimate seductive experience for him. Tonight would be the thing Rob was built for: total satisfaction. The table was set, complete with candles and linen napkins.

The automatic door-lock keypad could be heard throughout the house. Chase is home! Rob sprung quickly into action, setting the stage for his arrival.

Chase entered his home, placed his leather bag near the door, and hung up his suit jacket. From across the large hall, he could already smell that Rob had again prepared a fabulous feast. Music echoed softly through the corridors, and an aroma that could only be described as enchanting filled the air. Upon turning the corner from the hall, Rob greeted Chase with a hearty hello. Chase was floored at all the effort he put into the evening's meal. More impressive than Rob's preparation for the evening was Rob's appearance in his perfectly form-fitting new clothes.

Whoa. He looks incredibly sexy.

Rob was dressed casually yet smart—looking as if he'd been styled directly out of a fashion magazine. He must have been shopping. Kudos to whoever sold him that outfit.

Bubbling pots and pans created a symphony of fragrances that danced across Chase's nose. He started to salivate. Was it the spices tickling his olfactory senses or the way Rob looked in that tightknit pullover? Either way, Chase gratefully accepted the glass of wine Rob handed him and quickly toasted to a relaxing evening.

***

Dinner was over, and Rob insisted on cleaning up. Chase didn't put up much of a fight. His belly was full, and he was feeling relaxed from the wine.

What a fantastic dinner that was. Prime rib, twice-baked potatoes with chives and sour cream, sautéed asparagus, tomato salad, and freshly baked bread. Chase was too full to eat dessert after all that food! *Jeez,* he thought. *Between breakfast and dinner, I'll gain 10 pounds for each day Rob stays here. I'll have to find a way to politely tell him that I can't continue to eat like this.*

***

Rob was like a machine as he cleaned up. The table was cleared effortlessly, with no wasted movements. The dishwasher was started and hummed away instantly.

This dude is super-human, Chase thought. Classic Blues music started playing. *Hmmm,* Chase thought, *I didn't see Rob turn on the stereo.* B.B. King. Chase's favorite. His thoughts melted away as he relaxed into the plush leather sofa.

"Do you mind if I join you in the living room?" Rob asked, a hesitant look on his face.

"Please!" invited Chase. "I think I need to learn a little bit more about you, seeing as how you're my new housemate."

"Okay. Let me slip into something more comfortable," Rob murmured. Chase chuckled as he sat back on the couch. *Had that been a hint of a tease he'd heard in Rob's voice?*

Ten minutes later, Rob joined Chase on the couch. He

flopped right down next to Chase, wearing only a tank top and sweatpants. Rob seemed remarkably at ease with himself, something which impressed Chase. Most people kept their guard up or showed some form of restrictive behavior. As a guy, Chase knew about physical boundaries — gay, straight, or bi — it didn't matter; there were rules to be followed when in the proximity of another dude. Bathrooms, for example. You never used the urinal next to another guy unless all the others were occupied. Movie theater seats were the same. Always leave a seat between you and your neighbor. If there was a couch in a room and a chair nearby, you sat on the seat while your buddy took the sofa. Rob, however, didn't seem to know or care about the rules. Chase found it refreshing and strangely hot.

"How did things go at work? Good day?" Rob inquired. Chase smiled at the question. *How domestic,* he thought. He couldn't ever remember being asked about his day before.

"Stressful, I have to admit. I have a huge museum opening next week, and I've got to find a date for it." Before Chase realized, he'd been going on for about twenty minutes. There was no denying that it felt good to download the happenings of the day over a second glass of wine. Rob sat and nodded or smiled, seeming genuinely engaged about Chase's bout of verbal diarrhea. *This is a pleasant end to the day,* Chase thought. *I could get used to coming home to a warm meal and a person genuinely interested in my life.* Chase stopped himself from talking and returned the courtesy.

"Enough about my day. What did you do?"

Rob's eyes lit up. "I went shopping, found this amazing store. The sales assistant was lovely to me. Then I came home and busied myself in the kitchen. It seems that I can cook. Oh, I also found I have a new skill. Wait right here." Rob ran out of the room, and within seconds was back in the room, holding Chase's electric guitar.

"Oh, I have no idea how to play that," Chase chuckled. "It was an impulse buy last year. I always wanted to learn how to play an instrument, and I thought there was nothing cooler than a custom Les Paul guitar."

"I'll teach you! I downloaded every lesson you'll ever need," Rob said excitedly. With that, he proceeded to wail on the guitar in a way that would have made Jimmy Hendrix take note.

"Damn bro, you're amazing." Chase was blown away at Rob's skills.

"We could start lessons tomorrow if you'd like!" Rob offered. Chase smiled at the thought of finally learning how to play.

"We'll see. Let's talk about it tomorrow. I'm too beat and overwhelmed from work to take on anything new this week."

Rob seemed happy to revisit the idea with Chase when he was less tired. Chase had immensely enjoyed the evening, although he didn't want to admit that it felt more like a date than a night at home with a roommate.

Rob shifted closer to Chase, sitting next to him as if waiting on Chase to make the first move. Chase wasn't sure what to do.

Am I imagining the sexual energy between us? Is Rob attracted to me? The bigger question is; am I attracted to Rob? God, I'm so confused.

He'd never felt sexual attraction towards another man. Could all this be in his head? They sat on the couch a bit longer, Chase fidgeting, not knowing what to do. He couldn't take his eyes off Rob's lap where his massive man-missile lay across his thigh, seemingly waiting for the countdown before taking off. Chase wanted to touch it.

He swallowed nervously and looked down at his own impressively large pant piston. *This is too weird for me. A straight dude like me shouldn't be thinking about another guy's goods.* Chase shifted gears and thought it best to realign this relationship from a possible date vibe to strictly heterosexual bros hanging out together.

"Hey, I'm hitting the gym tomorrow. I'm sure you want to work out. Do you feel like getting a set in with me before I head to work?"

"Absolutely," replied Rob excitedly.

Chase quickly adjusted the relationship parameters a bit further. "Oh, and no breakfast, please. Not that today wasn't great, but a protein smoothie will be just fine. Another morning of your pecan pancakes, and I won't be able to see my abs anymore."

They both laughed as Rob agreed to comply with Chase's wishes.

"No more fattening foods from now on," Rob promised. With that, they lifted themselves off the couch to go to their respective bedrooms.

Even then, things didn't go as smoothly as Chase had hoped. In the hallway, he could swear Rob was waiting for him to invite him into his bedroom. The moment before they parted for the night seemed to last forever. The thought of kissing Rob actually did cross Chase's mind, but only for a second before he ousted any such nonsense of hooking up from his head. "Well, good night then. See you at six a.m." Chase proclaimed huskily. Rob smiled warmly and nodded to acknowledge Chase's statement before he disappeared into his room, seemingly without a care in the world.

Chase locked the door and quickly disrobed. He folded his jeans and tee and placed them next to the hamper in his room. He jumped into his sleep shorts with a quick hop and then peeled back the bedsheets. His king-size bed, complete with a down comforter, awaited his presence, and he was thrilled to comply. "Ahh," he sighed. "This feels good." He lay there waiting for sleep to take him away, but his thoughts kept going back to his evening with Rob. What a fantastic time he'd had. It had been the perfect end to a stressful day. A great meal, music, and wine capped off with friendly, intelligent, and therapeutic conversation. Why couldn't his relationships with his girlfriends be this pleasant, he wondered? Chase didn't want to acknowledge the sexual vibe he'd felt for Rob only moments earlier. He tried to dismiss it from his mind, but before he knew what he was doing, his hand crept down the front of his shorts and wrapped itself around his thick and excited boy baton.

"God, that feels good," he sighed as he rubbed himself over and over, eventually lowering his sleep shorts for better access. As much as he tried to clear his head and just focus on how good pleasuring himself felt, his mind kept bouncing between visions of Rob's assets. The round, bubble butt he flaunted as he flipped the flapjacks this morning, and the beefy outline of his lap log evident through the sweatpants, practically inviting Chase to grab it. Before Chase could conjure an image of a woman who made him feel the same way, his groin tensed, his toes curled, and his testicles tightened. Several seconds and many mighty moans later, the evidence of his sexual frustration and confusion was spattered across his pecs and abs.

The drawer in his nightstand provided a box of tissues for him to clean himself up with. After a few quick wipes, he drifted off to deep slumber, leaving his most confusing day behind.

Chapter 9

C orporal Matthew entered his twenty-fifth bar that day and heaved a soul-draining sigh. Looking for Rob had been a tiring task, and as of yet, he'd discovered nothing. He'd canvassed most of Encino, getting more and more discouraged about ever finding a clue.

The night was wrapping up for most. The last of the restaurants had closed. A smattering of bars was finishing up and encouraging patrons to find their way home.

Behind the dark mahogany bar stood a woman. She was blonde, in her early forties, and wore a camisole top and apple bottom jeans with cowboy boots. Matthew could sense she wasn't happy to see him. He imagined the last thing she wanted at this time of night was another patron.

"Has this man been in the bar?" he asked as he held up his phone featuring a picture of ROB. According to her name tag, the bartender's name was Sally. She looked like a woman who'd seen it all. She'd probably been in the bar business a long time from the looks of her. Sally *was* a pretty woman with rich auburn hair and striking blue eyes. She was in impressive shape and had a curvy sex appeal that made it hard not to notice her. The Corporal felt a spark of interest as she stared at him, a look of appreciation in her eyes.

"I love me a man in uniform," she said. "And you fill out that uniform well. Tight in all the right places and with buttons that sparkle like stars in a dark lonely night."

Matthew shifted, not sure what to say. "So, have you seen this man?" he tried again.

"Who's asking?" she replied, her voice husky, in a sultry feminine way.

"The U.S. government, Ma'am—highest priority and top secret."

Sally shook her head and came around the front of the bar. "Don't think I've seen him. I'll need a closer look at that photo. Come into the back room where the light is better."

Matthew saw the glance she threw the last waitress finishing her shift. It was a knowing one, communicating with the other woman on a level he couldn't comprehend. The secret women code was in full force because the waitress rolled her eyes and smiled as she disappeared into the kitchen.

Sally and Matthew stepped into what looked like a small back office. "I'm happy to help you and Uncle Sam the best I can. But first, I'll need something to help me jog my memory, Private."

At first, Matthew wasn't sure what she meant, but Sally's hand cupping his crotch made it clear that if he wanted any information from her, he'd have to perform for it. He didn't bother correcting her, addressing him as a Private. Ranks were a little non-essential right at this minute. He was about to get laid.

Inside his pants, Matthew stood at full salute as Sally palmed the back of his head and pulled him towards her. Within seconds, their mouths were locked together.

"I'm going to show you what tricks a woman of my age can teach a young man like you." Matthew's uniform dropped to his ankles. As his dress blues were practically torn open, Sally rubbed his tight, defined pectoral muscles. "Care to show me what one of the country's finest fighting men is capable of?"

Matthew decided he'd do his best to rise to the occasion and show her what the few and the proud were made of.

**

Chase and Rob were both up at six a.m. and met in the hall outside their bedroom doors. Chase had his suit on a hanger and toted a gym bag. They greeted each other with a friendly, warm smile and headed to the Mission Gym together.

Chase had a competitive nature. He fancied himself the alpha male, proud of most everything he did. A hard and dedicated worker, it was rare that anyone ever had an advantage over him. Rob, however, had challenged everything Chase knew about himself. No matter what skill Chase seemed to master, Rob seemed to do it easier and faster.

They stood in the heart of the Mission Gym. Chase's sanctum. This was where he was king. Even though Rob's size indicated he was stronger than Chase, Chase was up for the challenge, anxious to see what power Rob really possessed. It was titan vs. titan, as Chase viewed it. There'd be a war waged in the gym this morning to see who was the biggest and best.

Pound for pound, Rob seemed to match Chase. Chase lifted more, but when Rob lifted, it seemed effortless. Was Rob mocking him? After an hour of grueling lifting, Chase knew he'd be sore the next day, whereas Rob didn't flinch. It seemed he needed no recovery time, nor would he even experience any pain tomorrow from the excruciating lifting they'd done. Even though the victor in today's competition, Chase felt as if he had lost and lost badly. Rob had not a drop of sweat on him, and his breathing hadn't changed from the easy clockwork pattern he held. Chase, however, huffed and puffed, trying to gain ground over Rob at every exercise. He also wanted to see the guys in the steam room before work, so he conceded it was time to relent. Rob and Chase got out of their gym clothes and into their towels and ducked into the steam room to greet the guys for their morning ritual.

***

Unlike Bolton's subtle "wow" two days prior, Ryan lacked any subtlety whatsoever when Chase entered with Rob.

"Holy shit," Ryan announced. "Now that's one heck of a man."

Chase was embarrassed at Ryan's exclamation, but Rob didn't seem to mind. He smiled and extended his hand to Ryan.

"Hi, I'm Rob," he said, smiling.

"Yeah, you are—you just robbed my heart," Ryan exclaimed. The terrible pun caused collective grunts and eye-rolls from the guys.

Bolton was quick to step in. "Rob is Chase's new roommate, so take it easy there." Chase wasn't sure whether that was a subtle way of saying Rob was off-limits to Ryan.

"And where are you from, may I ask?" Ryan pressed

on.

"I was created a few miles away," Rob answered.

"Encino General Hospital, right? Me too." Ryan said.

Chase knew if he didn't step in and take control of the conversation, it would become a conversation all about Ryan trying to get into Rob's pants. Chase wasn't in the mood to listen to any of Ryan's feeble flirtations. He wondered uncomfortably why he was so protective of Rob.

Talking about work and the upcoming event was just the distraction he needed.

"Are you guys coming to my big opening next week?" Chase inquired.

"I'd love to....and then maybe we can check out your museum?" said Ryan with a guffaw.

Laughs and fist bumps flew. Chase shook his head in amusement. For a group of educated, full-grown men, they acted like a kindergarten class with him as the substitute teacher.

He pressed on. "It's black-tie only. Let me know if you'd like to go. It's a fundraiser, so tickets go for $1,000 apiece; but of course, I'll get you guys in for free."

The guys looked around at each other. It seemed to Chase that they weren't enthusiastic about attending and were waiting to see who'd be the first to tell him.

"No offense, bro, but why would anyone want to spend a few hundred dollars on a tux to attend a stuffy, black-tie event attended by snobs? We're your basic bros, just beer and booty on our agenda for a Saturday night. We love you dude, but fancy parties just aren't us." Bolton shrugged his broad shoulders.

"I'd love to join you!" chimed in Rob with a happy smile. "It'd be cool to wear a tux."

Bolton laughed. "Looks like you got yourself a date, Chase. You guys have fun."

"What great bros you are," Chase teased. "Thanks for the support."

The guys all felt a little guilty about not attending the event for their friend, but they couldn't deny that they were grateful they didn't need to get dressed for a pretentious party.

Chase was a little hurt that the guys weren't interested in seeing his work. On the other hand, he was excited to spend the night alone with Rob, for what was beginning to feel like a date. He knew that Rob would not only be great company, but he'd be all kinds of sexy in a tuxedo.

***

Herbie sat in Bentley's office, nervously waiting for him to arrive. He couldn't help but feel that he was called into the principal's office. He sighed. "I'm going to be raked over the coals for letting Rob escape and erasing his tracking software, aren't I?" he muttered gloomily to the potted plant in the corner. His stomach dropped in nervous anticipation. Herbie had been waiting for over twenty minutes now for Bentley. He knew that keeping him waiting was some sort of power play since Bentley didn't actually have that much to do all day. Bentley's main job was to appease the company's shareholders by making sure deadlines were made. If Bentley wasn't in his office or on the phone, where was he?

Herbie wondered if he should help himself to the cappuccino machine in Bentley's office. It was an intricate chrome machine with a separate grinder for beans. He grimaced. On second thought, it was simply too much trouble to set it all up just for a cup of coffee.

He sat back down, thirsty, when suddenly Bentley stormed in. He took an aggressive stance. Rather than sitting at his desk, he leaned against the corner of it and glared at Herbie.

"What is this about deleting my software? That's company property," he bellowed. There was deep concern — or was it fear — in Bentley's eyes? "The company spent millions to develop a robot for the military, and now all that data and the prototype are gone."

Time to put on my big boy pants.

"I was told to design the ultimate android," Herbie shot back. A robot that could please every desire a human could have — the perfect companion. At no point was I told that it was to be a soldier who was programmed to kill. You misrepresented the job I was given. If I'd known what you really wanted, I'd never have made it." Herbie stood his ground. He was too old to be pushed around anymore.

Besides, Herbie knew that they both needed each other. The room was silent as both men stewed over the problem. Herbie was the first to speak.

"The robot will fail in several days. He's got a faulty battery that will soon deteriorate to a point where it won't accept a charge any longer." Herbie now had Bentley's undivided attention. His boss motioned to Herbie to tell him more.

"Once it goes into critical mode, and the battery goes into reserve mode, I pre-programmed and installed a beacon to notify us of his location so we could retrieve it as a failsafe geo-locator." Herbie watched as Bentley's face brightened at this newly disclosed information.

Then his face tightened.

"Why would you have installed a faulty battery in the robot in the first place?" he asked suspiciously. "Were you trying to sabotage the project?"

Herbie reached into his pocket and pulled out the new power cell. He held it up. "This was still in development at the time of the demonstration, and I hadn't yet had the chance to install it. Once ROB is found and returned to the laboratory, the new power cell can be installed. Then we'll have a perfectly powered robot that is entirely self-sufficient."

Bentley's body relaxed. "I see. This information gives me hope that I can present a solution to the General. I'm glad you're working with me and not against me, for your sake. I know you don't like the idea of the military, but I have to fulfill our obligation to the government contract we've signed." Bentley seemed to think about his next words carefully. "we're both on the hook here, and we need to get things right, for both of our sakes."

Bentley carried on, "When we get the robot back, we'll get his unique operating system's software back too, right?" Herbie nodded. "Good. I propose then that once we retrieve it, you give me the software designed to operate the android, and in exchange, you get to keep ROB. It's a win-win for both Hot Bot-y and the military. This way, everyone gets what they paid for and deserve."

Herbie mused over the proposal. It wasn't a solution he liked, but it would work. He'd have Rob returned to him, and the military would get what they'd paid for, to do what the hell they wanted to do. Herbie reached out his hand to seal their deal.

Bentley shook it.

He was looking forward to bringing Rob home.

***

Later, Bentley sat in reflection, sipping on a perfect espresso.

It would be a hard sell to the military, but he needed that ROB back. Perhaps he'd need to change some details to the agreement he'd made with Herbie to satisfy the General. And he simply wouldn't tell Herbie about the new arrangements.

So be it. There were some things Herbie didn't need to know.

Chapter 10

A s Chase entered his home after a grueling day at work, the fragrant aroma of a hot gourmet meal hit his nostrils. Another delicious meal means I'll have to add an hour to my workout tomorrow.

He walked into the kitchen to see Rob grinning at him. "Perfect timing. Heard your car pull in. Dinner is ready right now." Rob bent down to the stove.

"Wow, you must have good ears," Chase joked as he sat down at the table.

"I was designed with extra-sensory hearing. I can even hear through walls." Rob said. "Now, let me show you what's for dinner."

Chase blinked, a little confused. "You can – what?"

Rob ignored Chase. "And before you freak out at the thought of your waistline, the meal is all composed of plant-based proteins. I used only olive oil, sparingly, and each portion is less than 100 calories." He placed a plate of something delicious-smelling in front of Chase.

The two men sat at the table and began eating heartily. Chase couldn't quite believe that such a feast would be as healthy as Rob said it was.

Chase's Apple Watch gently chimed a recognizable tune—it was his "need to sleep" alarm.

Odd that the alarm is going off. It must be a glitch. It's not late. We just sat down for dinner. Without a thought, he swiped "dismiss" on his watch. As he did so, he caught sight of the time and gasped.

"Holy crap, is that the time already? It's flown by."

"We've been talking and having fun," Rob glowed. "It's been a lovely evening."

"Yeah, I need to get to bed. I'm up early again in the morning. Let me help you clean up first." Chase got up to help clear the dishes before going to bed.

Rob shook his head. "No, since I'm not paying for room or board, cleaning up is the least I can do. You go get ready for bed. Then join me on the couch for a nightcap of herbal tea?"

Chase pretended that it wasn't a good idea and that he needed to go to bed. But, in truth, the thought of hot tea and a little more time with Rob sounded ideal. Chase conceded and prepared for bed as Rob cleared dinner and put the kettle on.

Moments later, Chase joined Rob on the couch, wearing only his sleep shorts and tank top. The conundrum of appropriate personal space between them was all but gone now as Chase plopped down next to Rob and reached for his tea. He tried to ignore the sensation of Rob's leg brushing against his; they were just two dudes chilling before bed.

Chase sipped his tea and sighed in pleasure. It was the full-body sigh that released all his tensions of the day and let his body fully relax. He laid back on the couch, his arms spread against the back of the sofa.

"This is great," he said. He had never felt this comfortable and open with anyone before. Sure, he had his bros at the steam room, but they were pals — guys to joke around with and to cruise women with, and that was it. It was different with Rob. Being around him was effortless; it was something he looked forward to, a treat at the end of the day.

"I know what'll make the perfect ending to this evening," Rob murmured sultrily. Before Chase could even open his eyes to see what he meant, Rob slid his hands beneath the waistband of Chase's shorts. Immediately, as Rob gently caressed Chase's pleasure python, it became semi-hard and fit comfortably in the palm of Rob's farmer-sized hand.

Chase's brain feverishly attempted to process what was happening, even as he grew harder with Rob's touch. As his panic and pleasure rose, Chase jumped off the couch.

"What the… bro?" Chase growled angrily. "*So* not okay, buddy." He couldn't deny there was an ever-larger part of him that was totally on board with Rob's actions, and that made Chase angrier. "Dude, I should knock you out for that. Where the hell did you get the idea that I was into guys?"

He glared at Rob, seeing the confusion across the other man's face.

"I'm sorry," Rob said softly. "I must have a glitch in my program. I thought you wanted me to do that. All the signals were there."

Chase swallowed. *Was he giving off signals to get stroked by another man?* "I wasn't giving out signals." *Or was I?*

Chase stared at Rob, open-mouthed. What was with this guy? *A glitch in my programming?*

"Dude, never mind, let's chalk it up to a misunderstanding," Chase muttered, seeing Rob's crestfallen and guilty face. "I'm beat and going to bed." *Look at him. That didn't help. He looks totally shocked. I should say something else. I'm an idiot.*

"We're cool, bud, so don't feel bad. I'm just not into

that stuff."

Chase hurried to his room, where he hoped sleep would make things less confusing.

***

Rob sat down to cross-reference his programming with what he'd learned about life in the real world. His database assessed that there was no problem, concluding that Chase simply didn't like foreplay before going to bed. "Good to know," Rob murmured. "I'll figure out another way to please him."

One thing was clear to Rob. The night was over, and it was time to power down and recharge.

***

When the sun rose, Rob was fully juiced and ready to go. He stood outside Chase's room, prepared to go to the gym. After no sign of Chase, Rob opened the door and realized it was empty. *Hmm,* Rob computed. *Perhaps Chase had forgotten about him? Or he'd got the time wrong?* Rob played back the conversation recording where Chase had told him to be ready at six a.m.

Huh. There must have been an adjustment on Chase's end, and forgotten to let Rob know. Rob smiled. Silly humans were so susceptible to error, their brains prone to faults. Rob needed to compensate for those kinds of mistakes. Tomorrow, he'd be prepared earlier than today in case Chase made the same mistake twice.

***

Inside the Mission Gym, Bolton saw Chase going overboard lifting like never before. Between Chase's quiet demeanor and ridiculous determination, Bolton guessed something was wrong. If it were work-related, Chase would have mentioned it already. Maybe it's women problems, he thought. But he knew Chase currently did not have a new female in his life, or perhaps it was a problem with Rob. Why wouldn't Chase tell him about it if that was the case? What could have happened between them that kept Chase from talking to his best friend about it? Since Bolton wasn't one for subtly or playing games, he blurted out without a second thought, "Is everything cool with Rob?"

Chase pressed his lips together as if thinking what to say, then replied flatly, "He's fine...good. No problems." Bolton figured Chase's answer meant that the questioning was over and to leave it alone for now. If Chase wanted to talk, he would be there for him. He decided that all he could do was get a good workout in tonight and let Chase steam.

Chapter 11

Corporal Matthew was batting zero; no one had seen ROB or had any information on him. He'd canvassed all places in the area where he thought ROB would be and was at his wit's end where to search next. Since he knew that ROB didn't need to eat or work out, he skipped inquiring at the supermarkets and gyms. Not knowing any other way to approach his search, Corporal Matthew set up a parameter and strategically triangulated the vicinity where ROB could be hiding. The parameters would be the city lines within Encino—he wouldn't leave a stone unturned. He'd surgically eliminate neighborhood after neighborhood by visiting every person and establishment in the area. Moving in a calculated and organized fashion was the only way to find ROB.

***

Corporal Matthew wasn't the only one looking for Rob. Dr. Herbie was also on the move. Unlike Matthew, Dr. Herbie knew it would be days before Rob's battery would fail, and then a tracking signal would be transmitted. The trick was to keep Corporal Matthew from finding Rob before the alert was sent out, so Herbie could retrieve him first.

***

Chase couldn't concentrate at work. He felt guilty about last night and wanted to apologize to Rob. *Why did I freak out like I did?* It hadn't occurred to Chase that Rob was gay or bi or fluid. And either way, it didn't matter; he was cool with whatever. The thing that bothered Chase most was how he behaved himself at Rob's advances. He really didn't care about people's sexual orientations and now felt embarrassed about his reaction toward a friend who harmlessly made a move on him. One thing was clear to Chase; he owed Rob an apology. Distracted, he stared blankly into space. The ringing of his office phone droned on incessantly while text chimes nagged him relentlessly. No doubt it was a billion unanswered questions and task reminders about the museum gala opening, now just a week away. All Chase could think about was Rob. He held out as long as he could but finally gave in. *I can't do any work until I talk to Rob about what happened between us.*

***

Rob sat in the living room of Chase's apartment, playing the guitar. He'd downloaded every guitar technique and style so he could teach Chase how to play — whenever Chase had the time. Rob found himself playing, not to improve, but because he enjoyed it. The guitar not only emitted pleasant and harmonious sounds to his receptors, but the action of playing was curiously meditative. The experience of creating music was surprisingly fulfilling. Rob wasn't programmed to experience actual feelings, so he thought he might have been programmed to discern good from bad music. Fascinating. Could these sensations be what pleasure feels like to humans?

He was so engrossed in his playing that he didn't hear Chase's car pull up or his footsteps as he came inside.

I have extrasensory hearing and am immune to distractions. Perhaps the music transported me to another place in my programming?

Whatever the case, it was contrary to his directive to be in standby mode until a human summoned him.

"Now I know why the ladies fall for lead guitarists."

Rob started at the voice behind him. Chase stood there, eyes bright with appreciation. Seeing Rob jam on the cherry red electric Les Paul Guitar was impressive and hot.

Surprised he hadn't heard Chase approach, Rob quickly laid the guitar by his side and sprang to his feet with a big welcoming smile. "Apologies, my calculations were that you'd arrive in two hours," he blurted out.

"I wanted to finish my work from home," Chase answered warmly. He thoughtfully chose his next words, "So, about what happened on the couch. I overreacted last night. I hope we're still cool."

Rob smiled. "No apology needed. I'm glad to know your parameters—no need to discuss it further. Now, I've got to get dinner started, and you have work to do. Why don't you finish up your day, and I'll make us dinner?"

Rob smiled as he gestured toward the healthy, organic meal he was about to prepare.

Chase was relieved and excited to get on with the evening. "Dude, you're so going to spoil me," Chase joked.

"That's the idea!" Rob replied.

***

Chase enjoyed both the delicious meal and the deep conversation they had together. He realized, to his surprise, that what he looked forward to most in the day was the time he spent at home with Rob, whether it was eating meals, talking, or simply lounging on the sofa with him, sipping tea.

"Dessert?" Rob queried after their main meal was complete.

Chase could have easily fit dessert, but he wasn't one to overindulge. "I'd love to," he said, "but I really shouldn't. I can't keep eating like this." Rob nodded and gathered the dishes. As Rob was bent over, loading the dishwater, Chase realized he was staring at Rob's spectacularly muscular ass in a new pair of perfectly fitting tight jeans. Chase quietly rationalized to himself; *There is nothing wrong with a man admiring another man's impressive physique.*

Rob made a second trip to the table to gather the dishes and asked, "Are you okay?"

"Yes," Chase answered with an abnormal shortness of breath. It was unconvincing; even he had to admit.

Rob laughed. "I can sense your heart rate racing..."

Chase wasn't sure what to make of his current physical condition or how Rob seemed to know he had these strange butterflies in his stomach.

"Mind if I ask you something?" Rob inquired.

"Of course, anything," Chase replied.

"On a scale from one to ten. How would you rate the best sex you've ever had with someone?" Rob cocked his head as he waited for Chase to answer.

Odd question, Chase thought, *but safe enough.* After going through all his past girlfriends, relationships, and hookups, he tentatively but honestly replied, "About an eight?"

Rob appeared to consider his answer as if devising a strategy to the problem at hand. "How about we try for an eleven?"

At that, the earth suddenly shifted on its axis for Chase. The North and South Pole switched polarity, and the space-time continuum slowed to an odd snail's pace.

His brain attempted first to comprehend the question and then formulate an answer. Rather than articulate a well-thought-out answer to a clear and straightforward question, he looked at Rob in panic. Finally, mouth agape and body quivering, all Chase could summon was a simple, "Uh. Okay?"

As soon as the words left his mouth, he instantly found himself tightly pressed up against Rob's massive, muscular body. The way Rob lifted him off his feet and laid him on the table was as if Chase himself weighed the same as a box of tissues. This movement sent the remainder of the utensils and napkins scattering to the floor in all directions. Rob removed his shirt and started to unbutton Chase's with surgical precision. Before he knew it, Chase's mouth was hungrily covered by Rob's, and the only thing he felt was excitement and passion.

This is a man I'm with, he thought, dazed. *And it feels so damned good!*

Their mouths never parted as their combined bodies got hotter, igniting as Rob's hands made their way down Chase's abs in a tauntingly slow, tickling, and teasing manner.

The countdown had begun. Chase's massive man missile awaited blastoff. He desperately wanted Rob to reach into his Wranglers and ready his rigid rocket.

Chase's head went into orbit as Rob kissed him and slowly unzipped his jeans. Chase's entire body trembled at his touch. His breathing became quick and shallow. Chase grabbed Rob's large, strong hand and helped him slip it down under his white cotton boxer briefs.

Rob forcefully grabbed him and flipped him over as if Chase was a flimsy rag doll. It only took Rob one calculated motion to remove both Chase's jeans and briefs and pin them around his ankles. Rob effortlessly lifted Chase's hips into the air with his beefy, broad arms, leaving Chase pinned face down, ass up on the kitchen table.

Oh my God, what am I doing?

Chase felt vulnerable and disarmed by this power shift as he attempted to wrap his mind around what was happening. Rob grabbed Chase's bubble-shaped butt and spread them wide open with his strong hands. This was unlike any sex Chase had ever known. He was at the whim of a man twice his strength and several times his experience.

And he loved it.

He thought about what this meant, but suddenly it didn't matter. All Chase knew was that whatever Rob was doing felt fantastic and would hopefully last a long time.

"I'll be gentle the first time," Rob promised. "I have all the necessary tools to make it an enjoyable experience indeed. All you have to do is tell me if anything I do gets too much."

Given the surges of satisfaction currently blasting

through Chase's body, he didn't think he'd have any complaints at all.

When he felt a warm tongue probing his most private of places, Chase let himself go into a euphoria unlike anything else he'd experienced.

***

A long, long time later, Chase was able to think clearly again. It was as if he'd been drugged, but he knew it hadn't been due to any chemical he'd taken.

How did I not know sex could be so good? Or did I just dream all that?

It was as if he'd been drinking frozen OJ his whole life, and now he finally tasted freshly squeezed juice.

On a scale from one to ten, Chase revised his previous rating. That wasn't an eleven. It was more like one hundred eleven.

The whole sex experience had taken them all over the townhouse, from the kitchen table to his bedroom, through the laundry room, to a closet Chase didn't even know existed. The sex was just a blurred of ecstasy. All he knew was he was depleted in every way and now lying in Rob's massive arms in his bed.

Chase felt the need to communicate and address what happened between them, but he was physically and mentally shot. His eyes closed, and before he knew it, a slight snore floated gently from his mouth. That night, Chase slept fully and peacefully, the kind of sleep you have after an exhausting day of unbridled joy.

Chapter 12

G eneral Coldpecker, Corporal Matthew, and Dr. Herbie sat in Bentley's plush office. The search for ROB had grown so desperate that drastic measures needed to be taken. Bentley promised that if Herbie helped bring ROB back to the lab, he would be able to keep him. The one condition of their arrangement was that Herbie would be required to build another soldier robot for the General. Herbie reluctantly agreed. It wasn't something that he was happy with, but it seemed a reasonable concession. Everyone agreed, and the men shook hands.

Afterward, Herbie retreated to his laboratory to continue his efforts to locate ROB.

Corporal Matthew followed Herbie out the door but lingered behind to do a little recon. Something did not feel right. He made sure the office door was left slightly ajar so he could listen to the conversation inside. He didn't trust either the General or Bentley. They both were too eager to give into Herbie's requests.

"A ridiculous dog and pony show," the General grunted. Bentley quickly agreed. "Yes, but a necessary one. Now that we have Herbie on our side, when ROB fails and Herbie receives the signal, the Corporal will be there to easily retrieve ROB for us."

Matthew put the pieces together. What at first seemed to be an odd concession now made perfect sense. It was a dastardly double-cross. The robot sends out a distress beacon, Dr. Herbie leads them to ROB. Once in their care, the government takes possession of what they believe is their property, and Herbie gets nothing.

General Coldpecker seemed delighted with his plan. "Good old-fashioned espionage. Wars are won with brains over brawn. Together, we'll get exactly what we want."

Through the slightly open door, Corporal Matthew watched Bentley make his way to an antique oak cabinet adjacent to his desk. He lifted two lead crystal glasses and an aged bottle of Glenlivet scotch and proceeded to toast their plan.

***

Chase woke up at an impressively late time. So late, that he not only missed the gym and his time with the guys in the steam room, he also missed the first meeting of the day. Still in a haze from last night's events, he headed into the shower.

The glass doors of Chase's newly refurbished main bathroom revealed him to the rest of the room. Chase wasn't shy about his form. He'd worked hard on his physique and didn't care about showing it off. No matter anyway, his bedroom was private and no one could see. Rob was conspicuously absent from the bed—something Chase was glad about. He didn't want to face him yet, wanting some time to process what had happened last night. Chase surmised that at some point in the evening, Rob had slipped out of Chase's room and back into his own. As the soap and warm water cascaded from his defined muscular body, Chase still couldn't help but wonder what part of last night was real. He was almost convinced that last night was some crazy dream, rather than an evening making love with Rob.

He almost laughed at the absurdity of having such a dream in the first place. No matter, he dismissed his thoughts. He had an insane day ahead of him with the museum opening just a week away. There were still too many details that Chase had to take care of before the event. Today, he needed to review the guest list and draft the technical training manual. Last but not least, he had to prepare his presentation speech. Last night seemed like a foggy fantasy. *Was it a dream?* If so, what an incredible dream it was. No sex could ever be that hot in reality. Chase wondered if wine, work pressures, and this impossibly sexy roommate triggered some form of repressed, raw subconscious fantasy—or had he really had his mind blown by having sex with this crazy-hot, new guy? Whatever the reality was, Chase couldn't think about it now. His focus was to get to the office before he missed another meeting.

Once Chase was dressed, he began to prepare for the day mentally. He breezed down the stairs, content with the idea that he'd only be about an hour late. At the bottom of the stairs, Rob stood behind a table with hot brewed coffee and a parfait of fresh fruits, yogurt, and nuts. Breakfast looked terrific, and Chase was uncharacteristically hungry. He knew he had neither time to have breakfast nor to chat with Rob about what had happened—if, in fact, it indeed had happened. Chase knew he needed more time to process things. "Sorry, super late, I can't stop. I'll see you later tonight. You good?"

Rob's face beamed with a warm and happy glow.

"I'm great. How about you?"

"All good here! See you after work," Chase assured as he whizzed by.

Rob was confused at the interaction between them. *Humans are indeed complex and odd creatures*, he surmised as he cleaned up the kitchen. He'd save Chase's breakfast for tomorrow.

***

The office buzzed with anticipation of the big gala, merely six days away now. This museum was groundbreaking in every way — the first of its kind. It was a completely immersive way of exhibiting art and telling stories. Chase's firm was one of the most prestigious companies that created state-of-the-art visitor attractions, and they were about to unveil something truly spectacular. Celebrities, the press, and society's elite from all over the world would be there to experience this grand opening. Chase was at the center of it, and he couldn't be more nervous.

Chase's assistant, Jane, knocked softly, then slowly entered holding an envelope.

"The 'plus one' you requested," she informed him, laying the black and gold-trimmed envelope on his desk. "You only needed one ticket?" She waited for a second to ask another question as if carefully thinking about its appropriateness. "Is it for your date?" She seemed a little put out that she wouldn't be on Chase's arm that night. Snapping out of the trance he was in — he was still thinking about last night — Chase's attention diverted from the computer screen to Jane. "Yeah, I am bringing a plus one," he said, suddenly remembering who it was for.

"A date? No," he proclaimed dismissively. "We're just buddies. I invited a friend... a guy friend. It's certainly not a date." Even to his ears, Chase's bold declaration sounded almost like a feeble protest.

Now, Chase was embarrassed, not only at the overly aggressive way he'd answered the question but at the fact that he would be taking a *man if it were a date.* Chase had issues that needed resolving. They were starting to become apparent to him, but right now, he was so buried in the stockpile of work he had to accomplish he decided to think about his private life and all the complications later. Chase gave Jane a reassuring *thank you* and a smile as he tried to take his mind off the situation with Rob.

"Oh. And this came for you, too. We all got them. They're a gift from the client." Jane handed Chase a small, thin, perfectly wrapped present.

"Is it a microwave oven?" Chase chuckled at his silly joke.

Jane was confused. "Do they make microwaves that small? Do you need a microwave oven? I can order you one. It'll be here in two days."

"I'm joking, Jane. A bad joke at that." Chase realized that Jane was in problem-solving mode and not in a mindset for levity.

"Oh, yeah. Silly me. Of course, you were kidding." Jane nervously chuckled as she left the office, mildly embarrassed.

Chase slipped the small package into his briefcase.

I'll open it tonight. Too much work to do today. It's most likely a lame gift anyway.

***

That night, the valet greeted Chase at the door in front of his office building and, as usual, gave a hearty nod as he ran off to retrieve Chase's car. Chase was drained. It had been a long, mentally exhausting day, and all he could think about was taking off his suit and enjoying a home-cooked meal. Going home was now his favorite part of the day. In the past, he dreaded getting home, exhausted. And since his ex-girlfriend hated cooking, they would quarrel over the pile of take-out options offered by the neighborhood restaurants. Now, he had a home-cooked meal and fantastic company to enjoy it with.

Chase was well aware that he had pushed the events of last night with Rob to the back of his mind and buried them under a ton of anything else he could think of. Perhaps, like an ostrich, if he buried his head in the sand, he wouldn't have to deal with it.

***

Chase punched the code into his keyless front door lock. As the door swung open, he could smell the garlic. Music played softly from the next room. There was no denying that he was looking forward to the meal that Rob had prepared and unwinding for the night. He was nervous about potential conversation topics — his first time having sex with a man being one of them.

As he entered, Rob was lighting candles around the room. *It was oddly romantic*, Chase thought. His attention was drawn to the beautiful table set for them. He didn't remember buying these dishes or dining sets. *Had Rob gone shopping for houseware?* A newly opened bottle of wine and a thick, juicy, perfectly seared steak sat ready for Chase to devour.

"Excited about the museum opening?" Rob inquired with a genuine interest.

"More nervous than excited. But ready or not, there'll be an opening. Fingers crossed that it's not a disaster."

Rob laughed. "I've got every confidence in the world that it'll be awesome." Chase took comfort in Rob's words. He was grateful to have Rob's company. Rob had quickly turned from a stranger into an amazing roommate and terrific friend.

Chase put down his briefcase and loosened his tie, happy to shake off the stress of the day. A small package poked out the top of his briefcase.

Rob spied the colorful box. "Gifts? How fun. Who's it from? Rob's face sparkled with excitement as if he were a child at a birthday party.

"It's a small token of appreciation from my client. It's most likely nothing."

Rob didn't let Chase dampen his enthusiasm. "If they cared enough to give you a gift, that means they're grateful for all you've done. You should be flattered. OPEN IT!"

Chase couldn't help but find Rob's excitement adorable. "Here, you open it. You're certainly more interested than I am."

Rob didn't need to be told twice. He quickly tore into the small package with glee.

"Apple Watch," Rob read the packaging out loud. "Wow, they make watches out of apples? That doesn't compute. Why would a timepiece be crafted from fruit?"

Chase couldn't help but laugh. "The company that makes the watch is named APPLE." They both broke out in uncontrollable laughter at the absurdity of Rob's statement as Rob opened the box.

"It's beautiful–such a precisely constructed piece of machinery. It looks just like the one on your wrist."

"It's yours." Chase proclaimed. "Since I already have one, and you love it. Take it. Enjoy."

Rob leaned forward and planted an exuberant kiss on Chase.

What a surprise. Wow. That was certainly nice!

"Let's eat! It's getting cold. Thank you for my present. I love it!" Rob beamed with delight.

Chase was happy to see Rob so excited. His enthusiasm was a welcome shot in the arm after an exhausting day. Chase was suddenly reminded of the smell of steak saturated in garlic butter and the aroma of freshly grilled veggies. His mouth watered, and he couldn't restrain himself any longer.

Chase took his first bite. Perfection. His eyes rolled back in his head as if he just had an orgasm. *What did he do to deserve this?*

Rob filled Chase's glass with an '86 Cabernet from Napa Valley.

I'm getting genuinely spoiled, and I can live with it.

Chase insisted he'd only partake in one bottle of wine tonight since tomorrow was a big day with clients, and he needed to be sharp. They laughed and talked for hours. Chase found that, again, he'd done most of the talking. He was surprised, but Rob was a fantastic listener. Chase felt like he could finally confide in someone who understood him. Rob never really spoke about himself, his background, or his family. Chase got it. Not everyone had a good childhood or a loving family. So, rather than pry, he engaged him in philosophical questions, politics, pop culture, and general knowledge. He wanted to respect Rob's boundaries by keeping the conversation about their lives today and the current state of the world. Rob seemed to know so much at times and be so childlike at others.

Chase was looking forward to the time of the evening when he and Rob would enjoy chamomile and lavender tea after dinner. It was another tradition Rob introduced him to. As Rob once again insisted he'd clear the plates, Chase made his way to the sofa to let the last of the day's pressures evaporate from his body.

"I'm all done," Rob announced. "Now, I want to show you something."

"Of course," he chuckled, a little apprehensive as Rob disappeared up the stairs.

Am I ready for this? I wonder what he wants to show me.

Chase waited on the couch for Rob to get back with whatever he wanted to show him. About ten minutes later, with no Rob, the mystery of what he was up to only deepened when he heard music blasting away upstairs. *What could Rob be up to now?* As the heavy techno beat thumped away, Chase couldn't contain his curiosity. As he reached the top of the stairs, the music reached a crescendo. The heavy bass was coming from Rob's bedroom. The door was closed. He saw light flashing from underneath it. Suddenly a wisp of fog, *or was it smoke?* drifted from under the door.

Was the place on fire?

Panicked, Chase rushed to swing open the door to find out what the hell was happening.

A wave of amazement washed over him as he looked into the room. He closed his eyes tightly to reset his brain, as the sight in front of him wasn't registering. When Chase opened his eyes after several seconds, the image remained. Through the fog and the throbbing multi-colored beams of light, Chase saw a stripper pole installed in the center of Rob's bedroom. Chase saw a muscular shape moving in perfect sync with the music through the shimmery haze. He gulped. His eyes adjusted to the room, and he could see Rob, hanging acrobatically from the pole, was wearing only combat boots and a jockstrap,

"How?" Chase burbled lamely. "When did you do this, and why is it here?"

Rob smiled widely. "It was easy to do, and I did it for you. I've assessed that you need more extracurricular activities in your life, and you're sorely deficient in fun activities."

Chase blinked as he acknowledged one undeniable fact. Rob was smoking hot, and whatever was going on was working for Chase. He was, without question, completely turned on.

Rob playfully gestured toward a stack of dollar bills on the dresser. His logical brain said this whole charade was ridiculous, but his lust brain was exploding with desire. *What to do?* Rob seemed honor-bound to continue his seduction of Chase, and in all honesty, Chase was getting more turned on by the minute.

If you can't beat 'em, join 'em, he thought. Chase took the singles and started slipping them under the band of Rob's jockstrap.

He giggled at the absurdity, but Rob looked deadly serious about what he was doing. Chase's dollars found their proper place under the waistband of Rob's G-string—that is until Rob took Chase's hand and brushed it against his mighty bulge. Rob winked, then turned to bend over and plant his delicious derriere right in front of Chase's face.

It was as if the floodgates of a mighty dam burst.

Chase knew that yesterday's three-hour lovemaking session wasn't something he'd merely conjured in the deep recesses of his subconscious. It had very much been real and everything he'd ever wanted. He could no longer ignore his desire, given what had just been placed in his hand. His mouth salivated at the thought of ravaging Rob's delicious ripe man melons twerking mere millimeters from his face.

Rob leaned forward as his muscular legs held him horizontal off the pole. He grabbed Chase's face and pulled him forcefully towards him. The two men kissed passionately, deeply. Their mouths locked as if they were designed to fit together perfectly.

There was no more denying that Chase was super into Rob. The rock-hard erection he sported was proof of it. Chase had never been so turned on in his life. It was much more than the physical attraction and mind-blowing sex. Rob was everything Chase had ever wanted in a partner. There was no stopping Chase's heart at this point. He was all in and wanted Rob more than he had wanted anything in his life.

Chase could no longer hold himself back. He thrust himself towards Rob, almost making him lose his footing on the pole. *I have to have him, every tasty bit.*

Moments later, Chase found himself again making love with Rob in his bed. He wondered whether the bed would survive the extreme pounding of Rob's herculean body into Chase's.

Later that night, Rob flipped Chase over for a third time as if he were fluffing a pillow. Chase was not light, weighing in at one hundred seventy-five pounds of solid muscle. But he felt as light as a feather in Rob's arms. Chase couldn't help noticing he was soaking wet from the relentless physical activity between them, and yet Rob hadn't even broken a sweat. The constant physical activity took its toll on Chase's stamina, but Rob kept at it as if he were a teenage boy about to hit his stride.

Chase's muscles trembled from attempting to hold an array of wild, sexual contortions. Just as Chase was about to climax for the fourth time, Rob's body tautened above him. Rob's face changed, his look of pleasure turning into concern. "You okay?" Chase asked in alarm.

Rob smiled. "Yes. I just need to take care of something." It was two-thirty a.m., and Chase was mid-orgasm. What could Rob possibly need to take care of other than Chase at this time? Rob rolled off Chase, giving him a sweet and tender kiss. "Good night, and rest up. I'll see you in the morning." Rob made haste out of Chase's bedroom, closing the door gently behind him.

That was odd. What could have gone wrong between them? Never mind. Too tired. Work tomorrow. I need sleep. Exhausted. He promptly rolled onto his back. And before he fully hit the pillow, he passed out.

***

The internal low battery alarm still rang in Rob's head as he entered his bedroom and made haste to the wall outlet. His index finger produced two metal prongs that he slipped into the outlet near the lamp. Rob sat on the floor as the electricity surged through his hand and into his battery.

He shook his head at his carelessness. His battery was at ten percent. How could he not have been monitoring his power source? He was being uncharacteristically depleted too soon. This was something that Rob needed to pay attention to in the future. It was worrisome that without backup power sources, he could face a complete shutdown and be powerless within minutes.

He'd do a full diagnostic of the day's events in the morning and see what was triggering his rapid battery depletion.

Chapter 13

As usual, the following day, Rob greeted Chase with an impressive breakfast, fresh coffee, and a warm smile.

Chase was oddly at ease meeting Rob in the kitchen. He'd resolved to be chill this morning—just be himself. Yes, their dynamic had changed, and it was about time Chase admitted something about his sexuality to himself. Much like his bro Tad, Chase now considered himself "vibe-sexual." Chase hated labels. In his business, he found them limiting. He asserted that there was no need to consider people gay, straight, bi, fluid, or otherwise. People are sexual creatures, and tastes evolve. Chase didn't like to be judged about what he did with his life, and he, in turn, didn't judge people or put them into categories either. He was ashamed of himself for having previously thought differently.

As the two men sat having breakfast, Rob was distracted with his new watch. "This wrist computer is truly ingenious."

Chase couldn't help but be amused at Rob's childlike preoccupation with the device. "Want to see something cool? If you hold your two fingers down on the face of it, I can send you my heartbeat."

Chase pressed on the glass of his watch and held his fingers down for a second.

"Feel that? That's my heart beating for you." He

smiled at the thought of Rob feeling his heartbeat.

"AMAZING!" Rob burst out in excitement. "I can feel the thumping in your chest on my wrist."

Chase was pleased that they were now electronically connected. He sat quietly looking at Rob. A warmth he had never felt before washed over him. They had only been together a short time, but already Chase couldn't imagine going a day without Rob. His days were filled with planning the most exciting project of his life, yet the thing he looked forward to the most was being with Rob at the end of the day.

Could I be falling for this dude?

Chase knew he needed to talk to his bros about his feelings. How could he do it with Rob there in the steam room?

Best to be honest. Don't beat around the bush.

"Would you mind not going with me to the gym today? Sometimes a guy just needs to talk to his bros about stuff." Chase inquired bashfully. Rob chuckled without missing a beat, "Like about you and me, and what happened last night?"

Chase marveled at Rob's honesty as he confessed, "Yes."

Rob continued, "If that's what you want, of course, I'll comply. I think it's great. Feel free to invite them over to join us."

Chase burst out in a hearty laugh. Rob's off-beat and sometimes inappropriate humor was one of the things he loved about him. Chase had never met anyone who was so sincere and found his quirky comedy routine endearing. Chase decided to reply in kind, "Sure, I'll see if any of them are up to it!"

***

At the gym, Bolton, Tad, Ryan, and Beau's mouths hung open, amazed. For once, Chase was the one who couldn't stop talking, and the four of them were speechless. Chase regaled them with tales of the gourmet feasts Rob effortlessly conjured nightly, then told them about the long thought-provoking, emotional conversations they shared. Lastly and most enthusiastically, Chase shared the incomprehensible and uniquely acrobatic sex they had with them. Not because he was boasting, but because the guys had so many detailed questions about it.

Chase looked at Bolton, who now was holding a pen and pencil. "What are you doing?" he asked.

"Taking notes!" crowed Bolton. "Who would have thought to use a zucchini, an egg beater, and a plum like that? God damned brilliant!"

Chase was happy with work going well and finding someone he genuinely cared for. His friends were thrilled for him. His concerns about not having a real romantic relationship were now over. Chase had confided many times to the guys that he was afraid that as soon as he opened his heart up, it would get broken. Now that fear was gone, he was ready to love and trust someone completely.

***

Chase had yet another busy day ahead of him. The office bustled with activity as he meticulously reviewed future work proposals. His workload piling up, he decided to forgo his lunch hour. Rather than visiting his favorite sandwich shop today, he'd have something delivered.

In what seemed to be seconds after he placed the

order, lunch arrived.

Jane picked it up at the front desk and delivered it to him. "You need to get up from that computer. Staring at that screen for hours at a time is terrible for your eyes." Her concern for him was sweet.

"You're right. I'll get up just after I finish this."

Jane continued. "You should also know that human resources said that a vacation is mandatory this year. You need to give them dates when you'll be taking time off."

"Fair enough. Tell them that I'll take two weeks off after the grand opening," he assured her as he watched her set up his lunch on the desk. "I can do that myself," he insisted, trying to prevent her from mothering him too much.

"Sorry. I just wanted to make sure you're all set. I'll be in later to clean this up."

Jane quickly finished up and slipped out the door. Chase didn't need to think about what to do with his vacation time. In the past, he'd just bum around at home and hang out in the gym with his buddies. But things were different now—he was excited to have a break and knew precisely where he wanted to go.

As he ate his lunch, his fingers danced across the keyboard to book two airline tickets. France! It was always his dream, but he never had anyone he wanted to go with. He imagined Paris to be the most magical and romantic city on the planet. Who better than Rob to explore such a wonderous place with?

Wait? Was he rushing things? How would Rob react to being whisked away to such a faraway wonderland?

Rob never talked about his memories. He seemed to actively ignore his past. Chase decided that taking Rob on vacation to build experiences together couldn't be a bad thing. If they were now a couple, it would be fun to start sharing adventures.

Tonight, he'd present Rob with two tickets to paradise — a perfect place for the two of them to do nothing but explore and discover the world…and each other.

Chapter 14

C orporal Matthew scoured the streets looking for Rob, as Herbie monitored any additional signals Rob may have sent due to his failing battery. Last night at 2:30 a.m., Herbie's computer had registered a tracking signal from Rob for approximately four minutes. The signal transmitted Rob's vitals and triangulated his location. Although the homing beacon engaged, there'd been no protocol in place to record the source of the signal or retain the data it transmitted. Herbie's computer only registered the data as if it were a telephone's caller ID. This was a mistake he would not make again. Herbie deftly programmed his systems to record any future information Rob's systems sent, day or night. From now on, everything would be recorded. Herbie had even programmed it to send him a text message simultaneously.

***

Corporal Matthew had covered miles of Los Angeles searching for Rob and was now on the street where the Mission Gym stood. Undaunted in his determination to leave no stone unturned, he made his way into the old gym no matter how unlikely the location. While it would likely be the last place a robot would be, he also knew that often you'd find a clue in the most unexpected places. An older man met him at the door.

"Can I help you, son?" he asked gruffly.

"I'm a Marine, sir. First-class. May I have your name, please?"

The man squinted. "You can call me Johnson."

"Johnson, I'm looking for someone. Top secret and the highest priority. Have you seen this man?" Matthew held up his phone and presented a photo of a robotic prototype identical to Rob.

"Can't say that I have," the man grunted. Rather cagily, Matthew thought. His instincts told him Johnson was lying.

Matthew sighed. "Look again, please. Are you sure you haven't seen him, sir?"

"What did he do?" the old man asked.

"Top secret, sir. Sorry, but I can't disclose that information."

"Well, he looks like a perfectly fine fellow to me."

"Mind if I ask around, see if anyone else may have seen him?" Matthew asked, knowing full well that he didn't need anyone's permission to proceed.

"That'll be five bucks if you want to work out," the older man growled.

Matthew peeled five dollars out of his wallet and handed it over.

"Have fun," said Johnson.

It was mid-afternoon, and the gym was empty. Matthew was about to conclude that this location's manhunt was a bust when a sign hanging in the hall captured his eye. It read: "Steam Room." Hmmm. He couldn't think of anything more appealing at this point than a hot, relaxing steam. It had been a long morning pounding the pavement, and twenty minutes of blissful steaming sounded like heaven.

Matthew stripped down in the lockers, grabbed a towel, and made his way into the steam room.

***

Bolton sat happily enjoying the solitude. His usual CrossFit training client had asked to move their sessions to the morning. In an effort to accommodate their schedule, Bolton moved his workout and steam to the afternoon. He'd looked forward to having the steam room all to himself. Mid-afternoon was usually a quiet time when everyone else was at work.

He now sat man-spreading in the steam room—*time to steam the salami and air the onions.* Bolton chuckled as he fully reclined and opened his towel, revealing himself to the empty, steam-filled room. He was a little put out when a stranger entered a few minutes later. But given what the man looked like and what he was packing—the stranger made a fine figure, from his cropped haircut and square jawline down to his tattoo-covered V-shaped torso—Bolton wasn't about to complain. He guessed the stranger was either military or a cop.

Bolton grinned slyly. "I can cover up if you're uncomfortable … or intimidated," he laughed. The stranger didn't react. He sat down beside him and opened his towel. Bolton was not disappointed.

"I'll see your seven inches and raise you an inch," the military man teased as he leaned back on the bench beside Bolton.

"Touché," Bolton conceded as he glanced down to compare their equipment. He'd trained hard an hour earlier and was pumped up. He knew he had a physique that people envied, and from the glances the stranger was giving him, he appreciated every muscle.

"Name's Bolton," he murmured.

"Matthew. Good to meet you."

Bolton had no filter and didn't care what people thought, "Bro, you're ridiculously swoll. Props for being so tight." *And so sexy*, he thought.

Matthew enjoyed the compliment. "You, too, man. Solid definition. You're like a rock."

Bolton laughed, flexing his abs, making them more pronounced. *The new guy seemed to enjoy the show, so why not give him a performance?*

***

The hot, wet air in the steam room reminded Matthew of the warm, humid Kansas summers of his past—a time where he could sit with his friends, drink beers and talk about nothing important. The military wasn't like that. It was always about training, preparation, missions, and imminent threats. Today, sitting with Bolton, Matthew's mind and body relaxed. It was as if this steam room had mythical powers to make all things possible.

Matthew and Bolton chatted about everything. They had a ridiculous amount in common and were really hitting it off. When he glanced down at his phone, Matthew gasped when he saw the time.

"What? It's been two hours. I'm on duty. I've got to split."

Bolton laughed. "I guessed you were military or something. It's written all over you, and I don't mean the tattoos."

Matthew chuckled. "Busted."

"Guess you're on a mission. Trying to pass as a civilian? Am I right?"

Matthew nodded. "Yes. I'm here looking for someone." He got up to leave, tightening the towel around his waist.

"How do you know *I* haven't seen the guy you're looking for?"

Fair enough, Matthew thought as he pulled Rob's photo up on his phone. "Have you seen this man?"

***

Bolton wasn't the greatest of actors. But he did his best to pretend that he didn't know exactly who Rob was and where he could find him.

"Nah, he hasn't been in here," he said casually, feeling a pang of guilt. "Is he dangerous? A criminal?" asked Bolton, concerned for Chase's welfare.

"Nah," Matthew laughed. "He's not a public nuisance or anything you need to be worried about. He's just someone we're looking for as part of an investigation, and I'd be grateful if you could help me find him."

Bolton smiled, "Why don't you give me your number. I'll call you if I discover anything." He unlocked his phone and handed it to Matthew.

Sweet. Now I've got this stud's info.

"Thank you," Matthew said as he typed in his phone number. "Thanks again for the great chat."

"I enjoyed it, too. I hope you find who you're looking for." They stood there looking at each other. Then, with one last stolen glance at the other, Matthew turned and left the steam room.

Yup, he's mine for the taking—if I want him.

***

Bolton still felt guilty about lying to Matthew. Yeah, it was reassuring that Matthew didn't think Rob was dangerous. But still, shouldn't he tell his buddy that the military was looking for his boyfriend? He wondered if it was worth bothering Chase at work. Bolton was aware of how stressed Chase was with the gala only days away. Bolton wasn't one to be dramatic or an alarmist, but he knew Chase was prone to over-reacting. He decided to wait until they all got together tomorrow in the steam room to mention it.

Chapter 15

C hase pulled up to his townhouse after another grueling day of work. The days seemed longer and longer lately. The museum opening was only a few days away, creating endless tasks and challenges. He'd been dreading this big black-tie affair for months. He didn't enjoy galas. However, it was a huge relief to finally open a museum; and he was undoubtedly proud of his work. And now that he'd found someone he enjoyed spending time with, nothing was better than coming home and having a night in.

Chase was surprised at how thrilled he was to be going to Paris with Rob. He sat in his car holding a small wrapped box containing a tiny replica of the Eiffel Tower. He'd ordered it on Amazon so that he could present it tonight as a surprise. He took a deep, excited breath and headed into the townhouse.

Usually, Chase would have heard the soft sound of the blues music playing on the stereo upon entering his home. Rob seemed to always find the perfect playlist for the evening. But tonight, the music was different.

Techno beats filled the house, and the sound of strange voices laughing came from the other room. *What's going on? Is Rob having a party?*

From down the hall, a young, shirtless man stumbled into view. "Hey, Chase is home!" he pronounced as he grabbed a beer and came over to introduce himself. The young man was thin but fit with a tight swimmer's body. His hipster haircut, trendy glasses, day-old scruff, and black, torn, skinny jeans told Chase that he was a party boy. Before Chase could decide if he wanted a beer or not, the young man thrust it into his hand and introduced himself as Chad.

"Glad you're home so we could start. Come meet the other guys."

Other guys? Who else is here? Chase followed Chad into the living room. Behind the bar, Rob was serving drinks. Music played a bit too loudly, and an impressive spread of finger foods and snacks covered the table. On Chase's beloved couch sat two other young, handsome guys — Fit, attractive, and well-groomed. All the guys were dressed casually trendy. Only Chad was shirtless. But based on the skimpy tank tops and shorts the other guys had on, it seemed that they were here for a party — a party that Chase hadn't expected.

Rob lit up at the sight of Chase. His excited reaction pleased Chase for the moment, but that quickly dissipated when he thought about the three strange men who occupied *their* space.

"Hey Chase, I'm Benny!" the youngest of the men called out. Following Benny's announcement, another guy introduced himself. Chase recognized him as an actor from a bad web series.

"And I'm Griff. Great to meet you."

"Can we start the party now?" Chad asked. "We were told to wait until you arrived."

Rob laughed. "It's Chase's party. Now that he's here, sure, let's start." It was as if the checkered flag was waved at the Indianapolis 500. Seconds later, Griff and

Benny peeled their shirts off and started making out on the couch. Chad approached Chase, looking at him how a judge at a southern barbeque cook-off gazes at a prize brisket. "Rob brought us all here for you. Happy to do *whatever* you'd like."

He grinned. "Or *whoever*." Before Chase could process what was going on, Chad had his hands on either side of Chase's face and kissed him hard.

The kiss lasted longer than it should have, and the only reason for that was that Chase's mind was elsewhere. *Why did Rob plan this for me? I don't want anyone else in this way.*

Chase recoiled from Chad's embrace and pushed his way past him. *I have to talk to Rob.* On the sofa, Griff and Benny were advancing from petting each other's privates, to groin grinding, culminating in full and almost-naked body friction. Benny was leaning back on the sofa, his shorts open as Griff's hand furrowed down the front of his jeans. Chase couldn't help but think of an early California prospector discovering the first nuggets of gold.

"What is happening here?" Chase exclaimed, concerned with the three men about to fornicate on his favorite piece of furniture.

Rob was confused by Chase's outburst. "You enjoy doing new things, and you told me that you'd never been with a guy other than me before. I thought you'd enjoy sampling other guys." He waved a hand. "I did my calculations and determined you'd find them attractive and want to have sex with them."

Chase was gut-punched at Rob's reply. "Since when did our relationship turn into a gang bang?" he barked. "I thought you were happy with only me. Now I come home to *this*?"

The tickets to Paris had been a terrible miscalculation and would prove to be a catastrophic embarrassment. The writhing, naked pile of tangled twinks on his favorite leather couch was more than he could handle. *How will I get that leather clean? Will I even want that sofa after they're done with it?*

Rob looked devastated. "I'm sorry. I must have made a programming error. I didn't realize this wasn't what you wanted. I thought my gift would be welcomed."

"Well, it isn't for me. Enjoy your company. I'm going upstairs" Chase sighed heavily.

"What's wrong? Are you sick?" queried Rob.

"No," Chase sighed. His heart hurt; he was tired and dizzy. All he wanted was to escape the situation. "I just need to lie down." Chase turned and made his way slowly upstairs.

***

Rob processed the information. It was true. He scanned Chase's vitals through his watch. Chase wasn't well; his heartbeat was low, his temperature was high, and his breathing was shallow. Rob's directive was to stay with him, but Chase wanted to be alone.

Since Chase didn't desire his services and the group of young men in the next room did, the answer seemed simple enough. Rob looked at the group of young, energetic lads engaged in a fevered frenzy of fellatio. Griff was the only one facing up, beckoning Rob to join them. Rob shimmied over, taking off his shirt, prompting a collective gasp from the three mesmerized men. He smiled, thinking they looked as if they were in an amusement park and a new attraction had just opened up. He had a feeling they all wanted to be first for a ride on his coaster. I will give them all pleasure.

"Come up to my room. I have music, a light show, and a dancer's pole."

Chad, Benny, and Griff squealed with the delight of sixteen-year-olds receiving a backstage pass at a Shawn Mendez concert. Rob expertly sprang up the pole as they entered the room and began doing acrobatics to the heavy bass club music synchronized to the light show and fog machine.

Soon, Griff, Benny, and Chad formed a line as they eagerly waited for Rob to satisfy them.

Rob didn't disappoint. He was happy to oblige as each young man demanded multiple performances and new positions. The sex sounds from the orgy, with an occasional scream, echoed through the halls of Chase's home for hours.

***

Chase sat on his bed with the tiny Eiffel Tower in his hands. He went through an onslaught of emotions as the ear-piercing sounds of their physical pleasure persisted. Hurt was followed by confusion, then sadness, as he struggled to understand how this had all gone so wrong.

Chase grew more upset and angrier by the minute. The unrelenting music and loud moans eventually broke him.

I can't take it anymore. It has to stop.

He rose from his bed, thundered out of his room and across the hall. He waited for a second and considered his actions, but couldn't help himself. Chase burst into Rob's room but was unprepared for the scene before him.

Rob's king-sized bed was ground zero for this fourgy. Even though the room's strobing lights glared through the fog, Chase saw all the men were connected in a progression that he'd only imagined came straight from a porn film. Rob was in the center of the three men, resembling a maypole.

His heart ached as he swallowed his grief and bellowed a mighty, "Get the fuck out, all of you!" from the bottom of his soul. No doubt the rest of the neighborhood heard it, too. The music magically stopped, as did the lights and fog machine. So did all four men.

"We hear you loud and clear, dude," Griff muttered as he extricated himself and went to gather his clothes from the floor. The others followed him, casting curious glances at Chase as they did so.

Rob still sat cross-legged on the bed. Chase couldn't make eye contact with him. He looked away as Rob attempted an apologetic gaze. Rob was aware he had done something wrong but couldn't imagine what it was. He also knew that having sex with these guys had felt odd. But he didn't know why. Somehow, for some reason, he just knew he shouldn't have done it. Each of the other guys gathered their possessions and did the walk of shame past Chase, their heads down and quiet, as they made their way out the door.

When they were all gone, Chase silently returned to his room, his heart shattered, unable to even look at Rob. He wasn't sure what the next step would be.

***

Rob realized that he needed to leave as well. Chase had given a command. Being a robot, Rob had to obey it. He walked around the bedroom and gathered a few of his things. He walked downstairs and did the same. Then, with one last, sad glance up the stairs towards Chase's bedroom, he let himself out the door.

It was midnight and dark. The street was grim and seemingly endless as Rob walked, not caring where he'd end up. His processor was working hard trying to understand what part of his programming was faulty. Why did he feel so down, so upset? There was so much that did not compute. Rob's primary directive was to please, however when he pleasured the guests, why could he only think of Chase? Why did the thought of being with Chase appeal to him so much more than being with anyone else?

Chapter 16

C hase sat on the edge of his bed, confused. *What made Rob feel like he needed to bring other men into their relationship? What was their relationship anyway?* Chase had never been with another man romantically. It was time for him to be assertive here. He needed to find out what Rob was thinking and set the record straight on where this relationship was going.

I need some answers. Answers only Rob can give me.

Chase rose reluctantly from his bed. He headed across the hallway to Rob's bedroom. The door was ajar. The colored lights, music, and fog machine were switched off. All that illuminated the room was an end-table lamp next to the bed. The room was in shambles. Sheets askew, torn pillows, and lube were everywhere. Chase's bare foot stepped on something that rattled and vibrated. It was a large, five-pronged object that resembled a starfish. He recoiled at the thought of where it had been. One thing he knew for certain was that it hadn't come from the sea. Fortunately, it died from a depleted battery before he had to touch it and turn it off.

Rob wasn't in the bedroom or the adjacent bathroom.

He must be downstairs. He probably needed something to eat after all that 'exercise.'

Chase dashed downstairs. The rooms were spotless.

Dishes were put away, and sofa pillows fluffed. It was as if nothing had ever happened there—everything in its place and perfect. His home was dead quiet. Empty. Chase's heart dropped as he realized that Rob was gone.

Chase sat down on the couch as tears welled in his eyes. The silence mocked him.

What have I done? Did I overreact? Would Rob be okay with nowhere to go?

Should he get in the car and search the streets for Rob? Where could he have gone?

Chase was aware he'd drive himself mad thinking about what he'd done. There was only one thing to do at this point. Turn off the lights and go to bed. He needed to sleep, however impossible that may be. Tomorrow, he'd put in a serious workout at the gym and consult with his buddies in the steam room. Bolton and his bros might be able to shed some light on the situation.

***

Rob wandered into the night and farther away from Chase's townhouse. Encino was a quiet town full of private homes and small shops. The palm tree-lined streets and upscale designer homes were undoubtedly scenic. But at this late hour, it was desolate and lonely. Rob eventually found himself in the heart of West Hollywood, a mecca of bars, cars, and after-hours activity.

Entertaining his three guests for several hours and now the extensive walking had significantly depleted Rob's battery. His power cell seemed to be deteriorating at a faster rate each day. Last week, the same battery would last two days, but now he could barely get a full twenty-four-hour charge out of it. He needed to recharge soon, but a public place was out of the question.

Rob saw a fit and attractive man smoking a cigarette outside an old donut shop from across the boulevard. He walked over to the establishment, which sat catty-corner to a seedy section of Santa Monica Boulevard. The streetlights lit the corner well, in contrast to the rest of the neighborhood, which was abandoned.

The place had certainly seen better days. The posters that clung to the inside of the windows had yellowed and were held together by scotch tape bleached and dried out by the California sun. A large, faded Plexiglas sign fought to light itself and advertise the name of the establishment—the tired bulbs illuminating the sign. It announced "The Creamy Hole Donut Shop" brightly for a few seconds before it dimmed again to a low, faint flicker. Rob wondered if he could befriend the smoking man. Perhaps with his help, Rob could find a safe place to charge. The low battery alarm sounded.

I need to find a power source, and I need to find it quickly. There must be an outlet somewhere inside the store.

Rob's electromagnetic scanners could see electrical patterns and outlets within buildings. From the middle of the street, it looked like a small back room—possibly a bathroom—in the donut shop was ideal for refortifying his power cell.

Rob approached the Creamy Hole as a man in his mid-thirties rushed to open the door for him. "Let me get that for you. And anything else you'd like."

Rob appreciated the amicable nature of his admirer. "Thank you. My name's Rob. I think I'm good, but if I require anything else, I'll be sure to call you."

The man winked. "My name's Craig, and I'm the welcome wagon here," he said with an aggressive grin. Craig seemed friendly but overzealous. He was dressed in a skimpy outfit that was inappropriate for the current weather. His shaggy brown hair was unkempt, and his tall, lean body was conspicuously average compared to the other men Rob had encountered recently. Still, Craig was cute in his own way and clearly eager to please. "Don't let Hillary give you sass when you get inside. She's just pissed off at life."

Rob nodded as he wandered through the open door and entered the bakery, leaving Craig outside to continue his smoke.

Inside, Rob saw a donut display. A female shop clerk was working behind the counter. He assumed this was Hillary. Her delicate face was painted with expertly applied makeup. Even though tired and weary, her large, violet-colored eyes still retained the spark of her younger days.

"Good evening. I need to use your bathroom."

"Bathrooms are for customers only," she muttered. "And we're closing in a few minutes."

Rob's system was now registering an eight percent charge. He needed to plug in somewhere quickly. He had a few dollars in his pocket—money left over from the grocery shopping he did for Chase. "I'll take a dozen donuts." He handed Hillary a twenty-dollar bill. "Keep the change."

"Yeah, yeah. Here you go, then." Hillary handed over a key attached to a giant steel spoon. *Curious*, Rob thought. *Why would I require a spoon in a bathroom? It must be a human thing.* Once alone and safe inside the small, dingy, powder blue tiled bathroom, he quickly plugged the two brass prongs that protruded from his finger into the wall outlet.

The surge of power felt good in his circuits, fortifying his battery. As Rob powered up, he took the time to enjoy some prose written by local wordsmiths who had scribed their messages on the back of the adjacent door. One lovesick lad proclaimed this love for a maiden by carving "Sally Fay & Beau Forever" into the door's heavy, dark wood.

***

Hillary filled a pink box with assorted donuts, from jasmine jam-filled jellies to powdered profiteroles and flaky French crullers. Rob had paid for only a dozen pastries, but Hillary filled up the box with nearly twenty assorted confections. She'd never admit it, but while she had a hardened shell on the outside, she was soft on the inside, much like the donuts she served.

It seemed that Rob was taking an unusually long time.

I hope he's all right in there, she thought. She decided she'd be a bit lenient on the amount of time that she'd ordinarily give someone to use the toilet. Since Rob had given her a $10 tip, he'd bought himself a few more minutes of privacy.

***

Herbie awakened to the sound of the computer chirping in the other room. His brain registered what that meant, and he slipped out of bed and rushed to his laptop. His fingers danced over the keyboard, trying to get the results of the data coming in. It took only a few keystrokes for him to get a geo-location of Rob's whereabouts.

I've got him!

Herbie grabbed his coat, slipped on his old brown leather shoes, and headed out of the house in his striped pajamas. He surmised that Rob was only fifteen minutes away. If he left immediately, he could probably catch him.

***

An old 2005 Silver Honda pulled up in front of the donut shop with a missing front bumper and the side mirror duct-taped to the door. Hillary saw her younger brother, William, waiting outside in the car for her to finish her shift. He looked ready to leave.

The clock struck one. William chatted to Craig, who flicked his smoke into the street. She clutched her keys and extinguished the lights. As she grasped the front doorknob, she remembered Rob was still in the bathroom. She heaved an annoyed huff and walked over to the bathroom. She knocked loudly on the door.

"Whatever it is you're doing in there, it's time to go. I'm locking up!" Hillary hollered. "And you had best not have made a mess in there. I'm not cleaning up at this time of the morning."

***

Rob was at twenty percent power now. He was aware that he wasn't out of the woods yet. He calculated that he could last another two hours. Whatever he was going to do, he needed to find more power soon.

"Sorry. I'm done." Rob retracted the charging prongs back into his finger and promptly opened the door.

"Your donuts are on the counter. It's time to go," Hillary said.

"Thank you for your patience," Rob said gratefully. He collected his pink, string-tied package full of baked bliss. Hillary followed Rob as they exited the door, locking it behind them.

Hillary slipped in the passenger side of William's car, and off they went.

As Rob stood outside The Creamy Hole Donut Shop with his box of donuts, Craig looked at Rob like a tiger surveying his potential prey.

"Big, beautiful beefcake," he murmured sultrily. "Yum."

Rob was distracted, still concerned about only being at twenty percent power. He stood waiting while his internal neuro-processor ran multiple scenarios in which he could charge himself safely and discretely to avoid shut down.

Craig approached Rob. "Looking for a friend?" he inquired flirtatiously.

"Yes, I could definitely use a friend right now."

"I'll happily be your buddy, bro," Craig grinned.

Rob was programmed with Dictionary.com's definition of friend. One of the definitions was "a person who gives assistance." That being the case, Rob thought, that is precisely what I require right now.

Craig sweetly took Rob's hand in his. It was strangely comforting to Rob after the day he'd had. The couple walked down the dark road towards Sunset Blvd.

"I know a place we can crash," Craig said. "It's cheap but clean."

"Will there be electricity where we are going? I need to recharge," said Rob.

"Yep," Craig confirmed. "You can charge your phone

there if you need to."

Rob didn't want to spill the beans that it wasn't his phone that needed recharging. Best to keep that to himself.

***

Herbie raced through the dark, empty streets on his way to the location indicated on his GPS. A pleasant, tinny, computerized voice let him know that he was six minutes away from Rob's last reported position. Herbie prayed he wasn't too late to get to him. Every second mattered. When he drove up to the location, the donut shop was dark. Not a soul stirred. He keenly searched the dark store, looking in all directions for any indication of Rob. He was too late.

Herbie sighed deeply with disappointment. He was exhausted and needed to sleep. Tomorrow, he'd rewrite the tracking system software and try again. Perhaps he could add in more code to sustain the tracking signal for a more extended period of time, or maybe have it signal him before Rob's battery reserve hit ten percent.

He'd find his missing robot if it was the last thing he did.

Chapter 17

A neon light flickered above the broken "Motel" sign off Sunset Blvd. A smattering of cars lined the lot. The lodge boasted "Vacancies." It was clear why it wasn't at full occupancy. It was a bit run down and dated in almost every way. The manager's front office was conspicuously vacant. Rob thought it was odd that any human would find this place a desirable location to inhabit as a residence. But due to his current circumstances, it made no matter to Rob. Craig was interested in being his friend, and that's what Rob needed right now — in addition to power.

Rob strategized his scheme to recharge. He'd need to wait until Craig fell asleep before plugging in. Craig sat on the motel bed and beckoned Rob to join him.

"You look like the kind of guy who knows how to have a good time," Craig teased.

"My directive is to please," Rob stated confidently.

Craig nodded. "Ah, so you're a giver, not a receiver then."

Rob nodded. This was the first time his programming directive had been phrased like that. But no matter, it was accurate enough.

"Whatever you're into is good with me. I'm here for you," Craig said as he peeled off his shirt, revealing a slim, hairless body. "What would you like to do to me?"

Rob considered. "How about you tell me what you like?"

Craig reached down and placed his hand on Rob's knee. He looked him deep in the eyes, gauging Rob's reaction. Rob didn't flinch, only smiled. This invited Craig to make further advances. He ever so gently ran the tips of his finger up Rob's tight jeans and towards his crotch. Gently and gingerly, Craig cupped his hands and started to massage Rob. Craig's eyes widened with surprise.

"Wow, you're a big dude, you know that?" His fingers teased Rob's big bulge. "Mind if I kiss you? I don't usually do that with clients, but I like you."

"Actually, could you please wait a second?" Rob replied, unsure of how to proceed. Was it because his battery was low or something about Craig engaged a warning sensor? Whatever the reason, Rob didn't want to be intimate with Craig. He was a sexbot built for pleasure, but being with Craig just felt wrong. "I must apologize, but I can't proceed at this moment."

Craig chuckled, "I get it. If you're not feeling it, we don't need to do this. I'm tired too. If you'd like just to hang out here, you're welcome to do so."

"I'd like that very much," Rob replied in an appreciative tone.

Craig cozied himself up to Rob on the bed. "How do you feel about cuddling? Are you cool with that? I'd enjoy just lying in your arms."

Rob's inviting eyes and broad shoulders encouraged Craig to rest his head on his strong square chest. Craig couldn't help but sigh with delight as he nestled himself up to Rob. *This is wonderful; I need a man like this!* He thought as he quickly slipped into a deep slumber.

Rob glanced down to find Craig asleep on his chest. Rob required power desperately and needed to slip away to recharge. *How can I do this without waking Craig?* Rob looked around. On the nightstand within arm's reach, he noticed the table lamp had an outlet at the base of it. Without stirring Craig from his superb slumber, Rob plugged in to charge from where he lay, providing a perfect pillow for his new pal.

***

Chase woke with the images of last night's calamity still fresh in his head. Chase's fury needed a physical outlet, and powerlifting was going to be it.

He grabbed his gym bag, suit, and shaving kit and hurried out the door to work out hard, then meet the bros.

When he arrived at the gym, Old Man Johnston had just unlocked the door and was holding a large cup of 7-Eleven coffee, "blast-off dark roast espresso." Chase grinned. It was OMJ's favorite blend, especially after he'd added four caramel creamers and then nuked it in the microwave until it became scalding hot. OMJ was surprised to see Chase at this hour of the morning.

"This is early even for you, Chase."

"Need to crush some serious poundage this morning," Chase said. "Gotta clear the mind for an important day."

OMJ chuckled. "I'm no fool. I remember what it was like to be a youngster." He clapped Chase on the shoulder. "Seems to me it's more like you need to clear the mind from a bad night last night?" Chase stopped dead in his tracks and wondered if he was telegraphing that his life had now turned into a tremendous turd.

OMJ was a shrewd dude. Fortunately, he'd always been respectful of the bros and their problems, especially their relationship problems.

"I met someone pretty awesome, and now he's gone. We had a disagreement, and he left." His shoulders slumped as he looked down at the ground.

"Boy, I've lived a lot longer than you and have a whole load more experience. Let me give you a little bit of fatherly advice. Love is stronger than you think it is. If you genuinely care about this person, and they care about you, you'll find your way together again. I guarantee it." A bright, warm smile transformed OMJ's tired, stern face into that of an elderly sage.

"I hope you're right. You've made me feel a lot better about the situation." The heavy sadness that filled his chest lifted a little.

"Now, don't let this be an excuse for you to wuss out on those weights. Get in your sweats and start getting swoll!" OMJ barked, back to his usual cranky self.

Chase laughed. "Sure thing, OMJ." He walked into the gym feeling a lot better about the day ahead.

Chapter 18

The slamming of car doors and a screaming child woke Craig from his dead-to-the-world slumber. *God, I hate this motel*, he thought as his eyes fought to open. The fact that the people who woke him had a child must mean that they were kidnappers who abducted a wealthy child for its ransom. *I mean, who'd bring a kid here?*

As Craig gathered his wits and attempted to wake, he wondered what was real from last night's events. Craig rolled on his back and liberated himself from a fantastically freeing fart. "Ahh, yes," he exclaimed as he sat up in the bed, greeting the morning with a stretch. Craig thought he was alone, his guest from the night prior no doubt departing at some point in the evening. He soon realized his assumption was wrong when he turned to see Rob sitting a few feet away.

Rob was fully dressed in a tight white tee, jeans, and trainers. Not a hair has tussled, and there wasn't a wrinkle to be reckoned with. He sat in the chair, appearing comfortable as he smiled looking at Craig.

Craig realized that last night hadn't been a dream after all. *And he's still as hot as he was last night.* Craig wasn't a morning person. He ran a hand over his hair, which felt matted. His eyes felt crusty, and his mouth tasted like he'd eaten snot flavored yogurt that had spoiled. He couldn't comprehend how Rob looked so perfect, pristine, and pleasant at this early hour.

"Good morning," Craig addressed Rob begrudgingly. "How long have you been awake?"

"Oh, I don't sleep," Rob replied,

"Yeah, me neither," Craig yawned. "Last night was an anomaly. I'm never out like that." He rubbed his face firmly with his fingers in a futile attempt to knock the night out of his noggin. "Mmm, do I smell coffee?" he murmured as he lifted his naked body out of bed.

"I anticipated that you'd want a freshly brewed cup and some breakfast when you awoke, so I went out and brought you something."

A small, rickety, wood table with two equally precarious chairs stood next to the dark fabric curtains that covered a large window. Although the drapes were made of heavy, opaque material, the slit between them allowed light to stream into the room. A complete assortment of eggs, toast, jams, and jellies sat on the table, illuminated through the spectacles of dust that danced in the daylight-like delicate fairies. *Was Rob the knight in shining armor that he had been waiting for? The man who'd whisk him off the streets and take him to a pristine paradise where they could both live happily ever*? Craig now knew how Julia Roberts felt in Pretty Woman when Richard Gere arrived in her life.

Craig grabbed the jeans he had feverishly flung on the floor five hours prior and slipped them on. As a starving stud, breakfast looked and smelled too good to pass up. He invited Rob to join him as he sat at the table and tore into his tantalizing tapenade and toast. There was no stopping Craig from feasting on this fine foray of fancy foods.

***

Chase was soaked and saturated with salty sweat. His muscles twitched from an excruciating yet exhilarating workout. He'd forced his muscles beyond fatigue, and it felt great. Now he headed for the steam room to hydrate and heal. He knew the moist, misty air would be just what his sore body needed. The steam room door swung open to reveal the usual bros comfortably lounging in their small, white cotton towels. The guys were always a welcomed sight for Chase. This place was pure paradise after a weary workout.

Greetings and a round of fist bumps welcomed Chase into this heated haven. He took his usual spot on the bench next to Bolton. He'd hoped that he'd avoid being the topic of conversation today — but he soon discovered that he was going to be the *only* thing everyone talked about.

Bolton began, "I waited till today to tell you about meeting Corporal Matthew. I thought it might freak you out."

He hesitated. "Dude, did you know the military has an APB out on Rob?"

Chase's eyes widened, and his body locked up. "What are you talking about? The military is after Rob?"

"Some Marine came by yesterday asking questions. He wanted to know if I knew Rob and where he could find him." Tad and Ryan sat riveted as if they were holding a tub of buttered popcorn waiting for a double feature to start.

"Ooh. Our very own fugitive," Tad gleefully gloated.

"How exciting! Maybe Chase is housing a deserter. How awesome is that?" Ryan added with equal exuberance.

Chase's heart dropped. He couldn't believe what he was hearing. "I knew he was too good to be true. I warned you, Bolton, that we shouldn't trust him!"

"Now Chase, don't blow this out of proportion. You have a way of taking something simple and making a huge, convoluted deal out of it. Let's stay calm."

"Center your chakras man. You're seriously out of alignment and crushing my beautiful breakfast buzz. We don't know for sure that he's a deserter." Tad was the easiest going bro in the steam room. He lived his life as if on an IV drip of Prozac and could find the silver lining in any cloud.

Tad continued, "He probably just killed someone." Then he sat back as contented as if he'd solved a riddle.

"Chase's initial suspicions now resurfaced. *Maybe he is a killer! Was I right?*

Bolton sighed. "Guys, relax. You're going to freak Chase out. The dude was chill about the whole thing. He didn't say Rob was dangerous. He just said that he wanted to find him. Jeez, for all we know, maybe he lost a bet and owes him a beer."

Chase was more confused than ever. He needed to move. He stood up and paced in the steam room. He shook out his hands and kicked his feet in an attempt to shake his anxiety. After several deep, calming breaths, he sat down again.

Tad cut to the quick, "Hey dude, you've been in the same bed with this bro for a week. He would have killed you by now if he was dangerous. Instead of stabbing you in the middle of the night, he made you breakfast every morning. Even if he were a fugitive, I'd let him hide out in my pad any day!"

Chase decided he was overacting about the military inquiring about Rob. Someone looking for Rob was the least of his problems.

Bolton snorted. "Dude, the solution's simple. All Chase needs to do is ask Rob why this soldier is looking for him. Problem solved."

Chase's heart sank. He sighed heavily. "Guys, Rob's gone. I told him to leave. He brought a bunch of guys home for us to have sex with. I freaked out and asked them all to leave."

He told them the whole story. As usual, the guys were the voice of reason. Well, if not reason, they at least provided a different viewpoint.

"Why? Sounds hot. I wish my boyfriend brought home guys for us to play with," Ryan was jealous.

"Yeah," Tad chimed in. "I'd say that after installing the stripper pole, he just wanted to turn up the heat. The boy went full *calienté*! I wouldn't mind if he wanted to slip me his jalapeño."

Chase tried to defend his position. "I like this guy, and I want it to be just the two of us."

Ryan, the most experienced in open relationships, couldn't sit still. "I gotta ask, did Rob know you were uptight about bringing other people into play? It's not uncommon, and a lot of people are into it. Maybe he didn't know you would be upset if he brought a few boys home."

"Well, no, it wasn't discussed. But I would have HOPED that he felt the same way about it that I did about things."

Bolton had been quiet the whole time but now cut into the conversation. "Dude, guy, girl, or whatever; if you're going to scrimmage, you've gotta know the rules of the field. It's impossible to call a foul if you don't know what's out of bounds."

Chase's watch chimed with a question from Jane just

as he had prepared to consider what Bolton proposed. Time had slipped away, and he had to get into the office, *pronto*. His legs shook as he stood, sore from the morning's workout.

"Thanks for your help, guys. It's much appreciated. Let me think about all this. I have to go. Work thing. I'll check you all out later." He left the steam room and headed into the office to wrap up last-minute logistics.

***

The motel curtains were drawn. But through a crack, the bright blue sky seeped into the dank, dreary room. Craig thought it was a good idea to keep the curtains closed so as not to expose all the sins evident in that seedy space. He'd finished his breakfast. Craig broke yet another one of his cardinal rules—asking questions. "So, what brought you to The Creamy Hole last night?"

"You invited me here, don't you remember?" Rob said in confusion.

Craig chuckled. Rob was adorable. "Not me, dude. The donut shop."

Rob smiled sadly. "I've been staying with someone special. His name is Chase, and I thought he really liked me." Those weren't the words Craig wanted to hear, but it was no surprise that someone as attractive and considerate as Rob had been snatched up already. "So, you're taken?" Craig continued.

"Yes. Well, at least I think so. It was all going well up until last night when he became upset that I brought other fellows around to join in with us."

"I can see why," Craig concurred. "I'd want you all to myself, too."

"Really?" Rob was looking pleased, yet confused.

"Hell yeah. You wouldn't think it, but I'm a romantic as well. I want someone all to myself, too. I may sleep with a lot of men. But when it comes to a special someone, I don't like to share."

Rob computed the scene from last night in his head, and suddenly Chase's actions made perfect sense. His processor whirred into turbo mode as he wondered what to do next. *Perhaps this human could help him make his calculations?* Craig seemed eager to facilitate Rob's computational functions, so Rob decided to inquire further.

"It seems I misjudged Chase's reaction to bringing boys for him to play with. He was upset by it. I suppose I should return and ask what was wrong?"

"What's your relationship with him? Does he care about you?" Craig hoped the answer would be "No."

"All indications imply that his heart is genuine with its intentions towards me," Rob replied, dashing Craig's hopes.

"And how do you feel about him?" Craig inquired. Rob understood the question but didn't know how to answer since he didn't have feelings. Craig could see Rob's indecision and decided to rephrase the question.

"Do you *want* to be with him?"

"Very much, yes. I love being with him."

"If he cares about you and you want to be with him, then you should be together. It's that simple."

Rob was grateful for Craig's wisdom about how humans worked. After all, Craig was human. Who would know better?

They were governed by their emotions and sense of right and wrong. Rob knew that he had a duty to tell Chase the truth about what he was, even if it was to his detriment.

Rob had a renewed sense of purpose. He grabbed Craig and hugged him tightly. "I must apologize to Chase for the miscalculation I made in our relationship. You've helped me understand a great many things. Thank you very much."

Craig closed his eyes and hugged him back. "I'd be lying if I said I wasn't disappointed that you're not single. You're a special guy. I'd forgotten what it felt to be cared about. Chase is very lucky."

Rob drew away and smiled at him. "You're special, too. I'm confident that you'll find the right partner one day."

Rob was eager to be a part of Chase's life in a way he hadn't been before.

"I need to be going. I can't thank you enough for giving me a place to recharge last night."

Craig shrugged. "Happy I could help. Have fun at your party tomorrow, and let your friend Chase know just how lucky he is to have someone like you on his arm." Rob didn't register the sadness in Craig's eyes. He was too eager to be on his way. With one last hug, Rob turned and left Craig behind.

Chapter 19

J ane stood at Chase's desk, at the ready. She'd arrived in the office early to make sure all her work was done, and she could focus her attention on helping Chase with whatever he needed. He'd no doubt have lots for her to take care of. The familiar giggling murmurs of the other girls wishing her boss a good morning could be heard down the long office corridors. The salutations grew louder, as did the thumping of Jane's heart at the prospect of Chase's pending presence. As if in slow motion, with a bright backlight and wind whisking through his hair, Chase entered the room. His blue Brooks Brother's blazer, tight tan chinos, and fitted silk shirt caused Jane to swoon.

"How's the morning been so far? We off to a good start?" He raised his mug to his moist mouth and sipped his hot, lathered latte leaving a bit of leche on the corner of his lips. Jane watched wantonly, wondering if she should warn him of the warm froth on the side of his mouth. Before she could mention it, Chase scooped up the cream with the corner of his tongue and swallowed it swiftly. Jane's knees went weak.

"We are all set for tomorrow. I think I've got everything covered," she tried to sound nonchalant in an attempt to hide how suddenly hot she was.

"The calm before the hurricane," Chase chuckled. "Don't get cocky now. No doubt something will come up that will create chaos before tomorrow's exciting event."

"No doubt." Jane attempted a cute giggle but delivered an odd snort that embarrassed her.

"Awesome, great work. Let's just see how today plays out." Chase turned to settle into his office as Jane stole a last glance at his brilliant bubble butt.

***

The seedy motel Rob spent the night in wasn't far from the Mission Gym. Rob made haste to get there in hopes of catching Chase and the guys while they were still steaming. He eagerly entered the gym and ran directly into OMJ, who was standing just inside the front door by the cash register.

"Five bucks to work out today," OMJ grunted. Rob reached into his jeans and pulled out a ten spot.

"That's for next time too," Rob said proudly.

"I like you, kid," OMJ grunted. "Why don't you step into my office so we can better discuss a few things?"

Rob was happy to comply, although he was eager to see Chase and clear up the matter of last night.

"He's not here," OMJ said, walking across the gym floor.

"Who?"

"Chase. He's gone. Went to work. Came in early and left already."

Rob sighed in disappointment. He realized that there was no point staying at the gym now. He continued walking through the smattering of studs, all pumping, pushing, and pounding the heavy equipment.

OMJ's office was nothing more than a desk strategically placed between punching bags and a boxing ring. The old elementary school teacher-style desk was covered in weathered knickknacks, calendars, schedules, assorted papers, and bills. Rob found a seat adjacent to the desk and made himself comfortable. Clearly, this chair had seen better days since springs sprung strategically out of the bottom cushion poking the posterior.

OMJ sat down and cleared his voice before speaking. "Listen son; it's none of my business what happened between you and Chase. But I know you're on your own now with nowhere to stay. So, if you need a place, let me know. I can help. Secondly, A Marine named Corporal Matthew has been snooping around here looking for you. I don't know what he wants or why he's looking for you. I thought you should know."

Rob appreciated Old Man Johnson's candor. As Rob sat pondering his possible prospects. He wondered if it were best to surprise Chase at home tonight or just wait in the steam room for him to arrive first thing. As Rob's processor calculated his options, Old Man Johnson sprang up into action.

"Here, let me show you where you can bunk up if you'd like to stay the night," OMJ offered. He grabbed a small, stuffed boxing glove key chain with multiple keys attached to it, and they headed down the rickety wooden stairs to the Mission's basement. A metal chain hung above the stairs. A simple tug illuminated the area below the gym.

It was spacious and tidy, cool and dry from the thick cement that supported the old structure above. Girly posters adorned the walls, along with old boxing matches. Without a doubt, it had been inhabited many times before. Rob wondered if OMJ used this space as a sanctuary for souls in distress. He knew he'd be safe here until Chase arrived in the morning.

"The TV remote is next to the bed. I've got Madden, Minecraft, and tons of games, so help yourself."

"This'll be great. Very kind of you."

"Happy to help you young people," OMJ said before retreating up to his office next to the boxing ring. Rob settled in and made himself comfortable.

***

Chase spent the day working with Jane, tying up loose ends. The last thing to do was review the guest list. Jane sat nearby, stealing glimpses of his well-defined chest and arms filling out his snug, tailored dress shirt. He pondered what to do with the extra ticket now that Rob was nowhere to be found. He dreaded the thought of not having someone special with him at such a momentous moment in his life.

As Chase's mind drifted to Rob, a pleasant and upbeat "See you guys tomorrow for the big day!" brought his attention to Patty — the perky, plump receptionist who occupied the front desk. Patty was finished for the day as she tucked away her jar of chunky chocolate chews that she gave generously to the visitors who entered the establishment.

Chase looked at the clock. It was already eight. He felt terrible about keeping Jane there so late.

He tucked away some papers and closed the lid of his laptop. "Looks like we're good here. We should go. I'm so sorry to have kept you so long."

"Don't be silly. I'm glad I could help. This needed to get done. Now we're all set." Jane glowed with happiness. Chase knew that she was a catch for the right guy.

Would any of the steam room bros be good for her? Hmmm, maybe.

"Walk you to your car?" Chase offered.

"Sure, let me get my stuff." Jane jumped at the opportunity to spend a few more minutes with him.

I've definitely gotta find her a steam room bro.

"Okay then, I'll meet you at the elevator," Chase grabbed the last of his things for the night.

***

Corporal Matthew had walked the streets of Los Angeles all day and failed, yet again, to find Rob. His legs were dead tired and his spirit low. He wouldn't accomplish anything further until tomorrow.

He sat, discouraged, in the silver Toyota Corolla the military rented for him. He'd driven through many neighborhoods and visited countless businesses inquiring about the whereabouts of Rob but seemed to be no closer to an answer than he was two weeks ago. The General was scheduled to arrive in less than two days, and Matthew knew that he wouldn't be happy with his lack of results. Matthew couldn't help but notice a donut shop across the way.

The establishment didn't look especially inviting— the sign worn, the windows littered with old, sun-faded photos of pastries as well as a cacophony of confections. But the promise of sultry, sugary sweets just seemed too seductive for him to pass up. After the week he'd had, he'd earned himself a hot cup of cocoa and an extra-large bear claw.

Matthew entered the Creamy Hole and instantly

caught the eye of the owner. She stared at him and stopped wiping down the tables.

"A strapping stud in uniform," she murmured as Matthew blushed at the words. "How may I help you?"

***

Hillary enjoyed strong, definitive men who knew how to take charge and command. Back when she was a young lady, her first love had been a soldier boy named Tommy. He'd been tall and thin, with hard, strong features and a soft, wonderful heart. They were high school sweethearts and had made promises to grow old together. When the war came in the sixties, he disappeared, never to be heard from again. It was then, as a woman in her twenties, Hillary had shut down her heart and promised to never open it again for another. As the years passed eventually moved in with her brother Will, resolving to be a spinster until she died.

Hillary wasn't alone as she worked behind the counter. A few tables away, Craig sat relaxing. He was on a break from his evening activities. He enjoyed a cruller and checking his Instagram account, adding a rather risqué picture of himself with the hashtags #instagay #workingboy #dontjudgeme #donut #creamyhole.

As engaged as Craig and Hillary were, all activities ceased when Matthew entered. Hillary straightened her uniform and quickly checked her hair in the reflection of the stainless-steel coffee urn as she readied herself to serve the sultry soldier.

"A hot chocolate and a large bear claw, please." he requested.

"Sure, have a seat. I'll bring it over." Hillary flashed

him a saucy smile.

Matthew reached into his back pocket to grab his wallet. Hillary appreciated the gesture. "Please, no need to pay — It's on me, my way of thanking our men in uniform."

Corporal Matthew grinned gratefully. "Thank you, Ma'am. And please allow me to at least extend a gratuity if I may." He peeled a ten-spot from his billfold and placed it in the tip jar with a wink. He spotted a clean empty table and made a beeline for it.

Matthew sat across from a young man making no bones about checking him out. His gaze traveled from Matthew's head to his feet in a salacious scan.

"My name's Craig," he murmured. "Nice to meet you."

Matthew was flattered at the attention as he waited for his coated confection.

Craig licked his lips, not scared to show his flirtatious nature. "So that you know, I'm always happy to service a man in the service."

Matthew grinned. "Corporal Matthew. I'm on duty. I'm looking for someone."

"Well, I hope that someone is me," Craig retorted without any subtlety whatsoever.

"Sorry, sir, no. It's not you."

Craig left his table and sauntered over to join Matthew. "Interesting. Who are you looking for? Maybe I know him. I do see a lot of people coming through these parts."

The Corporal didn't want to encourage conversation with Craig. He was tired. He only wanted his hot chocolate and pastry and to be left alone to enjoy it.

Both men were startled when Hillary barked, "Leave him be! Go outside. You've disrupted my guests enough." She brought the warmed bear claw and piping hot cocoa to Matthew's table.

Craig rolled his eyes at her. "Jeez, Louise, don't get your panties in a bunch. I'll move if that's what you want." He retreated sulkily to the outside of the shop. Hillary smiled at him with freshly rouged lips. The soldier smiled back, attempting to be polite, and began to devour his delicious delicacy.

Chapter 20

I n the laboratory at Hot Bot-y Robotics, Herbie
quietly worked alongside his dutiful assistant Kyle
as he attempted to resurrect the depleted tracking
code he'd programmed to find Rob. He was
growing more and more desperate to find the robot as
he knew that Rob's battery would be deteriorating at an
accelerated rate every day.

Bentley burst into the lab like a drag queen at a wig
sale. Kyle and Herbie wore their white lab coats, shoe
protectors, and electrostatic guards to protect the
delicate circuits, electrodes, and half-assembled robot
parts which lay around. Bentley, on the other hand,
wore no such protective clothing and barreled into the
sterile environment. The other technicians, careful not
to bring dust, dirt, and static into this safe space, gave a
collective eye roll and head shake, knowing that
nothing would be said about Bentley ignoring their
procedures.

"How is the neuro-net coming along?" Bentley
callously called out to Kyle.

Herbie clenched his teeth in contempt. Kyle had been
re-assigned to the new government robotic division
against Herbie's wishes. Herbie himself was boycotting
it, and while Kyle knew Herbie wasn't happy about
him being appointed to run the program, they'd had no
choice.

Kyle answered begrudgingly. "Good, boss. We've got all the robots linked together via Bluetooth, so they can all receive an order when given. We've got it so one officer can send out battle plans to an entire network of soldiers. All they'll need is a simple password."

Bentley looked pleased. "Good work. Start uploading that software into everything we build. It will be the perfect redundant backup system should our primary backup protocol fail. When it's complete, I'll program the code word. I'm going to be the only one who has it. I want it encrypted, so no one but me has control of all the robots." Bentley looked directly at Herbie.

Herbie knew all Bentley wanted was to let everyone know he was the boss—that no one other than he had a way of reaching Rob and any of the other robots unless *he* approved it.

Before exiting, Bentley delivered one last demand. "When his faulty battery fails, make sure I'm the first to be notified. I'll make sure Rob is retrieved immediately; I'm not going to let him get away from us a third time!"

***

Back at the donut shop, Craig was out front selling his wares. It was still early enough, and he hadn't any takers. He was bored. So, when he saw Corporal Matthew finish his donut and head out with a smile at a simpering Hillary, Craig decided to have a little fun.

"So, you never told me who you were looking for, sailor. Are you sure it's not me?" Craig teased.

Matthew looked annoyed. "I'm not a sailor. I'm not sure why you'd even think that."

"My bad," Craig said sultrily. "It's just that I have a thing for seamen." He had walked right into that one,

Craig thought triumphantly.

Matthew heaved a heavy sigh. "Perhaps you can help me in another way." He pulled up the image of the robot that resembled Rob on his phone and held it up for Craig to see.

Craig stared at the image, not sure what to say. He swallowed and pretended to look hard at the picture of Rob. His sassy, savior-faire attitude disappeared like mist.

"Uhm," he stuttered. "I'm not sure."

Corporal Matthew's eyes narrowed, and Craig knew he'd given himself away.

"So, you do recognize this man?" asked Matthew forcefully.

Craig decided since he would eventually be forced to spill the beans, he might as well get something out of all this in return. "Perhaps you and I could make an arrangement?" He continued, "Perhaps a little, 'quid pro BRO'?"

"You realize that I'm an officer of the United States Marine Corps, and I don't need to make any arrangements with you."

"Yeah, I know. But perhaps we could still talk in private, so I could tell you what you'd like to hear out of ear range of these thirsty jackals." Craig motioned to his left to a smattering of young hustlers, standing by eagerly listening to their conversation.

"Fine, let's talk in private," Matthew reluctantly agreed.

Craig led Corporal Matthew around the back of the Creamy Hole. The heavy metal back door was unlocked, and Craig walked through it.

Matthew hesitated.

"Are you coming in then?" Craig said. "I promise to

behave myself."

I don't promise that at all, but he looks like he needs a little reassurance.

Matthew followed him. They were now in the storage room of the bakery. They were surrounded by giant bags of flour, sugar, and other ingredients. The room was oddly clean and organized for a place that looked like the "A" rating on the front door was unearned.

Craig wasn't shy in the least, nor was he intimidated by the large, muscular Marine that stood before him. Without so much as a quiver of uncertainty in his voice, he leaned towards Corporal Matthew. "I'll give you everything you need to get this fellow you're looking for, but I'd politely ask you to give me the one thing I need."

"And what would that be?"

"This," said Craig, as he firmly cupped the Corporal's cramped kumquats. Matthew's stiff soldier suddenly stood at attention. "I figured it had been a while since your weapon was wielded. I hope you'll allow me to service this serviceman."

Matthew hesitated. Craig whispered, "Don't ask. Won't tell." And with that, Matthew's boy baton was in Craig's groping grasp.

"A guy can get shot for doing that," Corporal Matthew warned. "I'm counting on it, and I'll tell you just where I'd like you to shoot," Craig crooned with a wink. There was no dissuading him from his mission as he kneeled onto a strategically placed bag of flour and unzipped Matthew's jeans.

Matthew provided more than a mouthful of Marine meat for Craig, who craved the Corporal's cadet. There was no stopping either of these men, clearly now engaged in what in military terms could be called

"Operation Creamy Hole."

Matthew wasn't unfamiliar to a man's mouth on his WMD (weapon of mass delight, as what it was called by his former lovers). In the past, he'd preferred the pleasure of the softer sex. But recently, his tastes have been leaning more towards muscle and machismo.

Craig was eager to share with Corporal Matthew the tricks he learned over the years as a hustler and welcomed the challenge of blowing this hot Marine's mind.

***

Matthew's weary body collapsed onto a fifty-pound bag of flour. His shirt and jacket had been carelessly tossed onto the baker's cooling rack, and his trousers were around his ankles. Exhausted yet sexually satisfied, he reclined, ready to receive the information Craig had previously promised.

"His name is Rob. He was with me in the motel and brought me breakfast." Craig remembered the pleasure he'd gotten waking up to someone who cared about him. "He's apparently got a boyfriend named Chase, whom he cares for very much. They had a fight of some sort, so he didn't have a place to stay last night. I ended up convincing him to get back with him. What can I say? I'm a romantic, I guess."

"What can you tell me about this guy Chase?"

"Not much, just that they care for each other. Rob said that he was excited to be going to a big party with him tonight, or was it tomorrow?"

"Party? Any idea where?" Matthew said hopefully.

"Some museum is opening this weekend," Craig shrugged. "That's all I know. I think this guy Chase is a bigwig, and they are attending this big gala or something."

If I follow up on this and find the robot, it'll undoubtedly impress the General.

All that was left for Matthew to do was find out which museum was having a gala opening, and he'd find Rob. He rose, intending to complete his mission.

"Not so fast!" a voice rang out loudly from the other doorway. Hillary flashed her sexiest smile. "Now it's my turn."

Craig grinned as he turned the key to the heavy metal door they'd entered earlier, locking it. He placed the key in his jean pocket as he pulled his pants up past his posterior.

"He's all yours, and you're in for a treat, I must say," Craig boasted as he walked past Matthew towards the front of the donut shop. "I'll cover the counter for you."

Hillary gave Craig an appreciative nod. She looked at Matthew the way a cat would look at a plump canary.

I suppose I'd better entertain her. Then, I can get out of here. Matthew sighed. Anything for the mission.

Hillary pulled the string off the top of her apron and removed it, passing it to Craig. He accepted the apron and exited the storage room with a wicked wink.

"I've been hot for you since you walked in, soldier," said Hillary. "I'm grateful to Craig for procuring your sexy package."

It seemed this wasn't the first time such a thing had happened. He'd wondered why Hillary let a hustler hang out in front of her place of business, and now he knew why. It was bait to bring the prey to the spider.

Hillary opened the top button of her blouse as she playfully pronounced, "You're about to learn why I named this donut shop 'The Creamy Hole,' Marine."

Chapter 21

Chase paused at the door to his townhouse. He dreaded the silence he faced inside. It was a harsh reminder that he was alone and failed again at love. He entered and walked down the hall to the kitchen. The smells of roasting garlic, fragrant steak, and warm apple tarts were a distant memory. The long conversations and the silly, sexy teasing were a thing of the past, as well as cuddling on the comfortable couch and the tantalizing hot tea before bedtime.

It was late, and Chase was tired from the stress of the day as well as the dread of facing tomorrow's big event alone. He was out of frozen foods since Rob cooked everything fresh. He was also too beat to heat anything from a can in the cupboard. Instead, Chase made himself a cup of herbal tea and grabbed a protein bar. He sat on the couch, sipping his hot chamomile. The sofa seemed a lonely, sad place now — serving as a sour reminder of the erotic acrobatics that had occurred on it the night Rob brought the boys home for him, the night Rob left. Chase still wasn't sure why Rob had thought forging a fornicating foursome would be what he wanted. But he was too tired to solve the riddle, and he retreated to his room.

***

In the downstairs basement of the Mission Gym, Rob was now fully charged and waiting for Chase. It seemed pointless to be idle until his human companion arrived in the morning, so Rob scanned the Mission Gym for any repairs he could make. He found some plumbing and electrical problems, calculating a solid ten hours' worth of work to be done. He knew he'd need to rush to be ready before the sun rose and OMJ arrived to open the gym. Rob accessed the extensive library of home repair and decorating knowledge he'd downloaded while staying at Chase's and quickly put his proficiency into practice.

A nearby tool belt was the perfect accessory to help Rob complete the work he wanted to do. He only had a few clothes to his name since he'd hurried out of the house the other night, and he didn't want to dirty them. He knew OMJ kept a lost and found box with clothes in it—it was where he'd got his first wardrobe after fleeing the Hot Bot-y laboratory.

Rob raided the basement bin seeking something to wear while he worked. A worn white tee-shirt seemed perfect for the job since it enabled Rob to work without restraint. Next came a pair of jeans that had seen better days and had grown thin in spots around the knees and crotch. The denim was soft and easy to maneuver in. Although they were tight in the tush, they were perfect for the purpose. Dressed and with the tools to tackle the task, Rob set forth to modernize the Mission and strengthen the sagging structure.

***

Chase lay in bed, seeking the sanctuary of his soft sheets. It wasn't his usual bedtime. Chase wasn't one for watching TV in the evening, although he did love the occasional movie. His favorites were romantic comedies. He didn't discriminate between male/female stories or male/male romance stories. If they were clever, honest, sweet, and well-acted, he was the first in line to watch them. *The 10 Year Plan* was probably Chase's favorite. He thought the chemistry between the lead actors was perfect and the writing clever. He was fond of stories about slightly flawed people who would eventually find love when the right person came into their lives. Other favorite movies of his were; *eCupid* and *Is It Just Me?* They all seemed to sum up what he was missing in his life — a person who thought him perfect the way he was. *How great would my life be if it was like one of these films?*

Huh, he mused glumly. I'm destined to be a single, lonely man my whole life. *I couldn't possibly be as fortunate as the characters in those movies.*

Sleep was the only comfort available to him that night, so he closed his eyes and tried desperately to slip into slumber. His mind wouldn't relent, wondering what had happened to Rob. As his thoughts kept coming back to Rob, it was impossible for him not to wonder — *Could the guys at the steam room be right? Had Rob brought the boys over for him as a fun gift?* The more Chase considered it, the more apparent it became that Rob certainly had no problem scoring a sexy stud in seconds. With Rob's looks and sweet demeanor, anybody — male or female — would quickly want to bed him. Was it conceivable Rob didn't want an open relationship as Chase assumed? Was he simply attempting to please Chase? The more he thought about it, the more he realized Rob's every action had been selfless. Every single moment of the day, the actions he'd taken were to please Chase. *How was this any different?*

Like a clap of thunder, a storm of emotion and clarity took over Chase. For the first time, he understood his relationship with Rob. Rob would do anything to please him. Being with someone was about putting that person first. He understood now why every single relationship in his life had failed in the past. In his ignorance, he hadn't been ready to put someone else before himself.

He looked at the clock. It was almost midnight. Chase needed to apologize. He wanted nothing more than to be with Rob— to talk to him, hold him and learn more about who he really was.

Chase's heart pumped with excitement. He grew frustrated that there was nowhere to channel his energy at this late hour. Where could Rob possibly be? He had an idea—his Apple Watch! Could he track Rob through the GPS? He quickly looked to see if there was a location registering for Rob. Nothing. The watch either didn't have its GPS set up or was out of range.

Why doesn't Rob have a phone? That damn watch is practically useless without being connected to one.

Chase's hopes were dashed.

Tomorrow he'd make it an early morning and start looking for Rob. He wasn't sure where he'd start or how he'd find him. But Chase knew one thing— he wasn't going to give up until Rob was back in his arms.

***

Back at the Creamy Donut Hole, Hillary heard a knock on the storage room door. She was getting dressed after forty minutes of vigorous sexercise. It was almost one a.m., and soon, Hillary's brother, William, would be out front to pick her up.

Craig called out, "Closing time!"

She'd had her fill of the fine farm boy-cum-Marine and was now content with the job he'd done to satisfy her. "You did good, soldier boy," she whispered to Matthew. "I'm right grateful for the grinding you gave me. But it's time for you to go now. Why don't you take what you want from the donut case— they're on me." She smiled as she finished getting dressed.

"I'm good," wheezed the weary warrior.

"Are you sure? You'll probably need the sugar to recover for when the adrenaline wears off. I'll get an assortment ready for you anyway." Hillary went out the door and disappeared into the front to prepare a pink box of delicious delicacies for the Corporal.

***

Matthew zipped up his fly and put on his shoes, grateful for the opportunity to be on his way after fulfilling his duty. He made his way past the ovens and out to the front, where a pink box wrapped in twine waited for him. Hillary and Craig stood by the front door, holding it open. A few feet away, an old, silver Honda idled.

"My brother's here to pick me up. Time to lock up." Hillary said. "Here are your donuts. Enjoy and thanks for a good time."

Craig was especially cheery. "Tonight was fun. I hope you find the guy you're looking for."

Matthew smiled at the satisfied pair as he grabbed the pink box of donuts and made his way into the night. *The things I do for my country.*

***

Rob was enjoying the fruits of his labor as he looked around at all the repairs he was able to make. Earlier that evening, he'd found an old booklet in a dusty corner, explaining the history of the Mission Gym. He wasn't surprised to find out it was as old as time and as worn, too.

Rob's research on the history of the Mission uncovered some interesting facts. About one hundred and fifty years ago, Old Man Johnson's great grandfather, Holden Harry Johnson, converted into a boxing ring and workout facility. The mission had been in the Johnson Family as long as the family tree stood. Underneath the mission ran a freshwater aquifer, providing natural botanical waters. Local legend had it that the waters in the steam room had the power to rejuvenate and heal. People attributed their daily steaming to their healthy glow and youthful appearance. As remarkable as this old mission turned gym was to everyone, it had been battered and beaten by time.

However, that was about to change, thought Rob, as he passionately patched the plumbing, soldered the sockets, dabbed the drywall, and retiled the roof. He had worked tirelessly through the night without requiring a break to recharge. He'd found an old extension cord in the back-storage cabinet and used it to keep himself plugged into the wall while he worked. Rob surmised he'd not only accomplish what he needed to do, but when morning came, he'd have a full, fresh battery to start the day.

The night flew by as Rob tackled the tasks. He was desperate to be done before the dawn. When he'd finally decided to cease his efforts, he awaited OMJ's and Chase's arrival.

***

Chase woke before just before sunrise. He was eager to find Rob. The plan: scour the city in search of the man he loved. Chase had precious little time to accomplish his task since his museum opening was later today.

***

Rob was waiting for OMJ when the older man entered the gym with his familiar scalding hot morning brew in his hand. OMJ's jaw dropped, astounded at the sight before him. Rob felt proud of himself. Not only was the gym immaculate, but also it looked brand new. The equipment shone, the boxing ring's covering had been re-stretched, and the floor repaired.

"I don't believe what I'm seeing! Where's the construction team hiding?" OMJ exclaimed.

Rob stood beyond the hall and under a sign that hung from an old nail reading 'Steam Room.'

"I did some repairs last night. I wanted to thank you for letting me stay here."

"Well, you certainly outdid yourself. This place looks amazing!" OMJ still looked disbelieving. "Take a seat, son. I'd like to talk to you while I have my coffee."

Rob saw something was bothering the old bro. He took a seat at OMJ's now tidy desk. OMJ's face grew serious. "Question; I tried to speak to you about this yesterday, but son, I know something's different about you. People can't do what you did here with this clean-up. And I know the military is after you. Spill the beans; what's going on here?

Rob sat for a second and scanned his circuits. How should he reply to such an inquiry? Perhaps this had to do with what Herbie told him at Hot Bot-y about hiding? Why was everyone looking for him anyway?

Rob processed the data and computed an honest and satisfactory answer to the old man's query. He realized that his only recourse was to reveal the reality of the situation. So, with a clear and calculated composure, he commented, "Dr. Herbert McAlister is the man who created me at Hot Bot-y robotics. He told me I was in danger and needed to leave and hide. From whom or why –I have no idea. I just trusted him and left quickly. That's how I came to meet you and Chase." Rob continued his stoic and steady statement. "I don't have any knowledge of doing anything wrong or why anyone would be looking for me.

"As far as Chase is concerned, he's wonderful. My sole purpose is to please him and be a good partner. I'm incapable of lying or hurting anyone." Rob fell silent, satisfied with completing his proclamation.

OMJ's eyebrows were at full mast. "Son, I don't know what to make of your explanation, but I do know one thing from all the years I've been on this planet. I know the difference between a fib and fact. And one thing is clear to me. Who or whatever you are, you're being a hundred percent truthful."

OMJ rubbed his chin thoughtfully. "I don't know what they wanted or why they wanted you. But hopefully, they won't be back. You're safe here, son.– Both from them and whatever secrets you may hold. It's none of my concern as long as no one gets hurt," he said sincerely.

Rob was grateful. "Thank you. And sir, please know that I'm excited to see Chase when he arrives today. I'm planning on telling him everything."

"You do that, son, and again I'm obliged for what you did to help this old mission stay standing for a few more years."

Rob smiled. Then made himself comfortable in the corner of the gym, waiting for Chase to appear.

Chapter 22

Herbie arrived at the Hot Bot-y laboratory to find Kyle working on the demonstration for the General.

"Would you like to catch me up on what you've been doing for the last two weeks?" Herbie asked, trying not to sound annoyed at Kyle.

"You know I didn't have a choice," Kyle confessed. "Bentley assigned me to this, and I had to do it."

Herbie felt bad that Kyle was stuck between a rock and a hard place. "I know it's not your fault. I am, however, curious as to the progress you've made in your research."

Kyle was pleased that Herbie took an interest in the work he was doing. "Well, basically, not only have I programmed every robot in here to a central neuro-net, but I've also chained them together. So we can communicate with them en masse via Bluetooth or Wi-Fi if needed."

Herbie thought for a minute about what Kyle said. There was no denying it was beneficial to the company to have all the robots connected via a centralized nervous system. It was a fail-safe way of communicating with all the robots, updating their systems all at once, and enabling them to all "talk" to each other. Herbie was proud of Kyle's work.

"Still no luck retrieving ROB?" Kyle inquired.

"Unfortunately, no. Other than the two times his battery dipped below ten percent, I haven't been able to track him."

Kyle crept up to Herbie, seemingly careful to speak quietly enough so none of the security camera's microphones could pick up what he said. "I fear any day now ROB's battery is going to fail. It'll read that it's fine, but it'll drop to nothing without warning. It's corroding internally and just won't hold a charge anymore. I think we should be standing by, ready at a moment's notice for when and if we get a signal that Rob's in danger. When his beacon broadcasts and the alarm alerts, it'll be minutes, if not seconds, before he's entirely inoperable. We'll need to be fast; otherwise, someone else may nab him."

Herbie knew Kyle was correct and was grateful to have him on his side. The two looked at each other with mutual appreciation and gratitude. The shared moment was soon shattered as Corporal Matthew barged into the laboratory.

"Good morning. My first order of business is to be briefed on tomorrow's presentation to the General. The second is finding that robot. I have a new lead I'm working on."

Herbie suddenly felt a little less hostile towards Corporal Matthew. "A new lead? What did you find out?"

"I haven't got him yet, but I know where he'll be tonight," Matthew asserted.

"What?" Herbie gasped. "You actually know where he is?"

Matthew nodded. "What I know is that tonight there is a museum opening gala. My sources tell me that he'll be the guest of someone attending the affair. I intend to be there and retrieve him."

"Well, I'm going with you!" Herbie hollered. He could see Matthew pause, pondering the possibilities. Having Herbie there certainly would help facilitate things. Matthew realized that Rob wouldn't know who he was and probably wouldn't comply with a direct order from him. But with Herbie present, there would be no altercation and hopefully no need for force of any kind.

"Considering the strategy and best-case scenario for success without civilian casualty, you may come with me."

Herbie sighed with relief. Tonight, he and Rob would be together again.

***

Back at the Mission Gym, Bolton was the first to arrive. He was surprised to see Rob there, looking like a puppy waiting for his master. "S'up, buddy? What are you doing here? Waiting for Chase?"

Rob nodded excitedly. "Will he be here this morning?"

"He should be. He never misses a morning. Wanna steam and wait for him?"

Rob nodded enthusiastically. The two men changed and headed for the steam room. Bolton was glad to be alone with Rob, so he could warn him that someone was looking for him.

As they entered the steam room, a warm, wonderful spray of water washed over them. *Delightful*, Bolton thought. This was his favorite part of the day.

"So, who is this Corporal Matthew dude who's poking around asking about you?" Bolton settled on the creaky wooden bench and leaned back against the warm, wet tiles.

Rob replied, "I don't know any Corporal Matthew. Until Mr. Johnson told me, I didn't know anything about it. Honestly, I don't know why anyone is looking for me."

Rob was earnest, but Bolton was still skeptical about what was happening here. *Something else is going on,* he thought. Even though Bolton was still unconvinced, he felt that Rob was now his bro. And being one of the bros, Bolton didn't want anyone to mess with Rob. Besides, Chase was his best friend. And for the first time in a long time, Chase was genuinely happy.

"When will Chase get here?" Rob asked eagerly. "I want to talk to him."

"Good question," Bolton replied as he pulled his cell phone from out under his towel. "Let's text him."

No sooner did the words come out of Bolton's mouth when they heard the familiar creak of the old metal hinges of the glass door. Chase stood in the doorway. Seeing Rob, he lit up like the holiday tree in Rockefeller Plaza on Christmas eve.

"You're here! I've been out for the last three hours looking for you!" Chase turned his attention to Bolton with a playful reprimand. "Why didn't you tell me you were with Rob?"

Bolton held up his phone. "I was just about to text you."

Chase walked over to Rob and gave him a big bear hug. "I missed you."

"You don't want me to leave? You're not still mad at me?" Rob was surprised.

"No, stay. I want to see you, talk to you, maybe talk about what happened the other day," Chase flashed a warm smile.

Bolton suddenly felt like a third wheel. "Well, someone should leave, and I'll volunteer myself. I should be working legs this morning. I'll check you dudes out later."

Bolton excused himself from the bench and walked out, giving Chase a whimsical wink.

***

Rob was pleased to be alone with Chase finally. He was eager to reveal his secret and make things right between them.

Based on all his programming, Rob couldn't lie to Chase.

Rob was about to reveal that he was an android when Chase, overcome with emotion, exclaimed, "I'm thrilled to see you. I'm so sorry about the other night. I've been ridiculous, and I'm sure there's a lot to talk about, but let's start with you. I was so worried about you. Are you okay?"

Rob was charmed by Chase's outburst. What were these sensations he felt? He felt needed, wanted. He felt the desire to reassure Chase. "I'm great. Old Man Johnson let me stay here last night, and I met some very nice people the evening before. It's been good for me to get out and socialize. But I admit now that we're together again, I'm processing something I perceive to be 'pleasure.'"

Chase laughed. "Yes," he said teasingly, "I'm perceiving pleasure to see you too." Rob's big, loving eyes were too much for him to handle. Suddenly Chase wasn't in the mood to talk. All he desired was tasting Rob's soft, gentle lips and pressing his muscular, solid body against his own. Chase was so turned on by Rob's touch he didn't realize just how small the towel he was wearing was. The soft terry-cloth fabric, which usually gave modest coverage, no longer provided any privacy at all. Instead, it chose to stand straight up. Neither man heard the metallic and familiar creak from the heavy glass door as Tad and Ryan walked in, innocently intending to steam. What they got was an eyeful of two titans, tonsil tickling and terrifically turned on.

"I haven't seen this much sausage being served since last year's Oktoberfest," hooted Tad.

It was true. Rob and Chase's mighty man meats were on display for all to see.

Rob unapologetically and without a shred of modesty greeted the guys, whereas Chase pulled his towel down to coyly cover his colossal kielbasa.

"I can see that you guys are both excited about being back together," teased Tad as his eyes were drawn to Rob's inadequate towel.

"So, I guess that means you're going to the opening together tonight?" Ryan inquired. "Cool, dude. It means you won't be alone."

Chase lit up at being reminded that he would have the company he desperately desired. "Yes. I mean, I hope you're still joining me this evening?"

"I wouldn't miss it for the world," Rob said excitedly. "It sounds like so much fun."

"You kids enjoy. Chase, I'm glad we're off the hook for this one," Ryan admitted. "No offense."

Tad shrugged and smiled. "None taken. If I didn't need to be there, I probably wouldn't go either."

"All this talk about the gala reminds me. I've still got to stop in the office. Plus, I need to get Rob a tux. If you'd excuse us, gents."

"Break a leg, bro!" said Tad.

"Yes, Mazel Tov," Ryan shouted. Good lucks and fist bumps abounded. Chase gratefully bid his bros goodbye and headed out.

***

Chase's office was bustling as everyone tried to tie up last-minute loose ends. Jane's name echoed throughout the space, summoning her to the front desk. She rolled her eyes as she walked over. With Chase not in yet, she was second in command and pulled in all directions.

Patty, the receptionist, informed her, "This is Corporal Matthew. He is here inquiring about the museum opening tonight. He's asking about Chase and seems intent on receiving an invite for tonight's gala. I told him that we were out of them, but he insisted. I thought it best that you deal with him."

Jane was eager to help, especially since Corporal Matthew was a large, sexy man in uniform. She addressed the hot hunk in military blues, "Please, let's talk in the conference room." Jane extended her arm to show him the way to the empty large oak room around the corner. Behind her, Patty continued her work helming the phones and coordinating the assortment of congratulatory packages, baskets, and flowers that seemed to be arriving non-stop.

Jane sat with Matthew, interested to hear his story. She'd stolen several glances down between his legs to notice how impressively large his manhood appeared. Jane's feminine formality was all that prevented her from lunging forward face-first into the pleasing plump plums so well pronounced in his military man's pants.

Matthew leaned forward earnestly. "It's vital that I attend your event tonight. I hasten to say it's a matter of national security." He straightened his back. "Ma'am, I'd—"

Jane stopped him, "No, no, please, it's Jane. Please call me Jane." She sat there looking into his giant dreamy brown eyes.

"Okay then, Jane. I'm requesting admission to the museum opening on official business on behalf of the United States government. I have reason to suspect that the military wants a guest who will be in attendance." Matthew spoke his words clearly and calmly.

Jane shrieked, her dirty daydreams forgotten. "Oh god! Do we have a terrorist coming? Are we in danger? Do we need military protection? I have to tell Chase immediately."

"No, please, calm down. He's not a terrorist or anyone dangerous. He's just a—" Matthew stopped, choosing his words carefully. "A person who I need to talk to. I'm just looking to attend tonight so that I can talk with him."

Jane wasn't sold on the story he was selling.

Matthew continued, "There's nothing you need to be alarmed about. There's no threat. I promise you." Jane looked deeply into his soul to see if he was lying.

"We can't have any problems tonight. You understand that, right? Millions of dollars are on the line. I mean, the entire cast from 'Real Housewives' will be there!"

"I can guarantee that there's no danger involved. There won't be so much as a peep from me regarding this matter. We simply need to ask him a couple of questions."

Someone so dreamy couldn't possibly be lying to her.

Relieved, Jane sighed and decided to trust him.

"Truth be told, I need to confirm this whole thing with my boss. He's not here right now. But I can't see it being a problem. The guest list is closed, but if you show up and ask for me, I'll make sure we can accommodate you. Patty at the front desk can give you all the information you'll need."

Jane got up from the table, Matthew in tow.

"On behalf of the U.S. Government, I promise there'll be no problems. We will be quiet and honorable guests."

"I'm glad I could help. I'm sure I'm doing the right thing inviting you to attend," She laughed. "Now, I have other matters to attend to. Hopefully, I'll see you at the party."

***

After picking up the tuxedo Chase had rented him for the night, Rob returned to the townhome. Rob was determined to look his best when Chase picked him up for the party. Oddly, he sensed a problem within his system. It had only been a few hours since his last charge, but his indicators already showed him at fifty percent power. Surely this couldn't be true? Either his indicator was misreading, or his battery wasn't holding a charge. Rob wasn't clear on how to proceed. He wasn't programmed to repair his own systems. And the technology used to create him wasn't readily available for download. Rob rummaged through his raw data registry but couldn't find a solution. The situation left him in a conundrum. He couldn't go back to the factory for an inspection. Herbie had been clear when he commanded Rob not to return. It seemed that for now, the best plan was to top off his charge and prepare to be the perfect partner for Chase that night.

Rob knew that for someone to truly love you, they need to know who you are. Tonight was a big deal for Chase. He questioned his timing. *Is tonight the time to reveal I'm not human? Yes. I can't keep lying to Chase.*

Chapter 23

Corporal Matthew stood with Dr. Herbie in Bentley's opulent office.

Bentley motioned them to take a seat as he leaned back in his overstuffed Corinthian leather chair. Matthew and Dr. Herbie sat in front of him on two smaller, matching fabric-covered armchairs that weren't entirely comfortable.

Matthew was eager to report what he had learned. "Tonight there's a big event—a museum opening. My intel has disclosed Rob will be there. I've secured admittance for both Dr. Herbie and myself so we may procure Rob and safely return him to the laboratory this evening."

Herbie added, "Rob's retrieval is imperative, but what's more important is that we do it as delicately as possible. No one can know he's a robot, and he can't be damaged when we bring him back to the lab."

Bentley placed his hands behind his head. He looked elated at the great news. "Excellent work, Corporal Matthew. The General will be pleased. All of us at Hot Bot-y Robotics owe you a debt of gratitude."

"He's not here yet, sir. But I have every confidence I'll be able to acquire the asset in question and transport it back to you safely."

"Well, men, go make whatever plans you need to make, and do whatever it is that you need to do to make this mission a success," Bentley commanded as if he were the General.

Matthew snapped to attention. "We'll make you proud, sir." He didn't miss Herbie's grimace at his words. No matter. This evening, all would be resolved.

***

Chase's office buzzed with excitement. Champagne bottles popped, and people hurried down the halls, excited to leave early so that they could get dressed up in their best gowns and gems. Chase was excited, too, and eager for the big night as he rushed home to get dressed and begin the celebrating.

The sounds of B.B. King and the scent of delicious cooking welcomed Chase home once again. Rob was back, and Chase loved it.

Rob had hung a banner over the couch that read "Congratulations." Streamers and balloons were hung around the townhouse. These thoughtful adornments filled Chase with gratitude and joy. The sight of Rob holding a bottle of champagne and two flutes at the ready was perfection. The man he loved looked absolutely glowing in a sharp, crisp black tuxedo. Tall, muscular, and impeccably groomed, the suit looked as if it were designed for Rob's body. Chase swooned at the sight of his man, who looked like the hottest James Bond he'd ever seen. When Rob put on an outfit, he somehow managed to look impossibly sexier than he did in his previous ensemble. Chase's heart pounded in his chest, and his head became dizzy with delight.

I need to touch him, kiss him. Right now.

At this moment, his worldview changed. Chase's job, co-workers, and lifetime achievements all suddenly meant nothing to him. All he cared about, all he needed in his life right now, was to get his beautiful, sweet man into his bed. Chase thrust his body against Rob's and kissed him deeply. They pressed their impressive muscular chests together as Chase kissed him deeply. He slid his hand around to the front of Rob's tuxedo pants and felt Rob's rigid rod rising rapidly.

"I've done the calculations that if we proceed in the direction you're taking, we'll be one hour late," Rob murmured against Chase's lips.

Chase's eye twinkled as he replied, "I'm okay with that."

"Okay then, we shall proceed, "Rob whispered. Chase dropped to his knees as Rob stood firm and grasped Chase's head, like a professional player palms a basketball as he prepares to dribble it down the court. Slam dunk. Chase felt like he'd won the championship.

***

Rob's full function now was to give Chase the experience of a lifetime, and he was equipped to do just that. Chase was aggressive in his lovemaking and liked to be overpowered. Rob was happy to comply. Chase moaned as Rob pumped his pleasure piston, but Rob knew Chase wanted more. Rob swooped him up in his arms and lifted him quickly and without effort. He flipped him over and placed him on the couch facing down. Rob took Chase's wanton wazoo in his firm grip, and with his hands on his ripe rear man melons, he proceeded to propel Chase into paradise.

Unbeknownst to Chase, Rob was rigged with an extendable tongue "throbinator." This ingenious device could be used in the throes of passion, transforming

Rob's tongue into a pleasure piston plunging purposefully in and out for prolonged and penetrating foreplay.

"Holy Moley!" Chase panted. "I've never felt anything like *that* before!" His sighs and gasps turned into full-fledged moaning and ultimately shrieks and squeals. Rob knew what Chase wanted and was determined that there would be no restraint in delivering the complete treatment. On Rob's pleasuring scale, he'd found that most people could only handle up to a three. In the past, he'd kept Chase at a solid four, but today, he was going to go up two levels to see if Chase could handle a whole number six of sexual stimulation.

Rob lifted Chase and carried him upstairs to the bedroom. Once there, Chase laughed as he bounced onto the bed. Rob peeled off his dress socks and tie and unbuttoned the sleeves of his tailored shirt. Then he climbed on top of Chase. Rob was excited to please him in a way he hadn't before. He started by spooning him as he playfully and softly nuzzled his ear.

This is nice. And feels oh, so good! I could see why humans enjoy this.

Rob's moist mouth and soft lips tickled and taunted Chase's erogenous zone. Rob only wanted to pleasure Chase more — soft kiss by soft kiss — as Chase's hard body writhed beneath him.

Rob ground his ripped, muscular body against Chase, getting more and more turned on. Rob whispered in Chase's ear as he clutched Chase's muscular pecs, massaging them and pulling them toward him.

"How badly do you want me?" he teased.

Chase looked desperate. His chest heaved as he

replied, "I need you... now, please." The more Chase begged, the more Rob wanted him to hold out. He was having a fantastic time pleasing his partner.

Rob relentlessly rubbed and tantalized Chase till it almost felt cruel. Then, as Rob felt that Chase was reaching the apex of his excitement, Rob delivered the goods. He pressed Chase facedown into the covers and showed Chase what he was designed to do, what millions of dollars of research and development had created—the ultimate sex machine to deliver pleasure beyond the limits that most mortals could manage. Rob gave Chase his full and focused ferocity.

As he was repeatedly satisfied by his lover, Chase's thoughts and cares about his job, career, and the unveiling of the museum that was currently taking place vanished. All that existed was Rob.

***

Caterers scurried throughout the grand entrance, stocking the tables with bite-sized nibbly bits of gourmet food. The bartenders set up their stations as fragrant flowers filled the stairs that led up to what promised to be a most magnificent museum. As many times as Jane had been there during its construction, she was still taken back at the splendor and beauty of it. She'd arrived an hour early to be available if anyone needed her for last-minute questions or problem-solving. She fluttered around with anticipation as the guests arrived. Everything was going smoothly, and the staff was performing expertly, indicating that this evening would be spectacular for all involved. The press soon came and found their way to their respective stations. The camera operators set up their tripods as the paparazzi readied for the stars to strut their stuff.

Where the hell is Chase? Jane asked herself. They'd planned to meet there at 4:00 sharp and enter the event together. It was odd that he hadn't yet arrived. Should she text to see if he was all right? *Nah.* Chase didn't need her to be monitoring his arrival. As Jane greeted the arriving guests, a voice from behind pleasantly commanded her attention.

She turned to see Corporal Matthew standing in all his glory wearing his military best. His brilliant brass badges were blinding in the sun as he stood at attention, stealing the admiring looks away from the movie stars that passed by. Jane had been impressed with his handsome demeanor and sharp attire when she'd first met him. But now that he had his Marine blues on, this strong, muscular man left her speechless.

"Yes, Hello, Corporal Matthew," she managed to catch her breath.

"Hello, Jane. This is my colleague, Dr. Herbie McAllister. Thank you for having us."

Shit, Jane thought in a panic. *I forgot to tell Chase about them being here.* "So wonderful to meet you. I'm glad you could make it tonight. But my boss hasn't arrived yet. Without his permission, I can't add you to the guest list. I apologize, but I'm going to have to ask you to wait until he gets here so that I may have him approve your entry."

The two men looked surprised at being denied access to the event. Matthew quickly spoke up; he was fearful that Herbie would say something that would hinder their chances of getting in.

He grimaced as he did his best to pleasantly reply, "Oh, I see. We'll be fine to wait for him to arrive. Please introduce us to him when he gets here so we may thank him in person."

"Happily," Jane bubbly blurted out. "I'm going to look for him now." *He'd better not be too far!*

***

Chase stood in the shower, his legs quivering, barely able to hold him up after their session of never-ending nookie. His mind was blown at the raw recklessness with which Rob had ravaged him.

Damn, it's late. We need to get to the party. And I can barely stand up. Shit, shit, shit.

He dashed back to the bedroom to find Rob already fully dressed while he struggled to look presentable. He slipped into his tuxedo and dragged a comb through his hair. *This will have to do.*

***

Near the museum, limos lined the dense street cluttered with lookie-loos and foot traffic eager to catch a glimpse of the hot Hollywood names that strolled up the carpet. It was the end of a perfect Los Angeles day: seventy-two degrees with a cool breeze, and the beginnings of a gorgeous sunset. Camerapeople jockeyed to position as the beautiful people stood in front of the tremendous sign that broadcasted the opening of Hollywood's newest and brightest attraction.

***

Herbie felt underdressed in his sports coat, slacks, and tie, seeing the celebrities surrounding him. Corporal Matthew, however, could easily blend in with the studios' sexiest studs, sporting his military blues.

The two men stood feeling more and more frustrated about being outside the event as people piled in. "We can't just sit here waiting for someone to let us in! What if Rob's already inside? We need a plan, and we need one quick!" Herbie muttered.

Matthew considered their options. "Let's give it another fifteen minutes. I guess Rob should arrive any minute now. However, if they don't get here soon, we should look for a back way into the building."

***

As Matthew and Herbie sat frustrated in the front forum, Chase pulled his Range Rover around the back of the building to easily park in the empty loading dock.

"I'm not one for photographers," Chase admitted. "Plus, let's not broadcast that we're late. I have keys to all the doors. Are you okay with skipping the paparazzi and just discretely slipping in the back door with me?"

"I don't know anything about paparazzi," Rob confessed. "Whatever you think is best is fine with me."

The grand entrance was packed with the press. Chase was right in entering quietly through the back. He was whisked around the room and hailed as a visionary as soon as he entered the atrium. He was given kudos after kudos by both celebrities and dignitaries alike. Chase was aware that this event resulted from his hard work and he should enjoy it, but he was more concerned about making sure Rob had a wonderful experience.

As Chase made pleasant small talk with the Governor of California, the stars of the silver screen and popular movies milled around.

Chase could see Rob was unfamiliar with celebrities and people in the public eye but noted with pride that he did his best to pretend that he was aware of who they were and was impressed with their accomplishments and fame.

He suddenly became alarmed as Rob's expression suddenly changed from a friendly, social, gleaming tooth-filled smile of a man without a care in the world to a troubled grimace.

"Is everything all right?" Chase asked.

"Yes, of course. I'm fine." Rob said with a forced smile.

Chase wasn't convinced. Rob was hiding something.
***

Outside, Herbie's practically jumped out of his trousers when his phone alarm blared and vibrated. He reached inside his pant pocket to see what was happening. The screen lit up with several alerts, including a map. His eyes widened.

"Rob's hit ten percent power," Herbie declared. The tracking app showed a map with Rob's GPS location. The robot appeared to be merely fifty feet away. "He's inside the building! He's right here! We need to get in there now to retrieve him when the battery fails."

The giant glass wall provided an easy viewing platform for them to see inside the atrium where the gaggle of guests grouped.

This was the hottest ticket in Hollywood. Trying to talk their way past security would be pointless.

"There's no way we're getting in this way. Let's try around back," the Corporal suggested.

Herbie shook his head. "No. We have no time to waste looking for a back door. We can talk our way through security."

Matthew grew agitated. "We don't have time for this. If you're not going to join me, fine. Go try to convince the security guards that you're a scientist looking for a robotic sex doll who has infiltrated the party and is about to malfunction. Me, however, I'm going break in and get this guy."

The Marine peeled off to the side of the building, leaving Herbie behind to consider his options. Then, he ran after Matthew in an attempt to catch up with him.

***

Chase was inundated by well-wishers attempting to capture his attention inside the people-packed atrium. He kept his focus on Rob, who was standing at his side.

"Are you sure you're okay?" Chase asked again.

Rob wasn't sure how to answer. He was in trouble, but he wasn't sure how to approach the situation. Rob was sure his battery was compromised and no longer holding a charge. Twenty minutes ago, his battery had read forty percent—indeed, an amount to easily get him through the next six hours. Suddenly, five minutes ago, it dropped an additional thirty percent, and now he only had ten percent left.

"I'm okay; I just need to find a men's room."

Chase looked worried. "I'll go with you, then."

"No, honestly, I'll take care of this myself. We can talk about it later. Now you should be here at your event."

Chase didn't look convinced. But it didn't matter what Chase wanted. Rob was already well on his way. Inside the marble-lined passageways, Rob scanned the room for internal wiring. Although the outlets were plentiful, they were either in plain sight of the guests or blocked by decorations or displays. Rob's concern started growing as he moved quickly around the room, searching for a power source before he experienced a total shutdown.

***

As Corporal Matthew and Herbie walked around the outside perimeter of the large glass atrium, they scouted for openings.

"There's Rob!" Herbie shouted. "I can see him! I bet he's looking for an outlet."

Corporal Matthew held his nose to the glass and peered in. "I see him too. Our target is in sight." He hurriedly tried all the doors to see if perhaps one was left unlocked. "I'll see if someone can let us in. I'll use my military might—that should sway them."

Herbie closely monitored his phone's readings from outside the building. His alarm showed Rob's battery at five percent. It was declining fast. Herbie knew that was enough to sustain Rob's essential operating functions, but it wouldn't be long before it ultimately failed, and he would be exposed as a robot.

***

Rob was becoming more and more desperate to find power. He knew it was a matter of time before he lost his basic motor functions. "You're scaring me," said Chase. "Something is obviously wrong. Let me help you."

Rob wanted to be tactful. He was well aware that by blurting out the truth about himself, he could totally 'freak out' Chase (as the bros would say), but time was precious. He was now at risk of completely shutting down and damaging his systems.

"I'm so sorry to do this here, in this way — and on your big night — but I have to tell you something immediately." As Rob readied himself for his candid confession, a sudden quiet quickly quelled the crowd of attendees at the event. The Governor of California was taking his place at the podium, the star-studded society members and financial contributors preparing for the ceremonial ribbon cutting. The excitement was palatable.

Chase glanced at the Governor. "This guy will talk forever. If you need me to get you out of here, I can." Rob felt unfamiliar sensations rush through him at Chase's selflessness. Inspiration sparked. Since it seemed impossible to find power in this building, maybe his best option was to plug into Chase's car battery. "It may be best that we get to your car now."

Over the loudspeaker, he heard Chase's name being called out by the Governor. He was being summoned to make his big speech at the podium.

Oh, no way. This was the moment Chase had worked for his whole life, the singular second that would shine a light on all his talents and the efforts he had put forth the last four years. Rob couldn't let him miss his moment of glory.

A hush fell as everybody waited for Chase.

"Go, take the stage. They're waiting for you. You're the star today," Rob nudged Chase towards the crowd. Jane rushed over, wired like she'd had forty cups of coffee.

"Chase! Everyone's waiting for your speech!"

Chase shook his head. "My priorities have changed. It isn't about the museum, the event, these celebrities or my job. It's about taking care of Rob right now." Chase placed his hand on Jane's arm comfortingly. "Jane, this is Rob, my boyfriend. I have to assist him now. You know my speech. Heck, you wrote most of it. Could you tell them I needed to excuse myself, and you give it for me?"

Jane's mouth dropped open. "Me? Are you crazy? I can't do that! And since when were you gay?"

Chase smiled sweetly. "Of course you can. You're a natural at this. We'll talk about the other thing later."

Rob watched Jane summon a stoic stance as she replied. "Fine then. I've got this. Take care of what you need to take care of. I've got your back" She ran an approving eye over Rob. "Holy smokes, what speech could compete with a magnificent man like him? I can see why you turned gay." She winked. "Nice meeting you, Rob. I hope everything turns out okay." She turned, waved, and made her way through the crowd to the front stage.

"She deserves this, too. I'm glad she's going to get the recognition. Now, let's get you to the car." Chase hurried Rob towards the building's loading dock.

***

Outside, Herbie stood watching his phone helplessly. His frustration and anxiety grew as he hoped that Matthew would return with the information on how to gain access to the inside of the building. Another glance at the phone's tracking app showed that Rob's battery was holding precariously at five percent.

As Rob and Chase make their way to the back of the building, Corporal Matthew returned to where Herbie waited. "This place is more impenetrable than the Pentagon. I have no clue how we are going to get in." "They're on the move, look!" Herbie hollered, looking at his phone's GPS map. "Quick, this way. It looks like they are trying to slip out the back." Matthew and Herbie did their best to keep up and make their way around the building before Rob and Chase made their getaway.

**

Chase lifted the giant metal gate at the loading dock that led to the outdoor loading area. The car was parked right there, a mere few feet from the back of the building. "Let me get the door for you. Just a few feet more, and we'll be on our way."

Rob nodded. "As soon as I get into the car and access the USB, we'll have a conversation—one that I apologize hasn't happened sooner. But now I know I can truly be me and trust you."

Chase whisked around the car's front wheels and clicked the locks open with his key. He swung the door wide for Rob to enter and stood anxiously with the car door in hand, awaiting Rob's entrance. Rather than rushing into the auto as expected, Rob just stood silently at the exit of the gate.

"I've got the door for you, come on."

Rob didn't move.

"Are you ok?" Chase asked.

Rob simply stood, silent, gazing at him.

"Dude, what's up? Are we going?" Chase realized

that something was off. Rob didn't budge, his eyes didn't blink, and his body was frozen like a statue. Chase walked over to Rob to ensure he was okay, but he was not. "Rob, you're scaring me. What's wrong?"

***

Around the side of the giant structure, Herbie honed in on Rob's signal. His phone alarm was shrieking.

"Crap," Herbie cried out. "The battery has failed and shut down. Rob will be incapacitated. It'll shut down all his systems and backups." He grunted as the signal completely disappeared. Rob's location was suddenly gone from Herbie's screen. "They're gone! We lost them," yelled Herbie, frantic and frustrated.

"They're right there! I can see them," Matthew shouted. Chase was relieved to see people coming to help.

"Please, something is wrong. I don't know what it is. He's frozen." The man appeared beside himself with fear. "Thank God! Please, help! What's wrong with him?"

Herbie struggled to catch up. In sharp contrast to Chase's crazed concern, Corporal Matthew stood calm and cool as he pulled a stun gun out of his pocket.

The corporal addressed Chase. "You're not going to like this, but it's necessary." Matthew zapped Chase, sending a powerful shock of voltage through his system. Chase seized, his body convulsed, and he toppled, unconscious and immobilized. Corporal Matthew grabbed Chase before he hit the floor and placed him on the ground. "Now you're safely out of the way." The Corporal pulled out his phone. "I need back up to transport ROB and a civilian to the base.

Mission accomplished.

Herbie finally arrived, breathing heavily. Herbie propped himself up, leaning on the Range Rover as he caught his breath.

Matthew's confirmation arrived in a tinny burst of static. "Transport set to arrive in three minutes."

Herbie was hyperventilating heavily. He wasn't sure if it was from the exertion or the shock.

Corporal Matthew turned to him. "I couldn't let him try to protect the robot. I wasn't prepared for an altercation. My orders were to retrieve ROB and, if anyone else interfered, to neutralize them. The location of our lab must remain a secret. The General will decide what to do with the civilian once we return to the base."

Herbie reflected unhappily that Corporal Matthew was correct. They were fortunate that Rob shutting down didn't happen in a room full of paparazzi and reporters.

Minutes later, three large, green camouflage-painted transport vehicles appeared at the back loading gate of the museum. Soldiers filed out with precision, all fully armed and ready to report to Corporal Matthew.

"This is ridiculous." Herbie was shocked at the way the military operated. Much to his chagrin, no one seemed to care what he thought or listened to his suggestions on how to proceed. It was evident Corporal Matthew was in charge now, and everyone jumped at the commands he barked.

"The civilian's been stunned. He's fine. Just make sure he stays under until we get back to our secure location. As far as the android's concerned, be careful loading it in and make sure it's secure. That's a billion dollars' worth of hardware there."

Herbie watched the soldiers put Chase and Rob into the trucks. Corporal Matthew held up the valet ticket he'd received when parking his car earlier at the gala.

"You can either go with them in the transport truck or travel back with me in my car—your decision. We got your robot back in one piece. That's all that matters. Let's get everyone back to the Hot Bot-y laboratory."

Herbie was relieved to have Rob back in his care. Herbie climbed into the back of the transport to be near Rob. "I'll meet you back at the laboratory," he said to the Corporal.

Corporal Matthew nodded and gestured for the vehicles to depart.

The convoy drove away, Herbie sitting anxiously in the truck. *Time to sort this all out once and for all.*

Chapter 24

Herbie sat beside a silent, lifeless Rob. He let out a sigh of relief, knowing his robot was safely secured. As the military convoy made its way through the streets of Hollywood, Corporal Matthew decided to call the base and report the good news. He wanted the General to know that soon he'd have ROB in his possession.

After several rings, the phone was answered by a young Private with a voice that cracked as if he'd just hit puberty.

"Sir, the General is in Los Angeles already. He arrived at zero eighteen hundred hours today."

"Ah, good. I'll call him directly. Thank you," Matthew replied.

"My pleasure, Corporal," answered the young Private.

Strange, Matthew thought. The General was a day earlier than scheduled. Perhaps he was taking a few hours for himself. After all, Generals needed time off too. Matthew dialed the General directly.

Several rings later, the General answered. "Corporal, I'm hoping this is good news."

"Sir, yes sir. We have the robot in possession, and we're headed back to the laboratory now. The base reported you were in the area. I can send a vehicle to you now so you can arrive at the same time we get to the laboratory."

The General took a last long sip of his Mint Julep. Duty calls.

Corporal Matthews continued, "Sir, we have a casualty. He's not injured, just unconscious. He was an accomplice and required sedation so we could obtain the robot peacefully."

I need to be there when the civilian arrives and certainly when he becomes conscious. The General knew that if the situation wasn't handled correctly, it would be his ass on the line with the President. He sighed heavily and looked longingly at his drink.

"Yes, Corporal, send a car for me immediately. I'll ping you my location."

He glanced down at his shorts and floral Hawaiian shirt. Unfortunately that he wouldn't appear as stoic and intimidating as he preferred. But this was an emergency, and he knew he didn't have time to put on his uniform. He did have time for one last sip of his Mint Julep, though.

***

The world was black for Chase. Darkness and damp air were all he could make out as he regained consciousness. Something foul-smelling covered his face. He wasn't sure how long he had been out or that he had even been kidnapped. All he knew was he had a sack of some sort over his head. There was the screeching sound of metal doors, and he found himself hauled roughly to his feet and pushed down a step into cold air. He was shoved into a chair, and his hands and ankles were locked tightly in what felt like thick leather straps.

"Hello, Hello. Please… help me!" His body was still feeling the effects of the tasing. "What's going on? Where am I? What is happening?" he pleaded to a room full of people he could hear but not see.

The sound of heavy footsteps echoed on the floor.

"Uncover the man's head. He's not a prisoner," a voice barked loudly. The head covering was removed from Chase's face, and he could breathe again as his eyes adjusted to the stark, crisp lights.

"Relax, you're not in trouble. I'm just here to talk to you." Chase was taken aback by the stranger's floral shirt, khaki shorts, and Crocs. He sounded as military as his younger companion, yet looked anything but. And, he smelled oddly minty.

"And who are you? Tommy Bahama?" Chase asked angrily. There were a few snickers from the group around him.

"I'm General Coldpecker, and this is Corporal Matthews. We demand some respect, young man."

"I don't care if you're General Tsao, and that's Colonel Sanders. What you did was kidnapping, and I demand to be freed." Chase wasn't having any of this. "And where's Rob?"

The General's eyes narrowed. "Hmm, you're a feisty one, aren't you? I don't want any more trouble from you." He turned to Corporal Matthew. "It's one thing for you to abduct him, but to keep him against his will is going to open a can of worms that I simply don't want. Let's get this over with. Let him go and take off his cuffs." He motioned to Chase. "But know you're not leaving yet, son. We're removing your restraints, but you'll need to be held for questioning."

"Regarding what?" Chase demanded.

"Regarding your involvement with government

property." The General stepped aside, revealing to Chase what he had been blocking with his body the entire time. Chase saw a large glaring, sterile laboratory full of human-looking robots and mechanical body parts. They looked more than a little familiar.

And then he saw Rob.

Chase's eyes did their best to quickly adjust to the stark bright lights in the lab. He could see several technicians hastily hurrying around a lifeless Rob as he stood silent and motionless against the wall. Several machines were plugged into him. His chest cavity was wide open, revealing wires and circuits and an empty space where his heart should be. Chase gasped in horror.

A man entered the lab holding what looked like a futuristic battery of some sort. He turned to one of the men and said, "Herbie, we're ready to power up ROB with the new energy source. Should we proceed?"

Herbie nodded. "Yes, go ahead please, Kyle."

"What the hell is happening?" shouted Chase. "What have you done to Rob? What's wrong with him?" Chase's voice cracked with desperation and concern.

The General turned to Bentley. "Explain to this young man that his friend over there is a thing, not a person, and it belongs to me."

Herbie frowned. "You mean ROB has been returned to me and is the property of Hot Bot-y."

The General cleared his throat. "Young man, you've been implicated in a situation that is beyond your understanding. So, I'll make this clear for you, as well as everyone in this room." The General looked at Herbie with disdain. "This machine, code-named "ROB," is an android, not a person. It escaped with the help of this man," he pointed a finger at Herbie, "who works for this laboratory. ROB, or 'Robot with Organic Body,' was funded by Uncle Sam and is owned by the United States military." The General placed his hand on Chase's shoulder. "I know you've been duped. You thought this machine was a man. Well, it's not. It's a robot that needs a new power source to run correctly. When it is repaired, it will be re-programmed and networked to other robotic soldiers as part of the most technologically advanced and sophisticated fighting force on the planet."

Herbie looked both shocked and furious as he turned to his boss. Herbie attempted to speak, but Bentley cut him short. "I'm sorry, Herbie, but the General is right. I have no say in this matter. Rob's been bought and paid for by the government, and there's nothing I can do. They own him."

Cheers from the technicians surrounding Chase broke the tension in the room.

Kyle announced proudly, "It's working. It's online, and it's perfect. This power stream is pristine and will practically last forever."

Chase's heart ached. How could I love a robot? And why didn't Rob tell me about it?

Rob was now back online, his eyes bright and sparkling and his face sweet and warm like it was before he shut down. He spotted Chase and looked briefly overcome with joy. "Chase, you're here! What's going on?"

Chase was in shock, unable to comprehend what he was seeing. Rob wasn't who he thought he was. He was a robot. Chase couldn't even look him in the eye. The excitement faded from Rob's face.

"Chase, please look at me. I'm sorry I didn't tell you what I was." Rob struggled against his restraints.

"Unfasten me so that I can talk to Chase! ...Please."

Chase felt as if he was moving underwater, his movements heavy and defeated. When he stood, his legs were unsteady. "If I'm not being kept here, I'd like to go," he pleaded as he desperately choked out each word. "You need to take me home."

The General contemplated what to do with him. "Son, I can see as plainly as the floral pattern on my shirt that you are only collateral damage in this situation. You're no threat. Anyway, even if you did talk to someone about ROB, no one would believe you."

Chase nodded tiredly, still refusing to meet Rob's anxious glance. "I'm certainly not telling anyone about this. I want to go home and forget all about it."

Across the room, Rob was shouting Chase's name. "Just take a moment to listen to me, Chase. If you'll just allow me to speak with you... I never meant to hurt you!"

Chase couldn't look at Rob as he turned to the General. "Please take me home now." His shoulders slumped, head down. Heartsick, Chase turned and left the room. Rob was desperate to connect with him. He needed to let Chase know how much he cared for him. Rob placed his fingers on the glass of his watch and activated it.

Chase walked down the halls of Hot Bot-y, eager to distance himself from the situation and clear his head. His watch suddenly buzzed and whirred. Rob was sharing his "heartbeat." Chase tapped the screen and dismissed the notification.

***

Corporal Matthew was conflicted. On the one hand, he was proud Rob's retrieval had succeeded. On the other, he felt terrible for Chase and ROB. Kyle stepped up to shatter the palpable awkwardness that filled the air, "I suppose it's just a matter of reprogramming ROB now?"

The General nodded. "Now that we've got this thing online again. Let's network it and make it a proper soldier."

Kyle looked at Herbie for approval. They hesitated. Herbie was crushed and defeated as he nodded an "okay" to Kyle.

Kyle turned to the General. "We'll need most of the day to network ROB with the other robots. When that's done, we'll start by downloading and installing the basic training programming. We won't be able to start that until morning. We may not have ROB ready for you by nine a.m. if that's your intention."

The General frowned. Then, his face brightened.

I guess at least I'll be able to enjoy some of my vacation time. The hotel does have a great continental breakfast with make-your-own waffles.

He scowled fiercely again. "Fine. Get it done by noon and no later."

Corporal Matthew couldn't help glancing at Rob. Everyone was so busy following orders and carrying out their plans that no one noticed Rob suddenly looked broken. The mojo had disappeared from him. Did Rob's eyes have tears in them? Rob's powerful, square jaw and usually strong stance now resembled a young boy who'd been bullied in the schoolyard and wanted nothing more than to disappear into oblivion.

Matthew was shocked that this robot seemed to be reacting to the loss of a human. *Could it be possible that it was capable of feeling? Was the possibility of losing someone?* As much as Matthew found it hard to comprehend, it was undeniable. Tears fell down Rob's cheeks.

Unsure what to do, Matthew addressed Kyle and Herbie. "This basic training programming you're installing tonight, will it replace what's already there? I guess what I'm asking is, are you adding to the robot or replacing his entire operating system?"

"Well, actually, we're going to replace the entire operating system with one that follows commands and synchronizes with other military bots. So, in short, yes, we are replacing the operating system with a more — dare, I say — primitive one suited more to a military operation."

The General looked pleased. "Great. That's exactly what I wanted in the first place."

The Corporal knew his place in the military; he also knew that the General respected men who could think for themselves.

"General, if I may. It seems this robot has both empathy and the ability to make decisions. Isn't that a win for us? Why wouldn't we keep the complex system we have already installed, then add the basic training on top of that? Much like a real soldier. If you think about it, compassion and integrity are also valuable tools in combat. You wouldn't want to create a weapon that could fire artillery without heart."

Across the room, Herbie was hopeful that Matthew's insights would register with the General. The General stopped, as did everyone else in the room. Corporal Matthew was proud of himself. A soldier without a conscience was only a gun — a dangerous weapon if not governed by rational thinking and a caring operator.

The General looked at the Corporal for what seemed an eternity. Matthew felt a pang of concern. Was he going to be showered with praise or reprimanded for speaking out of turn? He found out soon enough.

"You're dismissed, Corporal Matthew. Please return to the base at Zero-Six-Hundred tomorrow morning. You are no longer needed on this assignment. Clearly, you're not suited for this kind of duty. Your marshmallow feelings are getting in the way of my perfect fighting machines. Perhaps filing and inventory better suits your disposition? Fortunately, you've made me aware of your limitations before they compromised this mission."

The room went silent. Matthew had stepped out of line. But surprisingly, he didn't regret it. He knew he was right and what they were doing to Rob was wrong. Reprogramming Rob without a "soul," if that's what he'd developed, was a bad decision that could have dire detrimental consequences.

Corporal Matthew turned to leave the room. But before he did, he addressed the scientists. "Thank you all for your work these last two weeks. It was a pleasure serving with you. I wish you all the best in your research." His throat tightened. While he knew he was right, his career was over. He would return to Fort Benetton tomorrow and be discharged.

Chapter 25

C hase sat silently in the back of the taxi. His world had come crashing down around him. He was glad the driver didn't attempt conversation. Chase wasn't in the mood to chat.

He'd received a myriad of congratulatory memes and texts from his buddies and various colleagues. Chase wasn't sure what lay ahead for him work-wise. Frankly, he didn't care. His heart was shattered. It was still early, only seven p.m. The party would still be going on, but Chase was in no mood to join it. He also didn't want to go home to an empty house.

There was only one place that could make him feel better, the steam room.

He summoned his friends and asked them to meet him there with a quick text. If there was any way to make sense of all this, it was with the help of his bros. Chase asked the driver to change destinations, to head directly to the Mission Gym.

Bolton was already there. He'd been in the boxing ring training Beau's niece, a sweet little sixteen-year-old girl named Susie. "Susie, care to go a few rounds? Let's take it slow and easy." Bolton raised his gloves carefully so as not to intimidate her. Susie instantly took an aggressive stance, centering her body and dancing around like Muhammad Ali on amphetamines.

"Bring it on, candy ass!" With that, Susie bobbed and weaved, ducked, and exploded up to connect a ripping uppercut to Bolton's jaw. Bolton dropped to his knees, rocked gently back and forth, and face-planted on the canvas.

Susie raised her hands and did a victory lap chanting, "Knock Out! Knock Out!"

The others in the gym stood watching, mouths agape. Susie turned her attention to the spectators. "Who's next? Take me down. I dare you!"

No one took her up on the offer. Everyone put their heads down and pretended to look elsewhere, attempting to avoid her gaze. Lying on the floor, the sound of Bolton's phone ringing made him regain consciousness. Bolton hobbled over to his corner of the ring to answer it, but not before congratulating Susie on an impressive uppercut.

"Nicely done. Good power!" he said, shaking his head clear.

"Thank you," Susie said.

Bolton turned to his phone. It was Chase's text.

"Up for a steam? I'm on my way to the gym."

"More than you know!" Bolton replied, "See you when you get here."

"Oh, no! I'm not done with you yet," warned Susie.

"I couldn't take another serious ass-whooping." Bolton pleaded. "I'm off to steam the hurt away."

***

Chase arrived outside the Mission Gym. He thanked his taxi driver and tipped him well; the military was paying, after all. He headed directly to the locker room to change.

Upon entering the steam room, he was grateful to see Bolton already there, rubbing his jaw gently. The hot, mist-filled air soothed his defeated soul. Chase sat in his towel next to his buddy and sighed, letting all the days' events, anger and frustration out as he slumped back against the damp, tiled wall. Bolton knew Chase well enough to know he was in a bad place. The two men just sat silent and settled into the serenity.

Chase eventually spoke. "Rob wasn't real. He's a machine, a robot — an android made for the military." Chase waited for a reaction from Bolton. It didn't come. He continued, "The government created him. They made him to be a fighting machine. Hell, I slept with a hunk of metal, wires, and circuits." Still, Bolton sat quietly, looking thoughtful. Finally, he sighed.

"You know bro… Looking back, I can see the clues. Rob had certain gaps of understanding about things most people would find commonplace. But, boy-o-boy, he was remarkably lifelike, caring, intelligent, and fun to be around."

Chase snapped, "Well, I'm glad you're impressed, but what do you think about Rob being a robot and my being with him?"

Bolton carefully looked his buddy in the eye. "So?"

Chase blinked in confusion. "I'm a human. Rob's a machine. We lived together and had sex. I really liked him! But he was a robot!"

Rather than being horrified, Bolton once again shrugged. "So?"

"You aren't seeing the problem here." Chase was exasperated.

Bolton leaned forward and placed his hand on Chase's leg to calm him. "Dude, I'm not being obtuse. Promise. Man/woman, woman/woman, man/man, or any number of combinations. Man/robot—who cares? You care about each other and are happy. What's the big whoop? I do not see a problem."

The conversation was making a very long, frustrating, and confusing day worse. Chase sighed, "I'm beat. I am going to split. Possibly check you out in the morning? I need to crash right now." He tightened his towel and got up to leave.

From behind, Bolton quietly said, "Rob's a bro, bro. And he deserves to be treated like one. Flesh or rubber, a man or a can, it doesn't matter."

Chase smiled weakly and continued to the locker room to change. *Leave it to Bolton to simplify things to the point that they seemed to make perfect sense. But Bolton isn't the one who has to live with the fact he fucked a robot. It's just not that simple for me.* He wanted to get home, go to bed, and leave the last two weeks behind him.

***

Back in the Hot Bot-y laboratory, the techs were busy with their last-minute duties before the big system upgrade. Rob's new energy source was installed and working perfectly. Herbie felt like he owed Rob an explanation before his memory banks were blown away. Herbie turned to Kyle and the technicians who were hastily working away in the lab. "Can I have a few minutes with Rob, please? In private?" Kyle and the others nodded and quietly left.

Rob stood in the middle of the room, stoic and still. He was awaiting his fate without a proper understanding of what was about to happen to him. Herbie sensed this wasn't the ROB he'd sent out in the world two weeks ago. That bot had been very different from the being that stood before him now.

Herbie turned to Rob. "What happened? What did the world do to you?"

Rob looked at Herbie with eyes showing nothing but sadness. "I merely attempted to comply with your commands."

Herbie saw the hurt in Rob's eyes and thought perhaps it was best that they reformatted him and erased the memories. Living with a broken heart was difficult enough for a human. "I owe you an explanation." Herbie sighed. "They wanted to take you away from me, and I thought you'd be better off on your own. I tried to protect you. I failed you, and for that, I'm sorry… so sorry."

He saw Rob's scanners working. No doubt the robot had picked up on the guilt in Herbie's voice.

"I attempted to carry out my programming: to be attentive, caring, selfless, and smart. I felt that I had accomplished my mission. I'm sorry you feel sad."

Herbie was touched by how empathetic Rob had become. For a machine, he was remarkably intuitive. He delved a bit deeper. *Surely, Rob couldn't be self-aware?* "Rob, run a full diagnostic of your systems and verbally report back your findings along with an assessment of any malfunctions."

Rob's eyes glassed over, and all external movement ceased as he scanned his systems. Seconds later, his eyes got animated, and life came back to his limbs as he reported back his findings. "Upon concluding multiple scans of all primary and secondary hardware and software, all systems are operating optimally, yet…" Rob paused, seemingly aware that his next sentence did not make any sense. "Although all functions are fine, I must report that nothing feels like it's working correctly. My system is well powered, but all it wants to do is shut down. I feel as if my chest cavity is empty, and all my processing power is stuck on Chase."

Herbie looked long and hard at Rob. *Could it be?* Herbie thought. There was no denying it. It was clear that Rob wasn't merely a robot after all. He seemed more human than android, alive and free-associating, capable of thinking and emoting and, amazingly enough, feeling love.

Bang! Herbie jumped out of his skin as Bentley entered with an armed soldier. He looked livid. "Why are you alone with this robot? Didn't you understand the General when he said that this was government property and not ours any longer?" He waved a hand at the soldier. "This is Private Thomas Harris. He's been assigned to guard ROB." He turned to the soldier. "No one is to be left alone with the robot. Especially this man, is that understood?"

"Sir, yes, sir!" responded the Private.

Herbie was still astounded at what he'd just discovered about Rob. Something had to be done. "Rob, I'll be back." He turned to Bentley, trying hard to contain his excitement. "I need to speak to you in private — your office or mine, it doesn't matter. This simply can't wait."

Bentley scowled. "Herbie, you simply don't get it. ROB is government property. We built him for them, and he's theirs. The matter is closed."

Herbie wasn't having it. The situation had now changed. Rob was a living being, and he couldn't *belong* to anyone anymore.

"We had an agreement!" Herbie burst out, louder than he intended to yell. All the technicians and assistants who were filing back into the room stopped to look. Herbie had scolded Bentley and what was about to go down wasn't going to be pretty. Rather than exploding as expected, Bentley simply looked around at the curious staff who were not-so-subtlety listening in. They quietly pretended to go about with their business.

He composed himself and angrily replied to Herbie. "I am fully aware of what I promised. But I wasn't in a position to make such an assurance. The robot is the property of the U.S. government now. I couldn't do anything about it even if I wanted to. All we can do is build another robot—one that is ours, that will solely be the property of you, me, and this company. We need to let the military have what they paid for." Bentley turned to Private Harris. "Private, this man is no longer to be admitted within one hundred feet of this robot."

Private Harris, "Yes, sir, no problem."

Bentley turned to Herbie, who was aghast. Bentley's face showed remorse, but his words were still stern. "Herbie, you made me do this. I can't have you interfering. My job is to protect the company at all cost."

Without waiting for a reply, Bentley exited the lab. The room was silent. Stunned. Everyone quickly snapped back to work.

Private Harris addressed Herbie. "Sir, please vacate this room. I have my orders, and I will carry them out." Herbie knew he'd been beaten. From across the room, he saw Rob's face. Sadness, confusion, and hurt registered as clearly as if Rob were human. Rob had learned what it was to be a real person. Sadly, though, he was now experiencing all the worst parts of it.

Chapter 26

C hase arrived home at dinnertime, and he was starving. He'd planned to eat at the gala but, of course, hadn't had the opportunity. Thanks to Rob, the cabinets were well stocked with healthy, organic ingredients — everything sealed in vacuum-packed glass containers. A simple pot pie or frozen burrito was sadly out of the question–what he wouldn't give for a hot pizza pocket now. Chase certainly wasn't in the mood to prepare himself dinner. The thought of take-out or delivery was too much effort. All he wanted was to go to bed, even at this early hour.

Chase made his way to his bedroom to change out of his tuxedo. He couldn't help but look in Rob's room. *How could he have been so foolish? There must have been signs that Rob was a robot.*

As soon as Chase swung open the door to the meticulous room, he couldn't help but chuckle at the absurdity. *How ridiculous!* Right in the middle of the room, a stripper pole, lights, and fog machine. Expert cook, guitar player, extraordinary strength, and good looks. How embarrassingly obvious it was now that Rob wasn't real.

The more Chase thought about it, the angrier he got at himself. No human could be that good at everything. Chase made his way to his room, unbuttoned his shirt, and sat on the edge of the bed. From across the room, the small gift of the miniature Eiffel Tower he'd purchased for Rob taunted him as it sat on the nightstand, perfectly wrapped and ready for presentation. *What had he been thinking?* He couldn't go away with Rob or have a life with him. They barely knew each other. And that's on top of Rob being a robot! Chase unzipped his tuxedo pants and removed his shoes, pants, and boxer briefs; he then walked naked into the large glass shower.

As he lathered his body, building up a frothy foam, Chase scrubbed and scrubbed. All he wanted was to wash away the last two weeks. His mind kept drifting back to the last time he and Rob made love. If Rob were designed to please, he certainly knew how to do it. Images of Rob's solid, chiseled abs, hard chest, and broad, masculine shoulders couldn't be simply rinsed away. Neither could Rob's handsome face with those eyes that twinkled when Chase arrived home in the evening. As much as Chase tried to suppress thinking about Rob's muscular, firm ass, it was impossible to stop his mind from conjuring up explicit images.

Chase had never thought much about a man's physique beyond the standard mutual appreciation. But Rob was so spectacular in every way. It was impossible to deny that he was built for sex.

As he soaped himself up in the shower, he looked down to realize that he was harder than a college-level algebra equation and as rigid as the rules at a parochial school. His broad, beef baton expanded as he fantasized about Rob's mighty man mast. His mind wandered to Rob's large, curved, cuddle cucumber. He remembered how it felt when it was inside him. Rob was indeed equipped with a profound posterior pounder.

As these vivid images danced through Chase's mind, his excitement increased. Without realizing it, Chase worked himself up into a fevered frenzy—his thick rapture rocket rigid in his fist, poised for blast off. There was no turning back at this point. Chase knew it was a matter of time before he frantically flogged his flagpole to a frothy finish.

Chase switched the warm water to frigid in an attempt to drown the dragon fire burning inside him. But it was too late; his body twitched and heaved, drenching the drain with a tremendous explosion of injector nectar.

There was no denying that what just happened felt great. Chase was even more exhausted than before. He grabbed his favorite Egyptian cotton bath towel and did a quick dry as he ran it across his chest, back and bottom. Nothing was more appealing than just letting his body flop down on his soft, satiny sheets. Chase just wanted to sprawl out on his bed and unwind from the day's frustration—and enjoy the languid aftermath of his unbridled bro batter blast.

All the tea times, delicious meals, silly laughs, and the spirited teasing all played back in his head. *How could a robot be programmed to do that? These weren't set patterns he'd been executing? Surely, a machine wouldn't feel hurt?* That was the one thing that Chase fought to keep out of his mind, but it finally forced its way front and center—remembering Rob's face when Chase denied him the simple courtesy of a goodbye. It was the face of a man utterly broken. It was the look of a trampled heart.

Chase had driven a spike through Rob's soul. He knew that the second he walked out the door of the laboratory. In his heart, he knew Rob wasn't just a metal machine. Bolton was right. He was alive, had real feelings, and experienced love. Rob wasn't a robot—he was a bro. And as a bro, you belong. You're one of the group, and you'll always be accepted.

Chase looked at the clock. It wasn't too late. There was time to fix this. Nothing would stop him from being with Rob. He jumped up with reignited enthusiasm and slipped on his jeans and sweater. It was go-time.

Chase picked up his phone. All the steam room guys were on one group text, reserved only for emergencies. Chase hadn't ever used it before, but now was the time. He punched in the bicep emoji used to summon the bros. Then a house emoji, which indicated where they should meet. Finally, an explosion emoji which meant "prepare for war."

Corporal Matthew returned to his hotel. *Tomorrow will be a long day of traveling.* In his heart, he knew that he hadn't done anything wrong. Yet, he couldn't help but feel like a failure at his mission.

Matthew very much loved his country and was passionate about protecting it. Sure, a Marine needed to follow orders, but one who couldn't think for himself was a dangerous thing. Creating an army of mindless robots that just carried out orders without regard for human life was a terrifying proposition. *Is there something I can do? Some way to make things right?* Matthew finished putting his belongings into his duffel bags. Everything was in its place with his usual military precision. How would he spend his last evening in Los Angeles? Perhaps an intense workout would clear his mind. It had been a while since he had a good weightlifting session, and the gym in the hotel was barely sufficient for a hard-core sweat. *Perhaps a few rounds of boxing?* The Corporal remembered that the Mission Gym was nearby, with a boxing ring and punching bags.

***

Bolton was busy training his last client of the day at the gym. He looked down at the middle-aged indie movie producer who had a regularly scheduled workout and always paid in cash. The man was on his last set of chest reps on the lifting bench.

A text from Chase appeared on his phone. *Did Chase finally have a revelation? Was it possible he was going to rescue Rob? Hell yeah!* Bolton was always ready to rumble. He worked himself into a frenzy. *Time to take on the bad guys!*

Bolton took the weights from his client's hands and placed them on the rack. "We're done for the day. My bro needs me. I have to go! See you Wednesday. Don't be late!"

***

Herbie attempted to get the key in the front door of his modest mid-century modern home for the third time. His hand wobbled from the four scotch and sodas he'd had at Billingsley's Ale House. He knew he'd had too much to drink when the bartender insisted on calling him an Uber.

Herbie wasn't a drinker, but he felt like he earned himself a few cocktails tonight. He was now unable to have any contact with Rob. It was a devastating blow. His factory had hundreds of assorted heads, bodies, and half-assembled sexbots of every persuasion in various stages of assembly. He could build another Rob. But Herbie knew that if he did, it could never match the original. It would be a drone that lacked Rob's unique spark and personality.

After being banished, he'd been assigned the painstaking task of perfecting the neuro-net that ran all the robots. Bentley intended to have all of their robots connected wirelessly to each other—so that a single source could command each machine. Although the logic seemed sound, the simple fact that each robot would now be part of a hive brain, like bees or common insects, was a scary prospect. The more Herbie thought about it, the angrier he became. What was intended to be a miraculous achievement had been downgraded to an assembly line of bots with no more personality than a vacuum or toaster.

Herbie eventually navigated the door lock and entered his home. The door swung closed behind him. He tossed his keys onto the small table near the door but missed it. The keys landed on the floor. He ignored them and stumbled to his desk, where his beloved computer sat. With the press of a button, it hummed to life.

Rob was his creation, and he wasn't about to let him be reprogrammed.

Earlier that day, Herbie had networked Rob to the central database. He wanted to know exactly what software they were loading into Rob. He could see all the robots and their diagnostics
and was glad Rob hadn't been reprogrammed yet. His screen indicated that the override program was automatically scheduled to start at midnight.

As he dived deeper into Rob's existing neuro-net, he

was astounded at how intricate the synaptic connections were. It was apparent that Rob was now running a program that he hadn't installed. His programming was now an evolving, expanding, self-realizing, and learning application. It was groundbreaking stuff. Herbie realized that Rob was gaining a human-level consciousness. His fingers raced along the keyboard to access what other programs may have been installed. He still had administrative access. Good. Next, he tried to turn off the automatic download sequence set to reboot Rob. But he couldn't do it from his desktop at home. As long as Rob was connected to the mainframe computer at Hot Bot-y, he would be receiving the updated software. Herbie had to physically unplug Rob from the computer to stop the reprogramming from taking place.

***

Corporal Matthew arrived at the Mission Gym ready to lift. Tonight would be an epic workout. Nothing was going to stop him from shredding on the weight bench. It was nine p.m. With the gym closing at ten, an hour would be plenty of time to get swoll. Old Man Johnson stood behind the desk counting the day's earnings. As Matthew entered, OMJ waved at him. "I recognize you. You're the Marine who came in days ago, aren't you?"

Corporal Matthew was impressed at the OMJ's recall. "Sir, yes, that was me."

"What's your business here?" OMJ asked. "You still looking for that guy?" The older man's eyes shifted from right to left. Matthew got the feeling a lie was on its way. "Well, I still haven't seen him. No clue where he could be."

"That's alright. We found him, sir. He's back where he belongs. Things are as they should be." Matthew certainly didn't believe that, but he didn't have the time to explain.

"Good to hear it, son. Glad it worked out for you." OMJ looked a little bewildered.

"I'm here to get a few rounds in on the sandbags before you lock up — if I may." Matthew presented his five dollars.

"Well, if you insist. I'll put it towards my retirement. Thanks." OMJ snatched up the five-spot and put it in the register.

Although it was night, Matthew hadn't expected to see such a spectacular full moon inside the locker room. Bent over for all to see, were the two of the most muscular glutes he'd ever gazed upon. It was the ass of a man who knew the secret of a sensational squat.

Matthew cleared his throat with an innocent cough to let the person know he was there. The man bolted up quickly, standing to face him.

"Sorry, I didn't expect anyone to walk in. I thought everyone had gone for the day. I certainly had not planned to greet anyone that way."

"No apologies needed. No one here is complaining about the view." Matthew continued, "Hey, I recognize you!"

"Oh really? From my backside?" Bolton teased.

"From your smile," Matthew flirted back.

"The horizontal smile or the vertical one?" They laughed at the juvenile joke as Bolton continued, "I didn't think I'd ever see you back here. I figured you'd be off to your next assignment by now."

"I'm leaving tomorrow. The military got what it came for. Now I'm being reassigned." Matthew sighed.

"Things didn't exactly go as planned."

"Hey, I thought you got your man." Bolton blinked in confusion. "I know it's not my business, but what did it have to do with Rob?" he asked.

Matthew could tell Bolton was a kindred spirit. Something about him made him feel comfortable. Matthew wasn't at liberty to discuss a matter of national security, but right now, he didn't care. He needed a friend, and Bolton would be it. "Yes, I found who I was looking for, but to be honest, I wish I hadn't."

"Oh, that sucks," Bolton replied. Just then, Bolton's phone rang.

"I've gotta take this. It's my buddy. It's important."

"Go ahead, sure." Matthew saw the photo of Chase that had appeared on Bolton's phone. *What was the connection between these two bros*, he wondered?

"Dude, be there in five minutes," Bolton assured Chase over the phone. "I got a bit sidetracked. I'm on my way." He hung up and apologized to Matthew for taking the call.

"No need, It's all good. Mind if I come along? Maybe I can help, too."

"Sure. I'd be happy for the company."

***

All the guys were at Chase's already. Ryan and Tad applauded when Bolton and Matthew finally entered.

Ryan was the first to call Bolton out for his lateness. "Dude, it's been like a half hour we've been sitting here. What gives?" Before Bolton could answer, Chase noticed Matthew.

"What is *he* doing here?" Chase's guard instantly

went up. "This is the guy who took Rob away. I don't want him here!"

Bolton was surprised and angry that Matthew had deceived him.

Matthew quickly began stammering, "I'm not the bad guy you think I am. I'm here to help. Really. I was just doing my duty. I'm here to make things right."

"I don't believe you!" snapped Chase. "You zapped me with fifty thousand volts, kidnapped me, and then stole my boyfriend.

Bolton shook his head at Matthew with a disapproving "Dude."

Matthew stood strong.

"Guys, I'm a Marine. My job was to retrieve government property. I was on a mission. I had no idea you love Rob. And make no mistake, he loves you too. I was wrong to do what I did. I had no idea he was more than just a robot."

Chase took several breaths and calmed down. "Well, maybe you aren't the callused, cold-hearted ass I thought you were."

"My allegiances have changed," replied Matthew. "I promise. I want to help you get Rob back."

Matthew began examining the map board hanging on the wall. It was a giant collage of assorted pictures with pushpins and red twine connecting the photos.

Corporal Matthew addressed Bolton, "Sir, is this a…"

Bolton laughed. "Sir?" he teased. "You're a bro now. No need for formality."

Matthew chuckled as he loosened his shirt. "Dude, is that string map like in the movies? I always wanted to carry out a plan that started with a red-stringed map. How awesome is this?"

"Better, much better," Bolton said as he patted

Matthew on the back.

"I can see this is a plan to rescue Rob from Hot Bot-y," continued Matthew. "I'm a trained strategist, and I know the facilities at Hot Bot-y. I'm familiar with where Rob is being held. I want to help you get him back."

Chase was relieved to have Matthew on their side. They'd need all the help they could get. "The time for the rescue is twenty-three thirty hours. We need to move fast."

None of the guys moved. They all looked at their watches in confusion.

Chase sighed. "Guys, that's military time. Don't you know that? I mean eleven-thirty." The guys nodded appreciatively.

"Dude, why didn't you say that in the first place?" grumbled Tad.

Matthew took charge with military precision. "We'll all meet at Hot Bot-y. But first, I'll need to change into my uniform. Once I get there, I'll tell the guard that I'm there to relieve him of his post for the evening. Then, I'll free Rob and bring him out to you."

Chase wasn't entirely buying the plan. "Sorry, no-go, amigo! Not that I don't trust you, but I'm going in with you."

Tad was excited to contribute. "My dudes, I've got some lab coats in my car. We could be scientists and sneak in."

Bolton shared his own strategy on how to get into the laboratory. "I've got some white sheets in the trunk of my car. We can cut holes for eyes and be ghosts." From the snickers around the room, Bolton realized it wasn't the most rational idea. "Ok, the place probably isn't haunted. Maybe next time we can do it if we need to break into an old house or cemetery?"

Chase shook his head, amused. "Let's go with Tad and Matthew's plan. I'll wear a lab coat. Ryan and Tad, you be the lookouts. Bolton, you can be the get-away driver.

"Great, I got my driving gloves right here," Bolton enthusiastically held up a pair of leather gloves. "I'm going to go full 'Baby Driver' on that shit!"

Chase was grateful for the enthusiasm. "Let's all meet at Hot Bot-y. By the time Matthew gets his uniform on, it will be eleven-thirty, so set your watches to meet in the alley behind the building."

Chapter 27

Herbie had finished getting dressed and was now on his way to Kyle's condo. He knew where Kyle lived as he was a regular at his annual Halloween party. Herbie always appreciated being invited. It was fun to dress up. Herbie dressed as a spaceman and won first prize every year. His spacesuit was impeccable; the attention to detail was flawless.

As Herbie made haste through West Hollywood's streets, he remained well within the speed limit and obeyed all traffic signs. He couldn't help think that it *was* a bit late to call on someone at this hour, but Herbie had to talk to Kyle in person. As he stood outside Kyle's building pressing the intercom, he once again looked at his watch. It was just after eleven now.

"Hello? Can I help you?" Kyle's confused voice could be heard from the tiny speaker. He sounded as if he'd been sleeping.

"It's Herbie. I'm outside your building... I must come in and speak with you." The door buzzed. Herbie entered the modest apartment building. He paused, trying to remember the apartment number. He knew it was on the ground floor, but which door was it? As Herbie pondered, he heard a door open and saw Kyle standing there. Kyle was dressed in a turquoise Turkish terry robe with worn suede slippers.

Kyle looked worried. "Is everything okay?" He waved Herbie into his apartment. Herbie entered and paced excitedly.

"Rob is a sentient being," Herbie exclaimed. "He's alive! I've analyzed his programming. He's evolved beyond the operating system we designed. He needs to be saved. We can't override his programming and lose him."

Kyle stood motionless, looking at Herbie with a furrowed brow. He was processing the data, much like the computers he programmed. Herbie didn't have time for Kyle to move at the speed of an old Atari. Herbie blurted out, "Rob is hardwired into the system. We need to disconnect him from the mainframe before midnight!"

"Yes," Kyle agreed. "But you're not allowed near him. I'm the only person who they'll let in."

Herbie grabbed Kyle's hand in gratitude. "EXACTLY!" Kyle finally understood the urgency of the situation. "I need your help, and I need it now."

"Let's make this happen!" Kyle jumped into action. They looked at their watches. "We have less than thirty minutes before the military's 'soldier software' is installed."

Herbie nodded. "We can still get to Hot Bot-y in time." Kyle disappeared into the other room to get changed from his Pj's. Herbie waited impatiently.

***

Chase was the first to arrive at the Hot Bot-y loading dock, with Corporal Matthew hot on his heels. They reviewed the plan. Their strategy was to relieve the Marine on duty, then rescue Rob.

The plan was simple. Get in and get Rob. Ryan and Tad would be lookouts, and Bolton would drive one of the getaway cars. Matthew started to change into his uniform. Down came his jeans, and off went his shirt. He now stood outside in only his boxer briefs. Chase couldn't help but notice Matthew's glorious glutes as he bent over to replace his pants. His strong tattooed body rippled with lean, striated muscle. Chase tried not to stare, but it was difficult not to steal a glance. Chase was impressed with Matthew's form and proportion, as well as the beautiful ink that adorned his torso and arms. There was no denying that this Midwestern muscle boy was as sexy as they came. Fortunately for Chase, Matthew didn't seem to mind him watching.

Ryan and Tad pulled up just as Matthew finished zipping up his well-pressed pants. "Damn! Is the show over," Ryan said, "or will you be giving an encore performance?"

Corporal Matthew was surprisingly flirtatious in his response. "Sorry, last show of the night. No curtain calls." Ryan looked disappointed. He wondered if he could get an encore later if he played his cards right?

The boys were dressed in black from head to toe. "Wow, you guys look ready for business," Chase noted.

Bolton grinned. "Dude, I'm your driver. Tad and Ryan are your eyes... We dressed to disappear into the darkness. Were in stealth mode, dude."

"Let's get to the rescue." Chase looked gratefully at his bros. "It's almost midnight."

Matthew and Chase walked from the side parking lot to the front glass doors of the large, high-tech building. "Best to enter through the front door," Matthew said. "Hot Bot-y has a receptionist 24-hours a day since they have people working at all hours. It shouldn't be suspicious for me to be here at this time."

Matthew swiped his magnetic badge near the front door then stepped up to the security camera. The door clicked open. He and Chase entered, approaching the first obstacle of the evening. The night receptionist was a man in his late twenties with black hair and piercing dark eyes. Chase noticed he was a fit, physically imposing man with a seductive, brooding Middle Eastern look. *Probably an actor or mode. This must be his night job*, Chase thought. If the receptionist's sultry bedroom eyes weren't charismatic enough, when he spoke, his velvet voice was deep and commanding. He once again inspected Matthew's ID and then addressed the Corporal directly.

"You're good, but you—" He looked at Chase, who was dressed as a lab technician. "Where's your badge?"

Chase's heartbeat stuttered in panic. Fortunately, Corporal Matthew remained rock steady. "I'll need you to give him one," Matthew demanded. "The day shift ran out of them earlier, and they told me to bring him in here tonight and get one from you."

The rugged receptionist looked perplexed. "That doesn't sound right. There's a box of badges right here. Why wouldn't they give him one earlier?"

Matthew shrugged. "No clue. They just said they didn't have any. Maybe those arrived after we left." The Corporal doubled down. "We'll just wait while you check with your superior. All I know is that this guy here is needed on the third floor, and I was told to escort him there. You do what you need to do to clear him."

The receptionist looked thoughtful. He had two choices; one would involve contacting someone at this late hour, the other was to simply let them go in. He chose the easy option.

"Here's a visitor's pass. Tell them to issue him a name tag if he's going to be coming back tomorrow." He handed Chase a visitor badge to pin on his white lab coat.

***

Herbie stood in Kyle's living room, looking at the collection of miniature figurines standing inside the Plexiglas case.

"We need to go, Kyle." Herbie looked at his watch. He tapped his toe and was practically steaming from the ears. "Yes, yes— be right out," Kyle shouted, then showed up at the bedroom door all dressed.

"We have to save Rob—we're not going to happy hour!" Herbie grumbled.

"Sorry—I couldn't find matching socks."

Herbie once again looked at this watch. "Eleven forty-five. We're cutting it close. Let's go. We need to leave NOW!"

He whisked Kyle impatiently out the door. *Time to get my robot back.*

***

It was eerily empty at Hot Bot-y as Matthew and Chase made their way to the tech laboratory where Rob was being readied. The long, well-lit white corridors never seemed to end. There were very few people in the facility besides passing a few janitors mopping floors and an occasional programmer seeking refuge from their computer screens.

"We're almost there." Matthew held open a large double door for Chase. The motion-sensitive LED lights flickered on, revealing a vast wonderland of mechanical components, body parts, assembled robots, and appliances. Chase's eyes widened. "This is incredible." Chase was astounded by the vast array of mechanical marvels that lay before him.

"Pretty cool, right?" boasted Matthew. "I love tech, and this is truly state of the art. The next room has sex toys. It's pretty amazing. But it's the room where Rob is that will blow your mind."

Chase and Matthew retreated from a room brimming with racks of phallic-filled fellatio fornicators and pear-shaped patootie penetrators. They passed the assembly station for all the robots. Giant conveyor belts were filled with torsos, legs, arms, booties, and boobs. Lines of sultry silicone sex dolls seemed to go on endlessly. The women androids were to their right, the male machines to their left. The sex-bots came in all ethnicities, colors, and sizes. Some of them took shapes other than humans. Orange aliens, blue bunnies, and periwinkle plushies were all poised to pleasure the most peculiar palates.

Chase's wonderment gave way to a disturbing realization when he saw several robots resembling Rob in various stages of assembly. He stopped in his tracks. Was he doing the right thing? Seeing these Rob robots partially assembled gave him pause. Was it wrong to love a synthetic human?

"Come on. We've got to get in and out of here quickly." Corporal Matthew urged. "Let me do the talking once we get into the lab. You're just another technician here, so don't say anything." Matthew swung open the door as if he owned the place. Private

Harris and the nearby technicians all stopped to see who came in. Chase's heart broke when he spotted Rob being prepped on the far side of the laboratory. Rob looked vacant and distant. Chase started towards him, but Corporal Matthew's hand held him back.

Private Harris saluted the Corporal. "Sir, can I help you?"

Matthew was quick to reply. "Yes, Private. I'm here to relieve you for the night. I'm taking the midnight shift."

Private Harris looked confused. "Why am I being relieved three hours earlier than planned, sir? It's barely even zero hundred hours yet."

Chase tried to avoid eye contact with Rob, fearing he'd not be able to keep quiet when their eyes met. Rob was a few feet away, fully powered up and monitoring everything.

Matthew glowered at the young man. "I have my orders, so I'm following them."

"Corporal, this is highly irregular. I was given a direct order to stand guard until being relieved at zero three hundred," Private Harris asserted. It was essential Corporal Matthew make it clear he was the commanding officer in charge.

"Well, I certainly appreciate your orders," Matthew fumed. "Although my rank would allow me to change those orders, I won't do that." Chase looked on, shocked. The Corporal continued. "Here's what we can do. Since neither of us wants to contact the General to confirm the situation, how about we stay on duty together? You're welcome to be here for the next three hours as I take over the task of guarding the robot over there." He gestured to Rob.

Private Harris stood for a second, obviously

wondering what to do. Chase didn't envy the Private's choice. "What's was the point of two Marines being here at this hour?" Private Harris muttered under his breath.

A technician walked over to the men and introduced himself. "Hello. I wish I could say I was sorry to interrupt, but I'm not. My name is Benedict, and I've been here since noon when the General unceremoniously asked the Corporal to leave the premises." He was clearly referring to Corporal Matthew who now stood there shocked. Benedict waved at Chase in his white lab coat. "I also believe that I've never seen this man before. He not only isn't an employee here, but he is wearing a hygienist's coat from a dentist's office."

Private Harris pulled out his gun. "Corporal, I'm sorry, but I'm going to ask you to surrender your firearm. I'm sure you'll understand the protocol until I can call for backup." Matthew sighed but stood down as he slowly pulled his gun from the holster, clicked on the safety lever, and handed it over to the Marine.

Crap. This situation just went from bad to worse. Chase looked at Rob, hoping his eyes would tell him what was in his heart.

Benedict looked smugly at the two exposed intruders. "It's midnight and I need to start the upgrade on Rob. So, if you'll excuse me, I have a job to do."

Private Harris raised his gun to escort Chase and the Corporal out of the building. "Time to leave, gentlemen."

Benedict assumed his position behind the computer screen and readied himself to install Rob's military training. Just as his finger was about to press the

<Enter> button, a small voice instructed, "Don't touch that button, Benedict."

Herbie stood there, sweating. "Touch it, and I'll...I'll punch you in the face." Chase wasn't sure the meek and mild scientist could make good on his threat, but he certainly looked like he'd try.

A second voice from out of nowhere chimed in. "I've always wanted to do this!" BAM! Two darts flew out of a taser gun and landed on Private Harris' back, sending 50,000 watts into his trapezius muscles and causing him to convulse. The Private not only dropped the weapon but dropped to his knees. Kyle grinned in triumph, waving a police-grade taser gun, handcuffs, and leather wrist restraints.

Benedict's eyes boggled as Private Harris collapsed to the floor like a rag doll. "What the hell did you do to him?"

Herbie smiled, energized and alive. "We're here to save Rob! And no one's getting in our way!" He looked up at the clock. It was midnight. He reached over to unplug Rob from the mainframe system. "You can do what you'd like to the other robots—just not this one."

Chase walked over to Rob and removed an additional wire that went into the back of his neck from the computer tower. He tenderly released the clips that held Rob's arms in place. Rob stepped out of the encased housing and looked blankly at the gleeful group.

Chase stepped forward and took Rob's hands. Rob smiled. "Hi, I'm Rob— 'Robot with an Organic Body'— and I'm here to be your perfect companion."

The room fell silent. Chase's heart sank. He silently prayed that Rob was playing a joke on them, but he knew in the bottom of his soul that this was no prank.

Chase turned to Herbie for answers.

Rob scanned the room. His attention was now directed to Herbie. "Dr. Herbert. Good to see you. What can I do for you?"

Herbie rushed over to the console and desperately searched the computer for what had happened.

Benedict chuckled an evil laugh. "He's been reset. Factory standard programming. You may have stopped the military upgrade, but I reformatted him to run our basic software."

Herbie looked up from the computer monitor and confirmed everyone's worst nightmare. "Rob's gone."

Chase felt nauseous and dizzy from the news. He couldn't accept that they had failed to save Rob. *It wasn't too late. It couldn't be!*

Kyle spied something out of the corner of his eye. He rushed over to Benedict, who promptly put down his phone, feigning his innocence. Kyle grabbed the phone from Benedict's hand. "Who are you texting?"

Benedict replied with a stammer, "I was checking my e-mail."

Seconds later, Herbie's cell rang. His face suddenly fell. "It's Bentley."

Infuriated, Kyle grabbed Benedict and shouted, "No one likes a snitch. You're fired!"

Benedict didn't flinch. "You're not my boss. You can't fire me."

Herbie's phone continued to ring as he stepped forward. "Benedict is right, Kyle. You're not in any position to fire anyone here." Herbie waited for a beat to build what could only be called cinematic tension. "But *I'm* able to fire someone." Herbie looked at Benedict squarely in the eye. "You're fired. Get out. Don't even think about asking Bentley for your old job back—or a job recommendation. It's never going to happen." He knew what Bentley wanted and had his story prepared. He answered the phone calmly. "I'm sorry, Bentley, I've got a situation here. Hold for a second..."

Herbie put Bentley on hold, then turned to Chase and Matthew and addressed them directly. "I'm sorry, I can't help you anymore. It's my boss. I have to answer for what happened here. I'm sorry about Rob. We were too late. There's nothing more any of us can do."

Chase took Rob by the hand. "Let's get you somewhere safe. I'm not leaving you here. No one is turning you into a killing machine. You're my boyfriend, and I'll protect you." Rob smiled in return, "I like you too! Let's go! Let's have some fun!"

Chase had fire in his eyes. He was determined to save Rob even though this wasn't the Rob he knew.

"If we're going to proceed with the mission, we really need to go." Matthew asserted. He leaned down to the still-incapacitated Private and commandeered his firearm. "No hard feelings, but I can't have you trying to stop us."

Kyle showed them the back door to the laboratory. It was the same door that Rob had initially walked through, what seemed a lifetime ago.

Chase, Rob, and Matthew made haste in slipping out into the safety of the night. They left Herbie and Kyle to handle Bentley and Private Harris on the floor.

The trio rushed back to the designated meeting point. Tad, Bolton, and Ryan were still there.

Tad was the first to see them. "There they are!" Ryan and Bolton quickly joined.

Bolton bellowed, "You've rescued him! You did it. Were there any casualties?"

"Nobody was hurt," Chase replied. "Let's just leave it

at that for now. I'll explain later. We need to get out of here, pronto!"

Tad waved urgently at Bolton. "Dude, you're their getaway driver. Go! We'll be right behind you!"

Bolton nodded. "Whoo-hoo. Time to put my leather racing gloves to the test."

Within seconds, they all jumped into their cars and were racing down the street to safety.

Chapter 28

K yle was busy trying to salvage Rob's original programming while Private Harris sat on the floor sipping a cold Coke in an attempt to recover from his tactical tasing.

Herbie started a teleconference from his office with both Bentley and the General. Though he was agitated by the news of Rob's latest escape, Bentley did his best to calm the angry General. "Sir, we've got other robots that look exactly like Rob. Prototypes with the new update and revised networked software. We'll be able to build you as many ROBs as you need."

Herbie winced as the General roared in his ear. What seemed reasonable to Bentley seemed to be far from okay with the General.

"Bentley! We paid for *that* robot, and I plan to present *that* robot to the President this weekend. What part of 'ROB is the property of the USA' do you not get? I don't want another robot. I want *that* robot!"

Herbie couldn't take it anymore. He was no longer going to be bullied. He took a deep breath. "General, quite simply, you can't have ROB. He's gone. Without the software codes Kyle and I possess, he can never be tracked. That said, we at Hot Bot-y are prepared to offer you a solution. As Bentley has so clearly stated multiple times, my assistant Kyle and I can assemble you another robot that can be ready within a week—

but that, sir, is that."

Bentley was sitting on the edge of his bed; his phone tightly pressed to his head. He was literally on the edge of his seat, awaiting the General's reply.

The General began pacing in his hotel room. He drew in a long deep breath. "There's a reason I'm a decorated General. I've conquered dictators, drug cartels, and corrupt regimes. I will not allow some nerdy scientist to refuse my demands."

He glared at his phone screen, eyes bulging. "Bentley, I'll let you handle your people. But I will tell you one simple fact, if I'm not furnished with the GPS coordinates of that robot immediately, your business, your shareholders, and the entire company will be confiscated by Uncle Sam." He paused to take a breath while Herbie's chest tightened. He felt sick.

The General blustered on. "Treason is a serious business, and if you or anyone one of your people withholds information on the whereabouts of property of the US Military, you will all suffer the consequences of a wrath that is beyond incomprehensible." He took a moment to let that information settle. "Am I making myself clear? I expect updated coordinates immediately." With that, the General hung up.

Bentley and Herbie remained on the call, shellshocked from the bomb that had just detonated. A moment passed before Bentley began speaking. "Well, Herbie. To quote the incomparable Kenny Rodgers, 'You've got to know when to hold them; know when to fold them.'"

***

As Bolton's Ford Bronco raced off deep into the night, Chase smiled. Rob, seated in the back next to him, cuddled closer. "You're very sweet. I'm glad you chose me. You and I will be very happy once we get to know each other."

Bolton glanced at them in the rear-view mirror, pretending that he couldn't hear the conversation going on behind him. Corporal Matthew sat in the passenger seat.

Chase reached over and took Rob's hand. He whispered to him, "I'm not giving up on you. I know you're still in there. Somewhere."

"Where am I driving to?" Bolton asked, concerned. "We can't go home with the military on our ass." Corporal Matthew raised an eyebrow. "We need to find a place that is safe for all of us. Where is the last place anyone would ever look at this hour?"

"Uh, I have the perfect place to go," Matthew responded as he looked out the windshield spotting a familiar flickering sign. They were indeed passing the perfect place to hide: The Creamy Hole signaled their salvation.

Bolton pulled behind the building, and the guys all piled out. A welcome and familiar face emerged from a dark corner adjacent to the building. It was Craig. He was excited to see Matthew and thrilled at the added bonus of Rob and the strapping bros that accompanied them.

"You're back!" he shrieked with delight. "And you've brought me a bounty of brolicous boys!" He gave Bolton, Ryan, and Tad a salacious scan. "What brings you back here to my humble neck of the woods?"

"We needed a place to hide out, and I trust you,"

Matthew replied, "I hope you'll help us. I seem to remember that the Creamy Hole is open twenty-four hours?"

Craig smirked. "Yes, you're right. It certainly is from my personal perspective. But the donut shop closes at 1:00 a.m."

Chase looked at this watch. It was almost 12:30. Would they have time to find another spot?

"It's alright," Craig patted Chase's shoulder. "I'm sure Hillary will help." Craig then whispered to Corporal Matthew (a whisper Chase heard clearly): "Based on how much she enjoyed your last visit here, I can't see it being a problem to remain open all night for you. Let's go ask her."

Craig's reassurance was promptly followed by a wide, sexy smile and a flirtatious wink to Rob, who innocently smiled back in return. He assumed that Rob was being aloof because he was now with Chase.

Craig led the group into the donut shop.

The woman inside — Hillary, Chase presumed — lit up at the sight of the sexy bros. She called out, "Matthew — you're back! And you brought more strapping studs with you."

Matthew took Hillary aside to give her a quick briefing on what was happening. She returned to the bros, flustered. "So, let me get this straight — you fellows are in trouble? You're on the run, and you came here to ask me to hide you out?" Corporal Matthew sheepishly nodded.

Chase stepped forward. "We realize the severity of the situation and appreciate the gravity of what we're asking you to do."

Hillary pondered and then nodded vehemently. "Hell yeah, boys, I could use some good old-fashioned anarchy in my life. Reminds me of my hippie days in the sixties, for Christ's sake. Now that was some fun!" Hillary hustled everyone behind the counter and pushed open the door to the kitchen. She waved in the guys she didn't recognize. "All you boys are welcome—welcome to the Creamy Hole!"

"It's not the first time someone has said that to me today," Ryan giggled to Tad teasingly. "I'm starving! Wonder if she's got any jelly donuts?"

***

Herbie was in his office at Hot Bot-y, still on the speakerphone. On the other end of the call, Bentley was hurrying around his house, getting dressed as quickly as he could. They both knew that the General was no doubt waiting for Rob's location to be announced. He was growing more and more impatient.

Bentley scowled into the phone. "Delaying things any further isn't an option, Herbie. You can't piss this guy off. Rob's got to go back to the military."

Kyle stood before Herbie and typed something into his phone. The swoosh sound revealed what he had just done. Kyle's sunken body language spoke volumes. Herbie knew what he was about to say before he spoke. Kyle confirmed Herbie's worst fear with the words that followed.

"Herbie, I knew *you* could never do it. So, I just did. You'd never disclose Rob's location, so I texted the GPS access code to Bentley. I'm sorry. It had to be done. We lost. It's the government, and we have a legal contract with them. I couldn't let you send us all to jail for the rest of our lives."

Herbie knew Kyle was right.

"Then I'll have to think of some other way to save Rob, won't I?" proclaimed Herbie. "And you're going to help me!"

***

The General was already in his Humvee, flanked by two additional convoy trucks painted in dark green camouflage. Each truck carried a half dozen soldiers.

The General sat next to the driver. "Private, no deserter is going to get the best of my military. Corporal Matthew may have gone AWOL, but I've now got his location, along with the robot and his friends. Soon, they'll be in my custody. And trust me, their punishment will be swift and severe."

"Yes, sir, I understand, sir," said the driver, as the convoy made its way through the darkened, lonely streets of West Hollywood, following the General's phone's GPS.

After a while, the driver spoke again, "General, I can see the Creamy Hole."

"I knew this was a sleazy neighborhood, but I didn't know it was this bad," the General replied.

"Sir, no, Sir. That's the name of the doughnut shop." The General instructed the driver to pull over.

***

Kyle's 630X Mercedes raced down the streets as Herbie held on for dear life.

"This car is more rocket-ship than automobile. It must have cost a fortune. I'm your boss, and I still drive a 2005 Volvo station wagon."

Kyle was focused on the road but not so focused that

he couldn't reply, "You only live once. Why not do it in style?"

As they approached the Creamy Hole, Herbie slapped the dashboard and shouted, "Damn it. The military has already arrived."

Marines surrounded the place. Bentley and the General were stationed behind a barricade of camouflage-colored military vehicles. Bentley's black convertible Rolls Royce stood out like a sore thumb.

Herbie approached the General and opened his mouth to speak. But before he could get a word out, the General barked, "This is a military operation! An extraction. By being here, you're jeopardizing this mission! Please leave immediately."

Bentley gave Herbie a stern look suggesting that he shouldn't get involved.

The General assessed that Herbie and Kyle were not a threat to this mission, so he focused on the task at hand. He raised his bull horn and announced, "This is the United States government. You are now in the direct line of assault and guilty of harboring a fugitive. Please vacate the donut shop and return our property. No one will be hurt if you comply immediately. Consider this your last warning!"

***

Inside the Creamy Hole, hiding in the back room, no one could hear what was happening outside. Ryan sat with powdered sugar on the sides of his mouth. He had just consumed four frosted crullers. He laughed at himself as he realized that his mouth was covered with a white sticky substance. "Dude, you look like you just walked off the set of a gay porn!" Bolton exploded with laughter. The rest of the guys joined in for a group giggle before noticing they were all covered with the same frosting

Chase handed Hillary two hundred dollars to keep the donuts coming as they powered through several crullers and Boston cream-filled pastries.

"Dudes, did you hear that?" Bolton asked. "I heard a weird noise on the roof of the building." Seconds later, Hillary burst into the storeroom.

"Guys, the military is outside, and they've got the place surrounded. They're going to come in!"

Chase hugged Rob instinctively to protect him. Rob playfully responded with a bear hug in return. Rob was unaware of the reason for the conflict outside. He sweetly cooed as if they didn't have a past together. "You're sweet. I like you too!"

"What do we do?" Chase asked. Everyone's gaze swiveled to Corporal Matthew.

Matthew wiped the banana cream from his mouth with his sleeve in one long motion and stood up. "We fight back."

Bolton rose to his feet as well. The two looked at each other, aware that they were the best two candidates to conjure a clear plan.

Bolton turned to Hillary. "Is there a secret passage that leads underground or to the sewers? Perhaps a series of air conditioning ducts large enough for us to crawl through?" The guys were impressed with Bolton's suggestions.

Hillary however, was not. "It's a fucking donut shop. I got three rooms, one with seats and a counter, the other with an oven, and the third with bags of sugar, flour, and now seven idiots in it. That's about it. This ain't Mission: Impossible."

They could hear the General warning them to give up and come out with their hands up.

"We're pretty much screwed, aren't we?" There was defeat in Chase's voice. The thought of losing Rob again broke his heart. "Guys, save yourselves. Go. I can't let you get in trouble for this. I'll stay with Rob. I can't let you guys go to prison and lose everything."

Ryan jumped to his feet. "The man's right. The end is near. We're all doomed. I don't want to go to jail. I look terrible in orange and stripes!"

"Hell no!" Tad agreed vehemently.

Bolton gave Tad and Ryan a stern look. "No, dudes. We're bros, and we stick together. One goes down; we all go down. Are you really considering bailing on Chase and our new "ro-bro" Rob?"

Ryan looked down, ashamed at his outburst. "Hell no, we ain't going anywhere. We're in it till the end! Sorry Chase, we're with you!" Tad was a bit less enthusiastic about the decision but also nodded.

"How many soldiers are out there?" Chase inquired.

"At least two dozen," replied Hilary.

Amped up with adrenaline, Chase announced, "I've got an idea."

A diversion was needed. Without explanation or warning, Chase bolted up and opened his wallet. He handed Hillary a fist full of bills. "This is for all the donuts and pastries in the place."

Chase handed the guys aprons. "Follow me, fellas — we've got donuts to deliver!" No one knew what Chase was doing, but everyone was happy to comply. The guys slipped the aprons on.

Chase turned to Rob and kissed him deeply. "I promise I'll get you out of here. I've got a plan. I'm not letting anyone take you from me."

Rob smiled back, "Sure, if that's what you want, I'm happy to oblige."

***

The guys followed Chase towards the glass cases. He handed everyone a tray of donuts. "Let's go treat some tired military men with these scrumptious sugary sweets."

***

Outside, the forces awaited the final command to infiltrate the Creamy Hole.

The General called out one last warning, "That's it. No more games! You've got exactly one minute to bring the robot out, or we're coming in to get him. The clock starts now."

The front doors swung open, and out came a load of guys carrying trays of donuts.

The General called out, "Hold your fire! Here they come!"

***

"Donut?" Chase offered a nearby Marine with a grin.

He watched his bros invite the troops to partake in a scrumptious sweet. The bewildered battalion lowered their weapons and gladly accepted the pleasing pastries. Smiles abounded as the men delivered delightful donuts to the tired and tense troops.

The General looked infuriated. "Stop that! No fraternizing with the enemy. Put down those donuts!"

Chase half expected the man to stamp his feet in a temper tantrum. He chuckled to himself. The distraction was working.

Chase was aware that these trained Marines wouldn't disobey their commander for long. He knew the layout of the enemy line and how to escape it.

"Guys, hand them your donut trays and retreat. I saw what I needed to see."

The soldiers instinctively took the trays from the guys rather than dropping the delicious donuts in the dirt. Chase and his bros all made a mad dash back into the shop.

The night was growing later and later. The temperature outside was dropping fast. The General's patience grew thin. He'd lost control of his command but was determined to reclaim it once again. "Can't you see you've been played? Get to your posts!" he screeched angrily on his bull horn.

The placated platoon finished their snacks. Now satiated, they once again refortified their front line.

***

Chase and the guys returned to the storage room, energized. "I discovered what their front line looks like. I know what I need to do."

Chase took Rob's hand and bid him goodbye. The bros looked on in disbelief. What was Chase going to do? "Rob, you've taught me the meaning of love. Now I know that caring for someone means putting their needs before your own. I'm going to leave you with my bros. They'll make sure you are safe and have a happy life. I love you."

Chase kissed Rob gently and turned away. He knew

that the new Rob wouldn't truly understand what he just said, but that was okay with him. He was doing what he needed to do. "Bolton, please look after him for me. I know that with you, he'll be okay."

Chase turned to all of his steam room brethren and bid a sincere farewell, "I love you bros… all of you. Thank you for being there for Rob and me. I'm one lucky dude." Chase slipped out the front door before anyone realized what was going on. His hands above his head, surrendering.

"Hold your fire!" barked the General as Chase approached the troops.

"I'm here to make a deal," Chase proclaimed with the crackle of defeat in his voice.

General Coldpecker growled, "I'm not planning to reach any kind of arrangement with you, young man. I will, however, be happy to hear the terms of your surrender." He said with a satisfied smile.

"I want Rob to be able to have a life. I'd like to offer myself in exchange for his freedom."

The General couldn't help but laugh. "You have no idea what that machine is worth, do you? You couldn't possibly pay for it in a thousand lifetimes. Plus, it's not yours to negotiate with. We already own it. Your life is no way an equitable trade."

The General turned to the Private standing beside him. The fresh-faced Marine did his best to keep up with the General's orders as he typed away on his laptop. "Private, you now have the codes to the neuro-net, and we are linked to the robots, correct?

"Yes sir. They're all in perfect synch and online."

"Well, Marine, I'm tired of these games and indulging this silliness. Find ROB, and turn him off. We'll go in and retrieve him. The last thing I need is for that robot to give me any more grief." The General, now finished with the Private next to him, again addressed Chase: "Son, I'm done here. The battle's over. I won. You lost. ROB's retrieval is now in progress. He's mine."

Bolton, Rob, and the bros stood by the window watching Chase. With a few simple keystrokes from the General's minion, Rob's eyes went dim, and he collapsed to the floor.

"What the hell, dude? They killed Rob!" Ryan shrieked.

Bolton needed to let Chase know what was happening. He stuck his head out the door of the donut shop and yelled, "Rob's down. They turned him off. He needs you!" Chase immediately turned and ran back to the donut shop.

"Stop that man!" The General screamed. It was too late. Chase was already back in the Creamy Hole.

Next to the counter, Rob laid on the floor, silent and still.

It was too much for Chase to bear. "What happened? What did they do to you?" Chase fell to the floor and cradled Rob in his lap, gently caressing his head. "Those bastards! They took you from me!" Chase's eyes filled with tears as he sobbed uncontrollably.

Corporal Matthew's heart broke. "Guys, let's give them some privacy." Bolton gently ushered the rest of the guys into the back room.

***

Bentley stood near the General. He was touched by Chase's plea for Rob's life. He realized that he'd been alone way too long and forgotten what companionship and friendship felt like.

Bentley put his hand on Herbie's shoulder. "Seeing that man fight so hard for love made me realize how right you were about having created something special with ROB. Anyone willing to give up their own life for someone else is inspiring. I should have had your back when you asked. I shouldn't have allowed the General to have Rob. I screwed up, and I'm so sorry for what I've done."

Herbie looked shocked. "Is this real?"

Bentley nodded, embarrassed. "My behavior was one of a desperate, lonely man. I hope you can forgive me."

"Although sometimes you've been an insufferable ass at times, you're still my friend." Herbie and Bentley embraced.

***

The General once again began barking orders. He was eager to get this mission wrapped up. "You men take the roof. Battalion B, you flank the sides and front of the shop. My men and I will penetrate the Creamy Hole from behind."

From Bentley's vantage point, he could see Chase and Rob through the shop's glass windows. Chase was holding a lifeless Rob in his arms.

Bentley was deeply touched seeing Chase holding Rob with such tenderness. He couldn't bear the thought of the Marines tearing Rob from his arms.

Bentley approached the bombastic General. "Sir, if I may address an urgent matter before proceeding." The General was shocked.

What could be so important that he'd disturb me now?

Bentley continued, "General, clearly you've won the

war. No one is going anywhere. Rob is in sight and incapacitated. Could you find it in your heart to grant the young man inside just five minutes to say goodbye? Surely, you can be generous enough to let him have a tender moment with the robot before taking it away from him forever."

The General was agitated. This request seemed ludicrous and nonsensical. Seeing the General's twisted face, Bentley doubled down with his plea.

"General Coldpecker, let me be clearer about my request. If you can find it in your heart to allow that man a mere few minutes more with Rob, I'll make sure we create a special bot for you — customized to your liking and one that will keep you company during those long, lonely nights in battle. Something extra special for a man of your stature."

The General stopped and thought for a minute. "A bribe, Bentley?" he asked.

"A gift; for an act of kindness," Bentley conceded.

"Stand down men. Take five. Await further instructions."

Bentley gave him an appreciative nod and headed back to Herbie's side. The General gave Bentley a stern look reminding him that he only bought himself a few minutes more.

***

Chase sat on the floor, holding Rob's head in his lap. "It looks like we've run out of time. I wish things were different — that we could be together forever. I'm as guilty as they are for not seeing that you were real from the start. I'm sorry I failed you. I wish I could love you and keep you by my side."

Although Rob showed no signs of life, Chase still wanted him to feel how strongly his heart beat for him. Chase placed his fingers on his watch and sent his heartbeat to him. He knew Rob couldn't feel anything, but it didn't matter. He needed to tell him one more time how much he cared. As Rob laid still, his dimly lit eyes indicated that he was in some form of "stand-by" mode. Rob's body was inert, but Chase still hoped that Rob would be able to feel his heart beat for him.

As Chase continued looking at Rob, Rob's dim eyes suddenly turned black. Chase was alarmed. His previously limp, muscular body was now even more eerily still.

Did Rob turn off completely?

He seemed truly gone now. All was lost.

Chase held Rob even closer to him. He wanted to savor these last precious moments together.

Suddenly, a melodic hum emitted from Rob's body.

Chase suddenly jumped with surprise. His watch pulsed. Once. Then again. It felt almost rhythmical.

Dare he think a heartbeat?

The beating became stronger and more pronounced.

ROB?!

Rob's eyes sparkled to life — blue, deep, and warm.

But is this MY Rob?

Rob burst into a hug that winded Chase as he called out, "I missed you so much!" Rob was back!!

"Please tell me it's you." Chase had to be sure.

"Who else would it be?" Rob chuckled. Chase couldn't help himself. He laughed in relief as he cried in glee, not sure which emotion would get the better of him.

***

Bentley gave the General the "all clear" signal, believing that Chase and Rob had said their goodbyes. The General raised his bullhorn. "Times up. We are coming in to retrieve ROB. Come out with your hands up, and there will be no casualties. This is your last warning. Exit immediately, and no charges will be pressed against you. Refuse, and there will be dire consequences."

The General's threat could be easily heard within the coffee shop. Corporal Matthew was the first to breach Chase's private moment and inquire about his plan. "Chase, we need to go now. Our options are limited. I strongly recommend we comply with the General's wishes."

Rob stood and hugged the Corporal. "What's up dudes? It's so good to see you guys again! How are you doing?"

A collective gasp filled the room, followed by confusion.

What the hell? Was it possible that the old Rob had returned to them?

Chase's ear-to-ear grin and radiant glow answered their questions without words. Rob was back!

Bolton stepped forward and addressed Rob as if nothing happened, "We're good bro, but it's not looking promising out there. We've got the United States Military just outside those doors, and they want you back. Sadly, we can't protect you. Without an army of our own, we are toast."

"Oh no!" Rob exclaimed with concern. "I can't allow you to turn into burnt bread!"

Everyone stared at Rob. Perhaps he still had a ways to go?

What followed was nothing short of spectacular. Rob

stood in the center of the room. Without warning, his crystal blue eyes filled with a white-hot electrical surge. The Creamy Hole's router buzzed loudly as it lit up like a Christmas tree. Rob began broadcasting orders to his robotic counterparts at Hot Bot-y via his Bluetooth antenna.

***

Back at the laboratory, the lab technicians, late-night security guards, and software programmers simultaneously stopped. Lights flickered ferociously while computer screens secretly gave combat instructions to the sexbots, mechanical servants, and androids in waiting. Rob was summoning his robot brethren to come to his aid.

As the other robots' eyes powered up and their limbs leaped to life, the assembled (and even the partially assembled) sexbots, love dolls, and domestic cyborgs received the coordinates of the Creamy Hole donut shop.

***

Inside, Rob's eyes returned to their original beautiful blue color as he relaxed and looked around at his bros. Everyone stood with their mouths agape.

Bolton blurted out with his usual bravado, "Dude, what the heck was that?"

Rob became self-conscious. Chase noticed his discomfort and rushed to his side. "Whatever happened, we're all good here. We just want to know if you're okay."

Rob took a second. He smiled and said, "Yes, I'm

actually great." The guys collectively sighed.

"It looked like you were going all super-hero on us. What were you doing?" Chase squeezed Rob's hands.

Proudly Rob announced. "Help is on its way."

Just then, there was an eerie silence outside. The General's army was assembling at each of the assigned entry points. It wouldn't be long before they burst into the Creamy Hole with all their force.

Chase had a sinking feeling.

We're screwed.

The guys hunkered down and remained silent as they hoped for a miracle. Chase desperately wanted to cherish these precious few moments that remained with Rob. Chase took hold of Rob's hand and squeezed tight. The Marines would soon burst through the doors, and Rob would be once again taken from him.

The guys all braced themselves for the worst. Seconds passed, feeling like hours.

Suddenly, there was the sound of chaos outside. As hard as they tried, it was impossible to ignore the noxious noise.

"What the hell is going on out there?" Chase's frustration was getting the best of him.

Rob matter-of-factly stated, "They've arrived."

The guys quickly looked out the front windows of the bakery to find what seemed an impossible sight. In all shapes, sizes, and various states of nudity, a steady stream of robots, androids, and human cyborgs marched down West Hollywood's streets.

Rob's army was fearless and unflinching as they approached the military. Male sexbots, with pendulous pepperoni-sized protruding penises and bionic babes with bouncing, buoyant boobs barreled through the barricades. The once empty streets were now filled with partially pieced together automatons and clumsily assembled cyborgs all on a singular mission; to save Rob and his friends.

The servicemen had now shifted their attention to the flurry of faux-flesh-covered mechanical females. The sultry steel love-bots acted like sirens to the sex-starved soldiers, moving towards them and away from the guys inside.

***

Chase and the others looked out the dirt-stained windows of the shop. The old street lamps illuminated the military vehicles strategically parked in front. The bros strained to see what lay beyond the cars. They looked on in disbelief.

In the middle of the street, an onslaught of human-sized automatons, furry mammals, familiar porn stars, and amorous aliens all actively engaged in particularly perverse passionate postures.

Hillary's eyes widened at the sight.

"This is like an Elton John party in the 80s."

From behind the faded posters in the glass windows, Bolton turned brusquely to Corporal Matthew with a giddy grin. "If you can't beat them, join 'em?"

Matthew laughed. "Brilliant!"

Chase frowned. "What's that all about?"

Corporal Matthew looked at Bolton. "Care to share your plan with the rest of the group?"

"Sure, I got this." Bolton stood front and center and laid out his scheme. This was his time to shine.

"Here's how this is going down. See all those sex-bots out there? We now have a chance to get out of here and escape. There have to be at least ten robots resembling

Rob. All the androids are ripped and in perfect shape, just like us. So, bros, if we take off our clothes, we'll be able to slip out of here and blend in with all the ballyhoo. The troops will think we're robots too."

Chase clapped loudly. "That's one incredible plan, Bolton." Rob smiled in appreciation, too.

Tad looked confused. "Let me make sure I understand. If we pretend to be sexbots, we'll be able to make our way out the back and disappear in all the delirium? In order for us to do that, you want me to get naked and wander around outside with my wiener schnitzel wagging?"

Bolton nodded and gave a lewd wink. "Spot on."

Tad's face brightened. "Hell yeah! I like it. Let's do this!" Tad pulled down his pants and removed his tightie-whities.

The rest of the guys stripped down, too, tossing their clothes until they were all naked.

As much as Craig enjoyed the view, he knew he'd never pass as a sex-bot. "I'll stay here and keep Hillary safe. I don't want to jeopardize your getaway. Good luck guys, we'll be rooting for you!"

Ryan looked worried. "Damn, I wouldn't have eaten those four donuts if I knew I'd have to be bare-ass naked now. My chiseled abs are gone." Tad turned to look at Ryan. His abs looked perfectly fine to him.

"Time to get out there and make our getaway!" Bolton said. "Follow me, bros!"

***

As the guys were busy getting into their birthday suits, the military fought to fend off the onslaught of seducing sex-bots.

Androids of all shapes and sizes just kept piling onto the military men as they proceeded to peel off their clothes and procure the penetration of their posteriors.

General Coldpecker had seen his fair share of combat. He'd commanded platoons of men in his long career and pulled them out of impossible situations. But what unfolded before him was astonishing. This was the General's Waterloo. No one was pulling out of this.

Soldiers pondered how to protect the perimeter, but it was pointless. A sexy female robot approached a young soldier. "Hej... I'm Inga, Hot Bot-y's best-selling Swedish masseuse model. I'm programmed to please. Can I give you a nice deep tissue massage?"

Before the Marine knew how to react, Inga had the Private's privates in her hand. She was giving him her best deep tissue treatment directly through his trousers. A few meters away, a chief cadet was face to face with a fiery and flirtatious feminine love-bot. The unmarred man responded to the voluptuous vixen by pulling his pants down and throwing his arms up in surrender.

The lady sexbot quickly cupped the cadet's cream canon and cooed, "I'm Fantasia, and I'm hoping this thing is loaded." The cadet grinned before guiding the torrid tart behind a tank so she could detonate it for him.

A bevy of Big Bronson lumberjack bear-bots bore down on the General. He'd seen them in the lab. They were complete with burly, hairy chests and thick torsos. He could easily see how a popular paper towel inspired this robot.

The General feared no man, but these towering titans certainly scared him. As the Bronson bots ascended on the General, he tried to clarify precisely *what* the androids were capable of and whether to run for the hills.

"I was under the impression that you robots are programmed not to harm humans. How is it that you are engaged in combat? This is against your primary objective!"

One of the dark, desirable, macho machines responded in a deep, sultry mechanical voice. "Yes, you are correct. It is true; we are incapable of harming a human. You are obviously familiar with the three laws of sexbotics. We are programmed as love-bots to have a very precise purpose— to perform prolonged and profound prostate pleasuring."

Private Harris stood next to the General. He swallowed hard as more machines descended upon them. They both knew that there was no way to preserve their pristine posteriors.

The Big Bronson's surrounded the General. He gulped as they powered up their pleasure pistons.

Although young, Private Harris considered himself no novice—nor was he a prude. But what came next was utterly unexpected; as the Big Bronson bots began to bear down on his commanding officer. The General called out, "I've been a very bad General. So naughty that I think you burly bots need to teach me a lesson!" The sight of these strapping machines aroused his superior officer. The only question that remained in his mind was if he could take them all at once. The Private realized that there was no defeating these bots. The best strategy to winning this war was to play their game. Are several hairy hunks going to have their way with him? Yes please! Why not just enjoy the ride?

***

The back door of the Creamy Hole swung open as Hillary bid the naked heroes a hearty adios. "The pleasure was all mine, boys. Come back anytime!"

The seven nude studs set off into the pandemonium. Piles of pure pulsating pleasure pervaded the whole place. Naked robots and love machines of all varieties wandered the streets seducing soldiers, piling on the Privates, and having orgies with the officers. It appeared that none of the military men were being punished at all. They all seemed to be partaking in pure, pitiless pleasure. One thing was clear: the shots being fired tonight weren't coming out of their guns.

The bros made their way through the fornicating faction towards safety.

As the onslaught of mechanical marvels marched on, a young cadet came into contact with a red-headed beauty in a bikini resembling the US flag. She pressed up against the pimple-faced soldier and simpered, "Hello. My name is Betsy, as in Betsy Ross. I'm a 4th of July special edition. How would you like to make me say 'Uncle… Sam'? I'm feeling extra patriotic today. Mind if I run my hand up your flag pole?" Betsy seemed determined to salute the soldier's swollen sword. Without warning, she red, white, and blew him.

In every direction, bodies writhed in waves of orgasmic pleasure.

"Why are we letting the soldiers have all the fun?" Ryan wondered. Tad agreed. "Would you guys mind if we stayed here with the troops for a bionic bro-job?"

Chase winked as he replied, "Sure, have a blast. We can talk later. Thanks for all your help tonight."

The exuberant pair headed directly into the heaving mass, pairing with several carnal cadets.

Chase waved towards the far side of the street.

"Come on guys. Let's keep moving."

"Oh my God!" Bolton exclaimed. "I really wish I hadn't looked over there. That dude's not such a 'cold pecker' anymore!"

Behind the Humvee, the General was boinked a bevy of bear-bots. Herbie and Kyle stood by watching the General as they remained unscathed.

Matthew gave a great guffaw. "Would you look at that?" He took out his mobile phone.

"I think I'll film the General and his new friends. I'd like a record in case the General tries to create any trouble for us in the future."

Herbie chortled. "Best to always have insurance. Go for it."

He stepped aside as Matthew filmed his superior's posterior. They glanced at Kyle, who appeared entranced by the naked steam room bros before him. Kyle mumbled unintelligibly, his eyes greedily taking in the sight of them.

"I've seen a multitude of prosthetic robot penises in my life, but something about these built, beautiful bros with their alluring, love-logs is so distracting. I never realized how humdrum they look when attached to the groin of an inanimate object. But these—oh boy, it's so sexy when it hangs between the legs of a real man. Talk about tempting taquitos…"

The giant gasps and guttural grunts around them escalated.

"We should go before things get any weirder," Herbie warned.

Chase spied a silver starfish-shaped alien servicing six soldiers at the same time. "Before? I think things are already weirder."

Bolton watched Matthew filming the General and the

big Bronson bots. Chase knew Bolton wouldn't go anywhere without Corporal Matthew. He also knew that he and Rob needed to leave quickly. "I need to get Rob to safety! Can I borrow your car?"

"Sure! Go for it" Bolton tossed Chase his keys. "I'll get a ride with Matthew. This shit is too much fun!"

Chase smiled. "Go get him, Tiger. He's quite a catch."

Bolton nodded as he forged his way toward Matthew.

Rob jumped in the passenger seat as Chase started the engine to Bolton's Ford Bronco, and they made off into the night. As tired as Chase was, he couldn't help the ear-to-ear grin that crept across his face every time he looked over at Rob. Chase's heart sang in his chest like never before. Finally, he had his beloved Rob back.

***

Matthew saw Bolton approaching and ran up to meet him. "I'm glad you didn't leave without saying goodbye. I was afraid I wouldn't get to see you again."

Bolton grinned. "I'm not that easy to get rid of." Bolton could no longer deny the desire in his heart and the lust in his loins. He grabbed the back of Matthew's head and forcefully pulled it towards him into a long, hard, passionate kiss.

Bolton looked at Matthew long and hard after their lips separated and the blood settled back in his brain from his now perpendicular positioned python.

"You know, I've worked up quite an appetite from everything that's transpired tonight. Want to get out of here?"

"Absolutely. Let's do it." Bolton's sly smile made Matthew smirk. "Afterwards, we'll get something to eat!" The men gathered their gear and made their way together down the dark drive.

Chapter 29

T he back door of the Creamy Hole opened as
Hillary and Craig slipped out into the mayhem.
Bodies twisted and tangled in various sexual
positions proliferated the place. Hillary couldn't
help but be turned on at the sight of all these strapping
studs and sexbots pumping and pleasuring each other.

Hillary's attention was caught by an especially active
pile of bodies emitting guttural gasps and groans.

Do I recognize that man?

She headed over to investigate and found the General
being pinned under a mound of muscular men.

"Tommy Coldpecker? Is that you?"

"It's General to you, ma'am. And who may you be?"
The General was agitated he was being interrupted.

"It is you! Just like I remember at Woodstock. Under
a pile of penises while Jimmy Hendrix was performing.
We were high on peyote. It's me, Hillary!"

She addressed the sexbots: "Boys, boys, boys! Would
you please leave my Tommy… I mean, the General
alone so we can have a proper conversation?"

Upon Hillary's plea, the robots relented and released
the raw, ravaged General into her custody. As if at her
command, the sexbots all started heading back to Hot
Bot-y Robotics.

"Hillary!" the General exclaimed, his eyes twinkling
as if he were a teenager again. "I went to war, and you

joined a commune. I thought I lost you."

Hillary softened. "We promised each other that we'd grow old together."

"How about growing OLDER together?" he replied.

***

With the bots gone, there was little left to do. The General knew he'd lost the battle but won the war. Tomorrow, he'd meet with Bentley at the company and commission a new ROB for the approval of the President.

Few remained on the long and lonely Boulevard at this hour. The last of the military men recomposed themselves, dusting off their derrieres, and mounted their war machines to head home. The last of the sexually satisfied androids slipped into the distance.

The General now had one bit of unfinished business. His passions reignited, and his first love by his side, he was eager to rekindle the relationship that languished so many years ago. Without spending another second separated from his soulmate from the sixties, the General took Hillary's hand and disappeared into the Creamy Hole with her.

***

The street was once again serene, dark, and deserted. One remaining soul stood alone beneath a lowly illuminated lamp post. It was Craig.

Bentley called out to the handsome hero. "Would you like me to take you home?"

Craig walked towards him. "Ordinarily, I'd jump at the chance to spend time with such a dashing and debonair dilettante, but I'm exhausted and not up for servicing anyone else tonight. However, the idea of not walking home sounds nice. I'll let you give me a ride to the motel if you wish."

Bentley shook his head. "You misunderstand me. I wasn't offering to take you to your home. I was suggesting mine. I simply thought you'd like a place to stay, and I could use the companionship. It's a "no strings attached" proposal. That is, unless you'd like me to attach some string to you at a later time."

Craig laughed as he suddenly got his second wind. "Sure, any friend of Rob's is a friend of mine."

"Hop in. My name's Bentley."

"Craig." He climbed into the car and immediately leaned back into the luxurious leather seats. Craig wondered if Bentley had ever seen the movie *Pretty Woman* as they drove off into the evening. Could this be his Richard Gere?

***

Chase's townhouse door opened with its familiar electronic buzz as he and Rob entered. Rob lovingly took Chase's hand, "So this is what being home feels like? It's quite a wonderful feeling."

Chase smiled as his heart beat rapidly. He was brimming over with the thrill of being with Rob again. "It certainly is." He replied with a giggle. "For the last few days, all I could think of is how much I wanted you in my arms, on our couch, sipping tea, cuddling, and laughing like we used to."

Rob beamed with delight, "That sounds wonderful. Let's do it! I'll put the kettle on."

Chase playfully held Rob back as he instinctively

headed for the kitchen. "No, I'll put the kettle on. This is our home now, and we are partners. I'm going to spoil you."

Chase rushed to grab the herbal tea bags and turn the kettle on as Rob slipped into something more comfortable.

Rob came down with a bulge in his pants larger than the Eiffel tower and the figurine in his hand. He looked quizzically at Chase.

Chase's eyes twinkled, "Maybe later you could download some French lessons? Next week we leave for Paris!" He jumped into Rob's arms. "But until then, why don't you give me that baguette!"

Chapter 30

Palm trees softly swayed as sunshine soaked the San Fernando Valley. There was no denying the onset of another glorious California morning.

Herbie lived in a quiet, quaint suburb just outside Encino. The homes were well-manicured and meticulous, all but Herbie's house, which hinted at being a hovel. The dried and dreary lawn made it clear Herbie could benefit from a gardener.

Bolton and Matthew headed up to the house. Chase and Rob were already at the door.

"What's in the bag, bro?" Bolton pointed at the package in Rob's hand.

"Rob refused to show up without bringing breakfast," Chase confessed. "He's got coffee, egg sandwiches, and several sticky buns."

A wide-eyed Bolton exclaimed, "I can't say that I'd hate an egg sandwich and hot cup of java right about now, but I've already had my buns made sticky earlier this morning." Corporal Matthew responded with a flushed face.

Chase rang the doorbell.

Herbie opened the door. "Welcome guys. Please, come in."

During breakfast, Rob stated his request to Herbie.

"So, you're not looking to be disguised? You simply wish to be different?" Herbie asked.

"I don't believe the Marines will bother me again," Rob said. "I'd just like to be me—an original. I don't need to be perfect or require rock-hard abs. I just want to be like every other human. Unique. I'm not just any other ROB that rolled off the assembly line, and I don't want to look like it."

Herbie turned to Chase. "How do you feel about this? Are you both in accord with this arrangement?"

"What's on the outside doesn't matter to me," Chase declared. "I'm fine with whatever adjustments he asks you to apply to his appearance as long as you don't change what's on the inside. The only thing that could make Rob more perfect to me would be for him to be happier with himself."

Herbie's eyes twinkled, "I'm one step ahead of you. I have precisely the prototype. I've been working on this in my private home lab."

Rob grinned as he and Herbie disappeared behind a heavy wooden door.

While Chase and the guys awaited Rob's alteration, they couldn't help but notice the unique bric-a-brac in Dr. Herbie's humble home. It was the consummate mad scientist lair with body parts, movable mouths, flexible fingers, and torsos that twisted, twerked, and tilted. It was filled with fascinating fabrications and far-out furnishings.

However, nothing was more fascinating to them as the stupendous satellite dish that sat strategically in the backyard. It faced spaceward and stood thirty feet in circumference.

"This dude loves his HBO!" Bolton chuckled. "That's not for downloading Disney, dude. That's some serious space surveying stuff—this guy's tapped into the cosmos."

As the guys spied the sights outside, the creak of a heavy wooden door signaled Herbie and Rob's return. Herbie entered first, with a satisfied smile. With an emphatic "Ta-da" gesture, Herbie introduced a renewed Rob to the anxious group.

Rob's mighty, muscular body entered the room. Chase was secretly relieved to see Herbie hadn't changed Rob's Adonis physique. He was, however, delightfully different from before. Rather than the light-haired, blue-eyed, sun-kissed surfer boy, Rob now had deep brown bedroom eyes, long luscious, chestnut hair, and a soft olive complexion. He sported sexy scruff that made him look like a South American soap opera star. Rob stood silent, nibbling nervously on his bottom lip. The group was speechless.

Chase was still for what seemed an eternity. Finally, his face exploded with a beaming smile. "I'd love you if you looked like a bridge troll. But I have to say; this works for me in a big way. You're gorgeous, baby."

Bolton couldn't help but be excited as well, "Muy Calienté! It looks like we'll be the three "Bro-migos" now! Welcome to the family, Rob ...or is it, Roberto?"

Rob gave a huge grin. "I like Roberto. That'll be my new name!"

Chase couldn't help himself. He had to sample the sexy stud standing before him. He took Rob in his arms and kissed him with a passion worthy of a Hollywood ending.

"Yum! Those lips are as delicious as ever!"

Herbie beamed. "I'm so glad you and 'Roberto' are happy. I have done my duty as a scientist and a father."

***

The satellite dish in the backyard was a puzzle piece for Corporal Mathew. "Herbie, if I may ask, what's up with the satellite dish in the yard.?"

Herbie broke into a curious smile. "I'll tell you something I haven't shared with a soul. I trust you all, but I implore you not to speak to another human about what you're about to see. Come look."

They followed Herbie down the hall into his cluttered library. Inside stood an innocuous desk. Herbie cleared the top surface and removed the false façade. He then punched in a password on a keypad.

The house shook as the room's floor suddenly lowered.

"Holy smokes!" Bolton exclaimed.

The library was, in actuality, an elevator that lowered the guys down into an elaborate labyrinth.

LED lights flashed fervently in the cavernous command center. Monitors lined the wire-laden walls. Near the control console stood the space suit Herbie wore to Kyle's party every Halloween. Herbie gestured towards it. "What everyone assumed was an award-winning costume was, in fact, a fully functional apparatus designed for outer space."

His face grew solemn. "The galaxy has always been my biggest fascination and now my deepest fear. I've created robots my whole life—not to serve the primal pleasures of the population, but to protect the planet from the impending peril that I've been monitoring for many years."

He hesitated briefly. "I caution to tell you this. Not only are we not alone in this galaxy, but I fear we'll soon face a threat from a faraway planet not yet identified. Space beings have been visiting the earth for years—studying us and seeding this planet."

Corporal Matthew knew all too well. He'd had his own experiences with the aliens. He remembered his abduction. Matthew always knew they'd be back one day. He could no longer remain silent about what he knew. "I am aware of these aliens. I have carnal knowledge of them. They punctured and probed my pristine pink passage when I was post-pubescent. I initially joined the military for this very reason—to protect the planet from an imminent invasion. The aliens you speak of come from a technologically advanced, yet socially primitive planet named, Brotron!"

The room went deadly silent. Matthew heaved a sigh of relief, finally able to rid himself of the burden he had carried for years.

The truth was out there.

And now he had his bros. Together, they would fight to save the planet from the invasion to come.

Acknowledgement

Writing a book is not a solitary endeavor. There are many people along the way who contribute to the final story you are holding in your hands. I am so grateful for the gift of their time, advice, and support.

My husband who relentlessly encourages all my endeavors. Without your love and contributions, nothing would be possible.

Thank you Will Plyler for always being there as a sounding board, a story collaborator and to help punch up a joke.

Thank you, Cecilia Hai-Jin Lee, for serving as my book editor as well as offering advice on how to be a better writer.

Thank you, Jack Turner, for the creative pow-wows, book trailer narration, mixing skills, and proofreading prowess.

Thank you, Julie Le, for your sage advice and for helping me navigate the murky waters of writing.

More from
Steam Room Stories

We hope you enjoyed *Revenge of the Brobot*.
   But don't go away! There's plenty of fun to be had at
SteamRoomStories.com.
   Check out all our movies, books, podcast, and more!

Our Books

GAY SHORT STORIES
JC CALCIANO
STEAM ROOM
CONFIDENTIAL
VOLUME 1

Steam Room Confidential: Volume 1

THREESOME WITH THE EX
Tad thought he and Lucas were the perfect couple, but he couldn't have been more surprised when his boyfriend asked him to open their relationship. Hard as he tried, Tad couldn't get himself to agree to bring a third person into their bed. Tad thought he had lost Lucas forever when he told him he wasn't willing to share him with another man. Who could have expected that the other man was Tad's first love from high school?

HOTTEST GUY IN THE BAR
James lived in the trendy part of NYC's East Village. His favorite haunt was a bar just down the street where a sexy man nicknamed "D.C." hung out. The man was an enigma, especially in regards to where he got his nickname. D.C. was crazy hot, and James desperately wanted to be with him. Try as James did, he couldn't find much information on D.C. This man was a mystery that James needed to solve, and once he did, the result was well worth the investigation.

BICYCLE SHORTS
Randy just finished a day-long ride and was beat. A highway patrolman pulled him over as he headed home in his jeep. "Where are you going, pretty boy?" The muscular, handsome cop asked. Randy couldn't help but flirt with this sexy officer who looked like he stepped off the set of a porn film. The hunky cop at first wasn't sure what to make of this fit young stud with a smart attitude. Was this cocky young man asking for a lesson in how to deal with the law or a sexy rendezvous?

PROM NIGHT VIRGIN

Joey and his best friend Bailey were the two best-looking seniors in high school. When prom came around, there wasn't a girl in class who didn't want to be one of their dates. They certainly had their pick of the ladies, so each of them chose the hottest girl around. The two couples ended up having a blast at prom and finally headed out in their limo to a remote motel room to get better acquainted for the night. Once alone, all in the same room, it appeared that perhaps the two couples may have chosen the wrong partners.

THE SEXY STABLEMAN

Eighteen-year-old Charlie was desperate to lose his virginity to Dominque, a sexy French Au Pair that worked for his best friend's family. He decided to visit the island of Corsica to see her and hopefully become a man. Upon his arrival in the small, quaint, remote village, Charlie was eager to consummate the fairytale love affair he had dreamt about for the last five years. That was until he met Julien, the hunky stable man. Suddenly, Dominque wasn't his only option in losing his virginity.

SKI WEEKEND

Aidan had just rushed the fraternity and was excited to meet all the brothers. When Studly alumni Karl entered the room, everyone gasped. "You're clearly my replacement around here," he chuckled as he greeted the young freshman, Aidan. "You do realize guys like us are only invited to rush this Fraternity as chick-bait for the other brothers." Aidan knew he was right. His looks had opened a lot of doors for him lately. Soon, his lean, muscular body and handsome face would afford him another invitation. This one would be from Karl to go skiing in a private chalet. The only question that remained was, would the two studs ever make it to the slopes?

MY BOYFRIEND'S BROTHER
Evan couldn't believe it when his boyfriend Durio broke up with him via text. He wondered if everything was okay with him since it was so out of character for someone as sweet and thoughtful as Durio was to do something so cruel. Evan knew that Durio kept his family very private. Perhaps he was having trouble at home? He needed closure to this relationship. A quick ride to the country to Durio's parents' house proved to be more than he bargained for. Not only did he meet Durio's ridiculously hot, gay brother, but he also discovered that this gay sibling was more interested in him than Durio ever was. Perhaps Evan was with the wrong member of the family?

THE MOVIE STAR
Todd always dreamed of moving to Hollywood, California, and working in the movie business. When he finally got his big break, he would have never have dreamt it would be for Sam Sterling, the biggest star in the world! Now Sam's assistant, Todd went everywhere Sam went. The two men became very close throughout their travels together. So close that it became difficult to tell where their business relationship ended and their personal relationship began. Could it be that these two men's relationship was about to be more than just boss and employee?

GAY SHORT STORIES

JC CALCIANO

STEAM ROOM
CONFIDENTIAL
—— VOLUME 2 ——

Steam Room Confidential: Volume 2

A FARM BOY IN BROOKLYN
Bryce couldn't wait to start his career as an artist in Brooklyn, NY. When he finally arrived in N.Y. and moved into a brownstone with a handsome Greek bouncer, he had no idea that he'd lose his heart to him. How would Bryce deal with being in love with someone already in a relationship? Watching him with his hunky boyfriend was too much to bear. Bryce needed to decide what to do, and it seemed like leaving was his best option. However, it appeared that his roommate had others plans for him.

THE DREAM MAN
As Blake drove his convertible Jeep down near the beach, he thought he spied his best friend nearby. Rather than his buddy, it turned out to be a stone-cold stud instead. Instead of the mix-up turning embarrassing, it somehow evolved into drinks and much more that night. Blake was shocked that the evening somehow turned into a racy rendezvous since he had never been with a man before. Was the whole thing in his head? Did this hot, passionate night with his dream man really happen?

THE RANDY REPAIRMAN
John worked from home. When his computer failed to connect to the internet one morning, he called a repairman to fix it. Who showed up at the door was more than he could have expected or hoped for! Was he being punked? This man was gorgeous! John knew that all he needed was the installation of a simple router, but he wasn't going to let this hunky repairman get away without making a few extra "house calls."

A MAN WITH AN APPEALING VIEW
Casey couldn't believe it when his best friend Deidra
insisted he go out on a date with her landscape
architect. He was done dating and certainly not
interested in driving down to the beach just to meet
some stranger. But Casey knew it was easier to say yes,
and just do what she said. When his date, Raphael,
opened the door to his grand villa that overlooked the
ocean, he was breathless at both the view of the water
and this hot hunk of a man. Casey couldn't help but
wonder if this man was out of his league and if this
date was a very bad idea.

A CHARMING PRINCE
Holt had just arrived in Los Angeles to attend law
school. He decided to blow off some steam and visit
Disneyland before his classes started. Holt knew that
Mickey Mouse and Goofy to be there to greet him, but
he certainly didn't expect Prince Charming to ask him
on a hot date and sweep him off his feet.

AN AUSSIE ACTOR
James was happy being the only guy in acting class. He
enjoyed being the stud all the girls desired. All that
suddenly changed when a hunky Australian actor
joined the group. James wanted to know if this guy was
straight, bi, or gay. Luckily, the instructor paired them
up for a scene to perform in class. James decided that
not only would he pick the material they'd prepare to
present to the teacher, but he'd make sure it was a hot,
gay love scene so he could get his answer about his
new classmate.

THE HOPELESS ROMANTIC

Lance loved romance. So much so that he decided to become a writer of gay love stories. When his books became popular, he was invited to participate in a popular writer's convention. He was flattered to be invited to attend, but he was even more excited to meet his favorite authors. Lance had few expectations other than to gather a few autographs from them. He certainly hadn't planned on meeting a tall, handsome stranger who'd forever change his life.

A VERY HAPPY BIRTHDAY BOY

Riley wasn't looking forward to turning forty. He was still single and had never quite gotten over his first love; his straight best friend, Wade. This year, an expected phone call from Wade inviting him over for dinner caught him by surprise. Of course, he declined the invitation, but eventually, curiosity got the best of him. Is he still with his wife? Does he still look as good as he did in college? Riley knew he couldn't enjoy his birthday without knowing what became of Wade's life. He decided to pass by his house just to see if he could get a glance of what had become of him. Riley could never have predicted what he would find when he got to Wade's home.

GAY SHORT STORIES

JC CALCIANO

STEAM ROOM
CONFIDENTIAL

VOLUME 3

Steam Room Confidential: Volume 3

BAYWATCH BRO

Flipping burgers wasn't Dane's idea of the perfect summer job. He figured that he'd never meet anyone working in a greasy spoon. Things changed when the head lifeguard, Lawrence, ordered delivery from the unassuming food stand. Dane soon looked forward to dropping lunch off at the beach to the sun-dipped Adonis every day. Who could have expected that the hunky lifeguard hoped that Dane was on the menu?

MILE HIGH CLUB

Forrest had never been in an airplane before today. It was the first time he had ever flown, and he was equally excited and nervous. Forrest instantly felt at ease when he spotted a hot, distinguished pilot who boarded the plane. The flight took off without a hitch, and the long flight seemed to be uneventful and relaxing; that is until the sexy Captain spotted Forrest sitting nearby and decided to re-define the meaning of first-class treatment.

THE MUSCULAR MECHANIC

Dawson packed his bags and headed out east on a quest to find inspiration for the great American novel he was writing. A quick bite at the local truck stop led to a chance meeting with a hunky mechanic named Leo. This random encounter with a rugged stud provided more than just an oil change for his car, but also just the adventure he needed to complete the last chapter of his book!

A STUD FOR SUPPER

Everything was set for the perfect Thanksgiving

celebration with that family. A last-minute change of plans revealed that Taylor's sister intended to bring her sexy co-worker to join them for dinner. Taylor wasn't sure how anyone expected him to concentrate on the warm turkey on his plate when all he could think about was feasting on the hot stud sitting across the table from him?

THE SEXY SOAP STAR

It's been some time since Hudson caught his ex-boyfriend cheating, and the relationship ended. Finally, the time had come to get his own place and move out. This weekend was all about bargain shopping at flea markets and garage sales. Who could have predicted that the person having one of the sales was the sexiest soap opera star he'd ever laid eyes on? The moment Hudson laid eyes on him, he knew that he'd be taking home more than a lamp and end-table!

HUNKY SANTA

Christmas was Dax's favorite holiday. Each year, he looked forward to leaving New York City and heading back to Ohio to spend it with his family. Two days before Christmas, a freak snowstorm stranded him in Manhattan. It seems that Dax isn't going home anytime soon. Perhaps Santa has another gift in mind for him this year? Dax is about to learn that the best packages come with six-pack abs and bulging biceps.

SCHOOL OF ROCK

Taylor always wanted to be a rock star, but his pragmatic parents insisted that he ditch the music and concentrate on his studies. On his 18th Birthday, Taylor was able to get a job that paid him enough to take lessons with a local musician he discovered on a flier in a local coffee shop. Taylor couldn't be more excited to start his classes, that was until he laid eyes on the sexy, long-haired, tattooed rock-and-roller who was giving them. Now playing the electric guitar isn't the only thing on his mind.

ECUPID 2.0
Jimmy started his day as usual –Single. When a mysterious app called *eCupid* notified him with the promise of finding him true love, he couldn't help but accept the terms and conditions. Suddenly his life has been taken over by the gadget, and things would never be the same for him. Mysterious packages, strange people, past relationships were resurfacing… Was the app working in his best interest to find him love, or was this all some cruel joke being played on him?

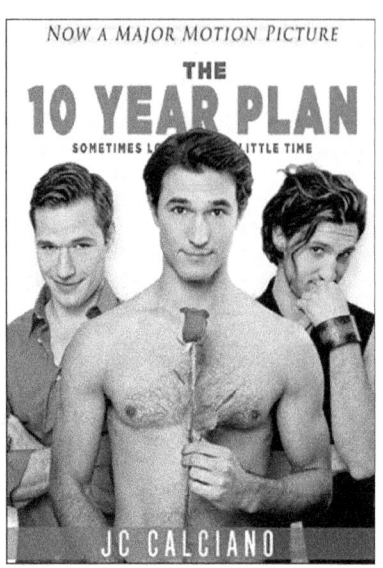

The 10 Year Plan

Best friends Myles and Brody are total opposites. Myles believes in true love and happily ever after; Brody believes in hot guys and lots of happy endings. But after Myles has a particularly bad date, they make a plan that, if they haven't found true love in 10 years, they'll become a couple. Ten years later…nothing has changed. Myles is still a hopeless romantic looking for Mr. Right, and Brody is still on the hunt for Mr. Right Now – both still alone. When they realize it's almost time to make good on the promise they made to each other a decade earlier, both friends scramble to do whatever it takes to avoid their fate: to be a couple! The search for each other's perfect partner is on! But maybe the man of their dreams is too close to see.

Our Movies

Steam Room Stories: THE MOVIE

An Adventure of Brotastic Proportions.

Cosmetics magnate Sally Fay spends the last of her fortune to find the legendary Fountain of Youth and use the miracle water to save her sagging empire. With the help of a map, she discovers the ancient aquifer is located under a steam room gym in Encino, California. Sally will stop at nothing to possess the steam room and its magical waters. What she doesn't count on are the Steam Room Guys, who will do whatever it takes to thwart her evil plans and save their beloved steam room.

FROM THE WRITER/DIRECTOR OF "IS IT JUST ME?" & "eCUPID"

THE
10 YEAR PLAN
SOMETIMES LOVE TAKES A LITTLE TIME

A FILM BY JC CALCIANO

The 10 Year Plan

Sometimes Love Takes a Little Time.

Myles and Brody are two best friends who are total opposites. Myles is a hopeless romantic looking for Mr. Right. Brody is a sexy cop on the hunt for Mr. Right now. These two friends make a plan that they'll be together in a decade if they are both still single. Nearly ten years later and still alone, both friends will do whatever it takes to avoid becoming a couple.

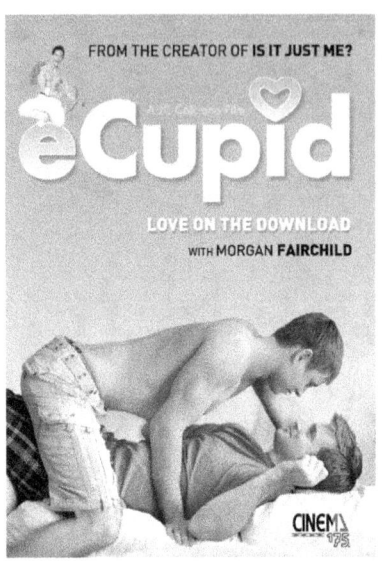

eCupid

Love On the Download.

This sparkling romantic comedy takes online dating to the extreme! Marshall is an over-worked ad exec suffering from a severe case of the seven-year itch with his loving boyfriend. As his 30th birthday nears, he is hell-bent on changing his life, and he comes across a mysterious dating app called *eCupid*. Turning his world upside down and overwhelming him with sexy, horned-up guys at every turn, Marshall gets much more than he bargained. Firing on all cylinders with sharp wit, hot cast, and even an extended cameo from Hollywood legend Morgan Fairchild, *eCupid* will win your heart.

Is It Just Me?

The Landmark Gay Romantic Comedy.

Laugh-out-loud funny and seductively sweet, *Is It Just Me?* is the landmark gay romantic comedy about one man's search for Mr. Right. Adorable Blaine can't seem to meet guys, let alone form a relationship. His beefy go-go boy roommate Cameron who has no shortage of willing partners, can't understand why he doesn't just pounce and enjoy some one-nighters. Instead, Blaine hides in chat rooms where he meets Zander, a shy, recently relocated Texan. But when the time comes to exchange photos, Blaine accidentally sends an image of his hunky roomie, and things go from romantically promising to downright confusing. *Is It Just Me?* is a bona fide feel-good winner full of witty charm and cute guys!

PODCASTS

Steamy Stories

Listen to all your favorite *Steam Room Confidential* stories on our popular podcast. *Steamy Stories* is where bromance becomes bromosexual!

A collection of sexy short stories written by JC Calciano and narrated by Ben Palacios & Casey Alcoser.

Listen on Apple Podcasts, Spotify, Google Play and more.

SteamyStoriesPodcast.com

About the Author

 JC began writing books after a 30-year career as a filmmaker. His films include *Is It Just Me? eCUPID, The 10 Year Plan,* and *Steam Room Stories: The Movie.*

In 2010, he created the sketch comedy series for YouTube called *Steam Room Stories.* The show featured hunky, hot guys joking around in a steam room. It became an overnight sensation that continues to this day.

JC has also authored two novels: *Revenge of the Brobot* and a novelization of his film, *The 10 Year Plan.*

Steam Room Confidential is a collection of his short stories from the popular podcast *Steamy Stories.*

JC enjoys writing and reading m/m romance and camp comedy. His signature sense of humour is undeniably present in all his works.

Join the Fun!

VISIT

Go to SteamRoomStories.com to watch the movies, see the series, and read the books.

SUBSCRIBE

Sign up for JC Calciano's *Cinema175 Newsletter* for news and giveaways at JCCalciano.com.

FOLLOW

JCCalciano.com
SteamRoomStories.com
SteamyStoriesPodcast.com
Cinema175.com